Embodiment of Evil

A Novel by Bill Hubiak

PublishAmerica
Baltimore

Hardcover 978-1-4489-3552-9
Softcover 978-1-4489-4071-4
PUBLISHED BY PUBLISHAMERICA, LLLP
www.publishamerica.com
Baltimore

Printed in the United States of America

For Carole

my wife, my friend, and the love of my life,
whose unwavering support and encouragement
made pursing my dreams possible.

Chapter 1

Robert Miller adjusted the rearview mirror, searching the dark road behind him for anyone who might be following. His frightened reflection stared back at him in the twilight shadows. In all his years as a psychiatrist, he had never been more cognizant of his own vulnerability nor experienced such a profound sense of evil. Fear slithered through him like a venomous viper. He frantically shifted gears, his foot grinding the accelerator into the floor.

In the confines of his Accord the air was thick with malignity. A sixth sense warned him that he was in peril. He glanced over his shoulder into the empty back seat of the car in order to put his mind at ease that nobody was hiding there.

"Take a deep breath and get a grip, Robert," he chided himself, hoping to gain control over his racing heart and accelerated breathing.

It had taken him months of sifting through an endless maze of paperwork and bureaucratic red tape to locate his client's mother. The prospect of speaking with the woman had energized him but, with the interview now completed, he felt a suffocating burden. The expression on the old woman's face compelled him to consider alternative explanations for his client's predicament...scenarios that stretched the bounds of believability.

He fingered the cassette recorder concealed in his jacket pocket. He had recorded his discussion with old woman, hoping later to confront Nick DeLucci with his mother's words. That is, if he could break through the psychological wall behind which DeLucci had retreated.

He rewound the cassette, stopped it, held it to his ear, listened briefly, then repeated the process until he found the poignant moment when Virginia DeLucci's words shattered like splinters his belief that humankind's capacity for inhumanity had limits.

"I am seeing your son on a regular basis to help him cope with disturbing dreams," Robert Miller's voice announced.

"Dreams? What kind of dreams?" Tension laced the old woman's voice.

"Unfathomable gruesome ones," he answered.

The woman's tone hardened. "He always had a highly overactive imagination."

Miller hadn't responded, allowing the ambiguity of his silence to work its magic. The mercurial creaking of the matron's rocking chair filled the void, escalating with the passing seconds.

"What did he tell you? What did that twisted little liar say?"

He had leaned forward, elbows on his knees, hands clasped authoritatively in front of him. The metronome of the chair's tottering amplified in his head as the silence around them thickened. He squelched his own emotional apprehension, instead scrutinizing the crone's haggard face, anticipating the moment at which the woman would surrender to her anxieties.

Her jaws clamped shut.

Say something damn it! His heart thumped in his ears.

The woman stopped her rocking. The contrasting stillness engulfed the room in an ambiance of hazard. The muscles around her mouth twitched. "He remembers!" she gasped in little more than a whisper. The fear in her eyes was unmistakable.

The words penetrated Miller's heart like shards of ice. Until that moment he had clung to the belief that Nick DeLucci's anguish was metaphorical. The old lady's response shattered that illusion.

"Remembers what?" he asked with professional calm even though his heart pounded in his chest so loudly he feared it might drown out his words.

The woman didn't appear to hear him. Her eyes turned wild and unfocused.

"Remembers what?" he repeated with more authority.

"No! No! No!" Her words came out like a moaning siren's blast as her body began to twitch and tremble in disjointed movements as if it was at war with itself. "There is no devil! There is no devil! There is no devil!" she wailed.

He had not been prepared for such a reaction.

Footsteps. The old woman's private nurse raced back into the room and hastened to her ward's side.

"What is it, Ginny?" her caretaker asked. "What's the matter, sweetie?"

"There is no devil! There is no devil! There is no devil!"

"Of course not, my darling. Relax. Everything will be all right."

"No, it never happened, none of it!" the older woman shrieked.

The blue-haired nurse turned to Miller. "Perhaps you had better leave, Doctor, while I try to calm her down. You can find your way out?"

"Yes, of course." He stood, bewildered. "I apologize for upsetting her," he added as he turned away. And that was when he noticed the portrait on the wall behind him.

The tape recounted Miller's hasty retreat from the retirement village Cape Cod styled cottage to a backdrop of hysteria.

Over the years he had learned that the most powerful force acting upon the human mind was fear and, as often as not, nothing was as fearful and terrible as reality. Nick DeLucci had withdrawn into catatonia after one of Miller's several failed attempts to probe more deeply into his recurring ghoulish nightmares through hypnosis. DeLucci lay motionless, like a zombie from one of his own popular horror novels. Now the reason for this unanticipated turn of events slapped the psychiatrist in the face.

This was unlike any case with which Miller, or his mentor, Tony Bralich, was familiar. When night fell each evening, his client reached for the obsolete portable typewriter that the little man had carried with him to every session, clutching to it like a security blanket. Miller had placed the featherweight Smith-Corona in DeLucci's room to accommodate his patient's macabre nocturnal ritual. Trance-like, the author worked at a feverish pitch for exactly one hour; typing gibberish, indifferent and unresponsive to his surroundings and his doctors' attempts to communicate with him.

"One hour every day. I write for exactly one hour every day. One hour, three hundred and sixty five days a year," DeLucci had informed him during one of their earlier sessions in a flat chant-like tone.

The ear-piercing shrieks of squealing tires snatched Miller's attention from his thoughts. The yellow dividing line vanished beneath his front bumper. Barricades, detouring a closed left driving lane, and a wall of oncoming traffic were in its stead.

He swerved further to the left, avoiding a fishtailing pickup. Blinding beams of light flooded his vision, obscuring the danger that a chorus of trumpeting horns made eminent, setting his every nerve on end.

When he stomped down on the accelerator, the Accord stuttered and the acrid scent of his fear assailed his nostrils. The engine kicked in just as the road disappeared beneath him and the vehicle launched into the empty night sky. A silent plea escaped his lips.

An eternity passed before the car again touched ground, colliding with the earth below in a jarring jolt that snapped his jaw shut. The coppery taste of blood washed across his tongue. His head thumped repeatedly against the top of the interior roof as the vehicle sped out of control on a roller coaster ride down a steep undulating embankment toward another thoroughfare.

Miller smashed the brake pedal into the floor but the Accord continued its course toward the speeding traffic below. He pumped the brakes, again and again but the pedal offered little more than a spongy resistance. His panic erupted, taking on a pulse of its own. At the bottom of the slope, he pulled the steering wheel hard to the right in a final attempt to avoid entering traffic.

*****

A gangly man with a hawk nose and brooding black eyes pulled his rust-pocked burgundy Corvair to a stop at the point where Miller's car left the upper road. He watched the psychiatrist's car fishtail, then erratically somersault into a series of macabre twisting rollovers.

Angry horns blasted obscenities as the runaway vehicle bounced into traffic, leap-frogging over the top of one skidding automobile before crashing into the hood of another. The two colliding cars exploded into flames while a host of other vehicles ripped through the smoke and flaring blaze, flirting with the scattered wreckage.

The spectator wiped the last traces of brake fluid from his hands unto his already oil-soiled pants before running his long bony fingers through his Mohawk mane. Turbulent emotion festered just beneath his swarthy skin.

"He's dead," he sneered in the direction of his companion still seated in the car.

The portly woman's face hinted of a perverse smile beneath an unnaturally thick mask of makeup, but she said nothing. Her eyes were the blue color of robin eggs but as impervious as a tinted windshield. She turned away. The man recognized this as a directive to move on. He tugged at his mustache as he contorted his gawkishly long body into the compact and drove off.

Chapter 2

A small Tiffany desk lamp offered the only illumination to the expansive meticulously appointed paneled office. Jefferson Thorne straightened his tie and cleared his throat. He could barely discern the outline of the figure seated behind the desk, obscured by shadows.

"Uh-hum, excuse me, sir. Here are the chapters you requested of DeLucci's latest manuscript. He submitted only six. It's been more than a month since I last heard from him."

A large arthritic hand with skin stained by time emerged from the darkness; an oversized red ruby banded on gold perched between the crippled knuckles of the ring finger. The hand issued a palsied, yet firm directive, tapping the desktop, then withdrew. Thorne placed the papers on the desk where indicated and waited further instruction. None came. He stared vacantly at the floor. To do more would be unwise.

His employer's hand reemerged from the shadows, shooing him away as it snatched the papers from the desk. Even in the insufficient light, the wrinkled skin appeared as translucent as waxed paper, a yellowish paw marbled with liver spots.

Thorne retreated toward the huge oak doors that functioned as a barrier between his employer's lair and the rest of the mogul's publication syndicate. Embodiment of Evil, he heard the old man croak with contempt. "Let's see what the ugly little bastard has come up with this time."

Embodiment of Evil
A Novel by Nick DeLucci

Stevie Cox resembled the Garden Grove, California, community in which he now resided, a man on the downslide. Blackened bags of flesh sagged beneath each eye, surrounding a bulbous nose, the focal point of the once masculine and attractive face. His thick black wavy hair had given way to a sparse covering of frayed tuft. Peppered facial hair hung from his chin like a tattered whiskbroom, framing puffy lips and yellowed teeth. The sparkle that once illuminated mischievous brown eyes and captivated audiences with elfish tales of daring and tomfoolery during their youth in the small hamlet of Cranford, New Jersey, now were vacant and dull.

Alan Ciani was unprepared for the transformation that his old friend had undergone since last they were together many years ago. He forced a smile and said, "Nice to see you again after all these years."

Stevie's stare was jaundiced.

"You going to invite me in or what?"

"You can come in if it's absolutely necessary," Stevie spat, his voice taut with anger. "That is, unless you intend to offer condolences regarding my dearly departed brother."

The huge, sad-eyed golden retriever at Stevie's side barked a friendlier greeting than Alan's host had offered. As he reached down to pet the animal, Stevie kneed the dog out of Alan's range and snapped, 'Shut the fuck up, Dammit," and walked away leaving the door open behind him.

Sidestepping mounds of clothing, magazines and litter, he followed Stevie Cox through a living room that reeked of stale beer and cigarette smoke. They entered the kitchen, which was in an equal state of squalor and disarray. Stevie grabbed a twelve-pack of Coors from the refrigerator, tore a can from its packaging, and tossed it in Alan's direction.

"Want a beer?"

Alan snared the airborne brew. Always a sure-handed athlete, his hands were unusually petite and mismatched his thickly muscled frame, a characteristic for which he had taken quite a bit of ridicule over the years from his fellow jocks.

"So what do you want?" Stevie asked, sitting down at the kitchen table with an open beer in one hand and the other hand guarding the rest of his stash of Coors.

Alan sat quietly across from him for a few tortuous seconds with his elbows stuck to the tacky table surface. The silence seemed to make Stevie even more irritable. The golden retriever, which had followed the two men through the house, placed her head on Alan's lap and looked up at him forlorn with her ears twitching for affection.

"Leave the guinea alone, Dammit, before he gives you fleas," Stevie snapped, yanking the dog's head off Alan's lap.

"What's your dog's name?"

"You're no smarter than I remembered. The bitch's name is Dammit, you dumb shit," he said without making eye contact. "I thought it might be less confusing when I call her. Get over here, Dammit! Go away, Dammit!" The obedient canine roommate started toward her master, and then reversed her direction, finally settling in the far corner of the room where she curled up on the floor looking desolate.

"I had a roommate in college who had a retriever named Ralph. The roommate's name was Spot."

Stevie didn't appear to find the anecdote amusing and said nothing.

Alan sipped his beer. "Guess that everything looks a bit bleak for you just now."

"Fuck you and the horse you rode in on, grease ball!" Stevie tilted his head back and poured the beer down his throat without pausing to take a breath. He popped open another can to the refrain of loud guttural belches. His rank and putrid breath wafted over Alan.

It occurred to Alan that grief and depression had taken hold in Stevie Cox's psyche, twisting and yanking until it snapped his hold upon reality. Alan choked on the emotion that surged in his chest for his tortured friend. Since the psychiatrists he'd watched on television tended to limit communication to mostly gestures and smiles, he decided to follow suit so as not to further antagonize his host. He hoped such a tact would allow for the prospect that his childhood friend might let out the anguish he had bottled up. Isn't that what a friend should do?

Stevie continued to drink at a fevered pace, saying little except for a spattering of undeserved insults. Alan could almost measure time by the empty beer cans. By the sixth or seventh beer, Stevie's earlier reluctance to communicate had dissipated, to be replaced by an incoherent series of hostile rantings.

When the opportunity afforded itself, Alan interjected. "I'm sorry about Danny, Stevie. I imagine that all the guys were equally shocked by his...early passing."

To Alan's bemusement, Stevie began laughing hysterically. It seemed to Alan contrived, vitriolic and melodramatic, as if performed by an untested and poorly directed B-movie villain.

Dammit sat up and tilted her head to one side as if to question her master's meaning.

"Quite a blow to the female population of the world," Stevie snickered, "but I'm sure there's more like him to replace the loss. The bastard deserves to rot in hell, but you can be certain that his unholy soul will revel there instead."

"Stevie, I know that your brother's death…"

"Spare me your bullshit," he interrupted with an expression spewing with venom. Then, the contemptuous expression vanished and the look of amusement returned to his face. "You really haven't a clue, have you?"

He shrugged his shoulders. "About what, Stevie?"

"Danny the Enchanter isn't dead, you idiot," he slurred. "Danny's kind doesn't die."

"What do you mean his kind?"

Stevie looked into his beer can. Alan asked the question again.

"Danny was the Devil, Al," Stevie retorted in an offhanded manner. "The Devil doesn't die, it just changes faces."

"What in hell are you talking about?"

Stevie jerked his head and shoulders forward across the table. His dark eyes darted around the room like an animal avoiding a predator. In a voice softened to a whisper as if his words should not be spoken aloud, he said, "Danny was from Hell. Yeah. That blue-eyed beauty, the paragon of physical perfection and the envy of all the kids on the block, was a demon straight from Hell.

"Surely you …?"

"Shhh! Some things shouldn't be talked about. It's dangerous." His eyes were feral and desperate.

Alan was speechless. He knitted his eyebrows and summoning every ounce of empathy he could, reached across the table for his friend's arm.

Stevie pulled away, squinting at him with distaste. He hurriedly swallowed more beer as if quenching an arid thirst, and then crumpled the can with his fist, and threw it across the room.

A thin but strained smile creased Stevie's face. "Danny was always special to Mom, they were very close. Unusually close," Stevie emphasized. His words were now badly slurred and his head bobbed up and down, back and forth as if it might roll off his shoulders. "It wasn't until after my Dad died that I realized the true nature of their relationship. I'm certain that Danny caused Dad's death somehow. I don't know how. Maybe Dad caught them together and that brought on the stroke."

Alan recoiled. "Caught them together?"

Stevie snorted his contempt. "The devil is in the details, isn't it old buddy. Do I gotta draw you a picture? Danny and Mom were very, very, very close. Mom knew that I knew. That's why she penciled me out of her life. She still won't even accept calls from me. She doesn't want to deal with it; with me." He chuckled. "Not that I really want to talk with the pathetic old hag anyhow," he added, a sorrowful, drunken smile painted on his face. "She's living in that retirement village in Brick Township. Refers to me as her crazy son. Yeah…I'm the fucking crazy one."

Alan hadn't seen Mrs. Cox since Stevie's wedding. She was quite a beautiful woman back then and like many of the other guys, she had found a way into more than a few of Alan's fantasies during his coming-of-age years. However, the thought that Danny had been doing his own mother was unfathomable, not to mention outright disgusting.

"Haven't seen Mom since my wedding day. She couldn't avoid showing up for that. After all, how would that look to the relatives and neighbors?" A sneer curled Stevie's lips. "My marriage, Danny took care of that too. Ya know, when I walked in on him and Katie at Danny's place, the two of them were all drugged up. She wasn't even upset I found them. She just smiled as if …if …" His expression softened. "I still think about her; the way the corners of her mouth turned up, and the tiny gap between her front teeth."

Stevie swallowed whatever bile was lodged in this throat. His eyes were fixed absently on the deteriorating kitchen floor linoleum, attempting to hide the tears that Alan had noticed welling up. "And you know what she says to me? She says, 'You should see the movies we made for you,' and then went right back to work on our golden boy as if I wasn't even there."

"You mean Danny and Katie …"

"Yeah, just another notch on his belt, and Danny captured it all in living color. Chronicling his conquests was a favorite pastime."

If true, that would have been a full time job, Alan thought to himself.

"My brother made lots and lo-o-ots of movies right there on Walnut Avenue. You'd be surprised at how many local celebrities we had and how much money there was in it for Danny. Humph! Not much happening at his place these days." He laughed. "Poof!" he said, miming a match being lit and a fire igniting.

"Danny made porno movies? How could he hide that from all us guys, Stevie? Shit, we'd have spent an ungodly portion of our youth watching them. He couldn't keep something like that a secret." Well, maybe then, Alan thought, but surely not today with everyone owning a plethora of electronic toys, DVDs and all. "Porn is a multi-billion dollar industry, Stevie. I mean, as pretty as Danny was, he would be as well known as...Brad Pitt. Somebody from home would surely recognize him."

"The devil has many faces. He never used Danny's face, that was his Pied Piper. Old Woody's a big star though. Bi-i-ig star!" Stevie said with a shit-eating grin, pumping his hips toward the ceiling with his arm way out in front of him, only slightly exaggerating the ampleness of Danny's maleness.

With another beer, Stevie sagged forward into a stupor. Dammit had come across the room and laid her enormous head on the table beside her master.

Alan felt raddled by his friend's vilifying revelations about his brother. No way could these things be true. Too edgy and bewildered to sit still, he absently meandered about the kitchen, then the living room. His friend's delusions were so bizarre and alien he felt a need to get his bearings, get a fix on a familiar object just to help him know that he, himself, was real. Episodes such as he just experienced were the stuff of horror books and movies, or nightmares, not reality.

Over the fireplace was a picture of Stevie with Katie and their little girl. That was ages ago. Stevie had long hair and a Fu Manchu mustache. Their daughter was an extraordinary beauty with jet-black hair and haunting dark eyes. On the wall in the hallway was another photo, this time of the little girl turned woman. She must be nearly thirty by now, Alan thought.

"Sam will be twenty-nine the end of October," Stevie said at Alan's back as he staggered toward him. Snatching the picture from the wall, he stared with longing at it, and then clutched it to his chest in a caress.

"She's been taken from me too."

Alan was hesitant to inquire how.

"Left for New York years ago," he said aloud but not really to Alan. "She's an angel, a goddess, everything that is pure and loving in this disgusting world."

"She's beautiful," Alan agreed. That was no lie, but then again she had been blessed with incredible genes.

"You don't know what it's like to lose your little girl."

Stevie looked past Alan teary-eyed and swallowed his grief. In an instant his expression hardened. "Do you still cook?" Without waiting for the response, he answered his own question. "You're an orally fixated guinea, of course you cook. How about going to the kitchen and pulling something together for us? I'm famished and there must be something in the cabinets you can work your magic on."

"Hey, let's get some fresh air. Come on, I'll spring for dinner at whatever your favorite restaurant is." Maybe a change of venue would help.

"What?" Stevie appeared to struggle with the suggestion. "Yeah, okay, let me throw some water on my face first. Go get yourself another beer." He turned to his faithful dog, which had followed him from the kitchen. With a big smile on his face he exclaimed, "You want to go out, girl?" As Dammit's tail begin to wag with excitement, he added, "Well, too fucking bad. They don't let dogs in restaurants. Get outta' here, Dammit." Despondent, the retriever bowed her head and beat a path back to the kitchen with her tail between her legs.

Seconds turned into minutes, and the milling about that had provided background noise to Alan pampering Stevie's mistreated pooch gave way to dead silence. The quiet grated on him. What was Stevie boy up to?

His impulse to call after his malingering friend was abruptly overruled by a loud blast from the back of the house that exploded into Alan's head like a monstrous wave crashing upon a shoreline. A breath lodged in his throat as he leaped from his chair. The anticipation of horror warped his perception of time, milliseconds protracting into minutes. As if in a dream, Alan floated surrealistically out of the kitchen, down the hall, toward the back section of the home as Dammit's barking echoed through the house. Navigating an obstacle course of discarded belongings, he collided into successive doorways. Pain exploded into his knee.

On the bathroom floor, a grotesquely quivering object flapped like a fish out of water, dark fluid oozing from one end. The walls moved, alive with red and ivory slithering worms. Alan thought his mind to be playing tricks on him until his eyes converged on the shotgun at his feet. A hand was attached to the trigger. The gestalt pattern came into focus. Stevie Cox's legs and arms kicked and bucked one final time as if in a futile attempt to fight off death, then went motionless.

Frayed by shock and tragedy, Alan's senses crumbled. An involuntary moan escaped his lips as flesh rippled down his back. His knees grew unsteady. Braced by the bathroom doorjamb, he slid down toward the tile.

Across the small room, he spied large uneven writing on the mirror over the sink that read: "fire at the river."

A burning wave of bile rose from his stomach, lodged in his throat, and then poured out through his mouth in discordant spasms. Time was fogged by delirium, becoming confused in a bottomless pulsating ache.

In another dimension of space, sirens further assailed his senses. Hard hands lifted him from the floor. Memories fragmented.

*****

A small circle of light spilled onto the manuscript pages as they were tossed onto the desktop. Dante Underland, the room's sole occupant and baron of the vast Underland Empire, chortled with delight at DeLucci's latest efforts. Anger and destructiveness were the guiding instincts in each of the twenty novels penned by Nick DeLucci over the previous two decades. "Bred for success," the ancient exclaimed aloud. He slapped his feeble and palsied fist unto the surface of his desk and with a sparkle of enthusiasm chuckled, "Bred for success."

Chapter 3

Tony Bralich clicked on the answering machine to retrieve his messages.

Beep.

"Tony? Are you there? Pick up." Pause. "I'll try back later."

Beep.

"This is Robert again. Are you there?" Pause. "I'm in New Jersey and just now leaving Dr. William Zent's office. He's the author of Satan's Foundlings. One of his cases is on our list from the Garden Grove Children's Home. Tony, I think I've located DeLucci's natural mother. She's down the Jersey shore in a retirement village. I'll leave my cell phone on while I'm in the car if you get a chance to call. Otherwise, I'll call you from Lakewood after I've spoken with her."

Beep. Beep. Beep.

Bralich ran his hand across what remained of the gray stubble atop his head. Sliding his glasses up on his forehead, he rubbed the bridge of his nose and yawned. It was late and he was too tired to worry about Robert Miller's obsession with the DeLucci case. Besides, he had to teach an early class at Columbia and had just concluded a demanding group therapy session that had left him drained. He dreaded the subway ride home. Pushing back from his desk, he summoned what little energy he had left to stand.

The mountainous frame of the hospital's chief administrator filled his office doorway. Because of his size, jocular nature, and oft-disheveled physical appearance, the uninformed at the psychiatric facility often mistook Wayne Alexander for an orderly. Chief Administrators were expected to be diminutive, napoleonic in disposition, and impeccably quaffed to compensate for ego deficiencies. Wayne always looked like he spent the night sleeping at the bus station or in the dryer at the

Laundromat. His massive stomach hung a good eight inches over his belt, forcing his shirttails out of his pants, and no matter how many times he tucked them back in, they found their way back out again.

Despite the wardrobe malfunctions, Bralich liked him; he was a good man to work for and didn't take himself too seriously. Bralich fingered his beard as he stepped from behind his desk. "Working pretty late for a paper pusher, Mr. GQ."

Alexander appeared uncharacteristically somber.

"What's the matter, Wayne? You look like shit." Of course, the pock-skinned, pasty-faced giant always looked like shit, he thought.

Alexander cupped his huge hand on Bralich's shoulder. "Tony, I have very bad news," he said softly, very unlike his usually boisterous ebullient self.

"What's wrong?"

"Robert is dead," he sighed.

Something deep inside shattered into fragments—shattered like a windowpane in a storm. The last remnants of energy drained from Bralich's limbs. Robert was more than just his protegee. The teacher-student relationship and many years of a professional association had evolved into kinship. He looked upon Robert as a son. Their closeness had helped Bralich rediscover the zest for living that had been stolen from him a lifetime ago when his own son had died in a Vietnamese death camp and, shortly thereafter, his wife Anna had chosen an overdose of sleeping pills over living with the loss. The remarkable physical resemblance between the two men had made the emotional bond enduring. Bralich steadied himself with the desk.

As if observing himself from somewhere outside his body, he heard his own shaky voice ask, "What happened?"

"A car accident...in Jersey. Tony, what the hell was Robert doing in New Jersey anyway?"

"Field research on a client."

"DeLucci, right?"

Bralich nodded and mumbled, "He left me a message on my machine."

"Jesus, I told him to back off a little, but he was so damn preoccupied with DeLucci!"

"He was going to speak with his client's mother."

"He located her?"

Alexander's subsequent comments were lost to Bralich. The shadowy depths of his oppressive grief swallowed him up. He sank down into the chair beside his desk. External reality faded into little more than a blurred etching. His thoughts flashed to Robert Miller.

"You say the intensity and frequency of DeLucci's dreams increased while in therapy, Robert?"

"Dramatically so, Tony, as did the incidences of paranoid withdrawal behaviors."

"And you began confronting him, believing the withdrawal to be a manifestation of his resistance?"

"Yes. Confronting the resistance only strengthened it, however. Hypnosis triggered a complete withdrawal."

"There's always that risk. Psychiatry isn't an exact science."

"I accept that, Tony. What haunts me is the content of his dreams...that we live in a world where such terrible things can even be imagined."

Bralich placed his hand on the younger man's shoulder. "Let's hope that neither of us become so callused that nothing shocks us. At times, mankind's inhumanity seems incomprehensible."

"I have to believe that his stories are metaphoric projections of a lifetime of internalized anger. They can't be based on reality."

"Whose reality, Robert? His or yours? The history of our species amply demonstrates that evil exists in the most extreme forms. Has DeLucci been in therapy before?"

"Not according to him. Why?"

"False Memory Syndrome. It's not unheard of that attempts to dig out exceedingly painful memories instead manufacture memories of events that never really occurred."

"If he had spent time in another therapeutic relationship, that would certainly fall in the realm of possibility. He has had to swallow a great deal of anger and pain...excruciating pain, over his lifetime, Tony. Loneliness seems to be the only permanent aspect of his existence."

"Tell me what stands out most in your mind about our little friend."

Miller reflected before commenting. "His skittish behavior. His reluctance to open up his past. He appears a well of suppressed anger and constantly on the alert, always watching out, as if no place is safe and no one can be trusted."

"Isn't that the natural inclination of someone growing up in an abusive environment? To be eternally on one's guard? The environment is always potentially hostile. From such a perspective, the past may also be the present...and the future."

Robert's pensive eyes showed the magnitude with which he considered these words.

"One needs a mental framework in which to place threatening memories, Robert."

"I'm horrified by the content. It has to be a total fabrication," Miller said.

"Never overlook the obvious. People hurt children."

"I know, Tony."

"Let's see what effect, if any, Samantha will have."

"Tony, are you all right?"

His mouth was as dry as cotton and he had difficulty finding his words. "I'm okay," Bralich responded, a hand pawing at his grizzled beard.

"Let's get you over to the couch and put your feet up. You're as white as a sheet."

Bralich didn't resist being assisted to the sofa. His mind was elsewhere. Had he been responsible for Robert delving so deeply into DeLucci's situation?

There was a question on Robert's face. "He's an orphan. The records indicate that his mother abandoned him at age six. He has no early memory of her and few concrete memories until his late teens."

"We both know that the typical human mind is psychologically fragmented," Bralich said. "While the conscious mind is making one set of choices, other fragments of the psyche, outside of conscious awareness, are choosing other things in order to protect the integrity of the whole being. In order to survive, Robert, some children dissociate, try to banish painful experiences...forget them."

"There is something much deeper here. Something sinister and hideous; I can feel it. It's as if out of an absolute necessity he has annihilated a large part of psyche."

Bralich paced. *"Sometimes one must seal off the horror and the pain from normal consciousness; hide it away in secret compartments of the mind. However, these horrors must resurface. In his dreams, perhaps."*

"Yes, without a doubt he is harboring deep hidden secrets. Okay, so his nightmares and writing horror novels are an outlet to release his personal trauma. But are these real and accurate memories, or fantasies and metaphoric distortions?"

"Perhaps, it's like Alice Through The Looking Glass. Writing is his rabbit's hole or magic mirror."

Miller's eyes widened with excitement. *"He steps through to find imaginary friends who will accept and help him?"*

"And the hidden horrors follow him. Nothing and nobody is what it seems."

"Tony, can you hear me?" Alexander covered him with a blanket.

"What?" Yes, Wayne I hear you."

"Is there anything I can get for you? You still keep a bottle of vodka in your desk?"

There was no urgency to respond. Yes, the bottle was still in his desk to serve as a reminder of how easy it was to surrender to life's assaults. More than once or twice he had gone as far as to pour a drink to steady his hands before passing on the temptation.

"Look at me, Tony? Shit, Old Man, don't slip away!"

"Never married. No children. No close friends. He has no apparent living relatives. Can one man be any more isolated from humanity than this little man, Tony?"

"What about his natural parents, Robert?"

"I'm working on that now." Robert Miller looked up from his notes. *"Jefferson Thorne, his agent, describes him as a loner, uncomfortable with people and suspicious of their intentions. He tends to avoid human contact and blends into the background as much as is possible."* He sighed. *"It's no wonder. I'm certain that people were content to let him do so. His deformities must target him as object of derision and scorn. Yet, the dialogue in his novels is so genuine, and often intimate and even humorous."*

"Isn't that the wonder of our work...that this fragile species is the cathedral for a mechanism as intricate as the human mind?"

Bralich's eyes focused on the worn area rug that only partially obscured the battered wooden plank floor beneath it. "Jesus Christ, Wayne!" You're shaking my brains loose, you goddam Neanderthal!" he exclaimed in a voice filled with brusque potency.

Alexander sighed with relief. A smile creased his worried face. "Thought you might be going into shock. You had me worried, Tony."

"That's why they pay you the big bucks. If you can't stand the heat, go back to professional football, if they'll have you. You're better suited to crushing unsuspecting quarterbacks than this kind of work anyhow," Bralich said, sitting up and rubbing his arm where Alexander had grabbed him. Rolling up his shirt sleeve, he added, "You bruised me, damn it! Look at my arm, you lummox."

The big blonde's smile lit across his face. The feisty old geezer looked better; surprisingly better as if the previous few minutes were just an illusion and had never occurred at all. "You better stay put, Tony. You've had quite a shock."

"I'll be fine," Bralich reassured him with steely resolve.

An awkward silence passed.

"I'm sorry, Tony. I know how close you and Robert were."

"I appreciate your concern," he said patting the administrator on the back as he walked passed him.

"Where you going?"

Bralich snatched his wire-rimmed glasses from atop the desk and slapped them unto his face. "I want to look in on DeLucci. If it's okay, I'll follow up with Robert's clients."

Alexander nodded his reluctant approval.

Chapter 4

When his private line rang, Underland laid down the DeLucci manuscript and answered the phone. "Yes," he stated with little emotion.

"Sorry to bother you so late," a woman's voice said through the line in a delicate English accent. "Thought you might be interested in knowing that there has been a fatal automobile accident in New Jersey."

"How tragic."

"Yes, indeed. It was very unfortunate."

"I thank you for your consideration."

"As always, it's my pleasure to be of service."

"Our friend, the implacable beanpole, is he behaving himself?"

"Matthew is doing well. I wouldn't be concerned."

"And the other matter?"

"We've found a suitable child. You'll be pleased."

"Fine, then. Good evening."

"And to you, Sir."

The line disengaged, Underland picked up DeLucci's manuscript and continued reading.

*****

Alan stepped off the plane under a late summer full moon and clear night sky, thankful to have his feet planted safety back on terra firma. A cacophony orchestrated by crickets inundated the crisp country air as his brain settled back into a more natural physiological positioning, and his other internal organs properly realigned for earthbound efficiency. He found few things less rewarding than the small engine shuttle from Pittsburgh, which he likened to an hour spent in clothes dryer. Thirty-five to forty weeks of the year in transit amplified the unpleasantness rather than alleviated the effect.

The ground crew, which consisted of one interbred yokel, had already unloaded the luggage from the compartment at the rear of the small aircraft and had placed it on the runway. Alan grabbed his bag and traversed the short distance to the waiting area inside the minuscule terminal. Evelyn and the kids were nowhere to be seen. His wife was late, as usual.

Artists run on their own schedule.

The one room terminal emptied quickly. Alan checked with the ticket agent at the counter, hoping that Evelyn had left a message explaining her absence. As expected, she had not. Getting angry was a waste of time and long ago he became disabused of any notion that confronting her disregard of his wants and needs would warrant her consideration. She would show in good time refusing to acknowledge that she had kept him waiting. Her good looks and effervescent personality had served her so well over the years that she hadn't needed to learn the art of compromise. That task belonged to Alan, who had raised acquiescence in the form of "Yes, dear" to an art. There were plenty of blue, hard-plastic seats from which to choose, so he selected one that looked less filthy than the others and planted himself in it.

"So, did you miss me?" his wife's voice echoed over the loud speaker.

When he opened his eyes, Evelyn stood smiling from the ticket counter with the agent's microphone in her hand. Alan looked up at the clock on the wall. He had been waiting almost forty minutes.

"Let's get those sweet Dago buns over here, Ciani. We got places to go and people to see," Evelyn said into the microphone, shaking her long dark hair off her delicate, tanned shoulders. The halter-top dress she was wearing showed off her figure. From across the room Alan could see the outline of her nipples protruding through the cotton.

Always the brash seductress.

He picked up his bag and closed the distance between them, for which he was rewarded a quick and dutiful hug and kiss—one that reminded him that he was missed but after twenty years of marriage and innumerable airport hellos and good-byes, not passionately so. They had tied the knot in a simple civil ceremony completely devoid of romance or pompous ritual, setting the tone for a feckless marriage void of emotional intimacy; she being deficient of gentler emotions and he, by necessity, keeping his hidden. As much as he wished that the mere whiff of her scent might take his breath away, he settled for finding refuge in knowing her sense of humor and delightful visage softened the sharp edges of their stressful reality together. Beyond the exterior facade of compatibility, the solitary feelings of abandonment were forever present just below the surface of his consciousness.

"Where are the kids?"

"Off being teenagers. There's no school tomorrow; it's a teacher's in-service day. The weekend beckons and their surging hormones heed the call. They've gone down to Pittsburgh to see the Rocky Horror Show again."

"You didn't let them take Tia?"

"She's been dying to go."

"Jesus Christ! That's your genes exerting themselves on my children!" he exclaimed only partly in jest. "If this backwoods state had required a blood test in order to get married, I'd have at least been knowledgeable about the psycho-cell anemia infesting your family lineage. Knowing that everyone here has been marrying his or her brothers and sisters for generations, I'm sure I would have quickly overcome my infatuation with you. How is your brother, by the way? Is he still slapping the monkey with his feet in a padded cell?"

Evelyn ignored him. In this relationship, only her humor was funny or merited laughter.

"Were you brilliant as usual at your seminar?"

"I'm not sure that 'brilliant' sufficiently characterizes my performance. I was..."

"Obnoxious?"

"That's a given but I was looking for something more ..."

"Irrelevant? Irreverent? Extemporaneously insignificant?"

"Well, now I feel better about the merit of my work. Thanks." He enjoyed her intelligent repartee but wished that she made better use of her intelligence than for the purpose of manipulation and deceit.

"Anything of interest happen during your stay in California?"

The mere mention of his latest sojourn elicited a ballast of dread that anchored him to the floor. "Not much, same old same old," he lied. "I'll tell you all about my travels after I've had a shower, something to eat, and time to unwind." He kept secrets out of necessity. His wife couldn't be trusted with the intimate details of his inner existence. It was not unlike her to use such information like a stiletto on the fabric of his psyche.

"You're taking me out for a late dinner tonight. I've made a new friend while you were away and she's invited us to her house this evening."

Alan frowned his disapproval.

"Linda is new to our little circle of artist elites," she reported, projecting a superior air that required no pretense since her idea of being an artist was acting like one instead of creating like one. With a touch of disdain she added, "The ones you pretend don't really exist."

"It's late. I've been in and out of airports all day. Had a God damn three-hour layover in Pittsburgh waiting for the shuttle. I'd appreciate a relaxing evening at home." He wanted to add, "And about the last thing I need right now is to meet another of your weirdo friends." To say so would prove futile, he knew, for his wife dictated their social calendar, and to Alan's shame, his emotions as well.

The last artsy friend to whom he had been introduced specialized in drawing nude figures with two sets of legs, no arms, and exposed genitals where one might expect to find a head and face. Somehow, the symbolism had escaped Alan and he could not elevate thoughts beyond "dickheads" and wonder at the possibilities for simultaneous oral and coital sex with persons of normal stature. When Evelyn had asked, "Isn't Cindy's work interesting?" he had feigned pensive introspection and fallen back upon his standard "Yes, dear," praying he would not be asked to expound upon what emotional arousal or conceptual enlightenment the work had precipitated. Of course, he could hope that just this one time Evelyn had found a friend who was a Milton Friedman economist, had a yen for the wholesomeness of "The Muppet Show" reruns, and recognized golf as a recreational pleasure and not a mindless activity in which Neanderthals, such as he, engaged to avoid meaningful interaction with the cosmos. The chances of that, he knew, were slim.

"This will be a good time. Linda's work is so interesting. She's expecting us. Okay?"

He could tell that nothing he said would change her mind. He bowed his head in submission and grunted his disdain.

He had been through this scene many times before. Another meal made from all sorts of natural herbs and trendy ingredients that resulted in unfamiliar and unspectacular tastes. Evelyn would "ooh" and "aah" everything just because it was different, and ask for his opinion and approbation, knowing full well that he was hating every morsel. The conversation would be about flying saucers, Wiccan words of wisdom, sexually perverted friends they held in common, and how misunderstood their artwork was by the ignorant American populace. He was about to embark on another evening in Hell.

He carted his own luggage unassisted to the car, unable to keep step with her brisk strides.

A few minutes later, they traveled across unpaved serpentine back roads with deep potholes. The tires spit up rocks and loose gravel at the underside of the Nissan Pathfinder. Evelyn appeared unconcerned by the unabated clanking and rattling, nor by their bouncing up and down, back and forth across the road as she sped hell-bent for leather over the insufficient roadway. Nor did she appear to entertain even a margin of concern that the thickly forested terrain obscured any forewarning of approaching vehicles on the continuously winding pathway. Alan held on to the seat for fear of his life and toyed with the radio dial to avoid confronting his wife with unsolicited and unwanted observations and appraisals of her driving performance and navigational abilities.

"So this is the road?' he fidgeted.

"Sit back and enjoy the ride, Jocko. I'm doing the driving here. By the way, clutching your seat with that panicky deer-in-the-headlights look only makes you look like a wimp. That's not very sexually alluring."

After a steady climb of several miles that required repeated downshifting, they crested the long-drawn, steep incline and began an even more dramatic descent into a valley so wooded that the moonlight had little chance to make its presence known. The road worsened, having been scarred with deep ruts created by numerous years of spring drain-off. As Alan approached the limits of his tolerance with the tumultuous roller coaster ride, and as the road had all but disappeared, Evelyn pulled the car to a stop.

"We're here," she informed him.

"What? Where? There is no here, here."

"It's just a little ways. We walk."

"Your friend lives back here?"

"Yes. Just down the path."

"What path? We're in the middle of nowhere."

Evelyn's smile was cryptic.

"It's pitch black."

"Grab the bag of goodies in the back seat, shorty."

A hundred yards down the narrow lane, they emerged from the cover of huge hemlock pine, ancient oak, and maple trees into a misted clearing flooded with moonlight and alive with the aroma of the new fall season. They walked by an old barn that was home to a large community of cats.

"The in-laws?" he quipped. "Aunt tiger is looking a bit under the weather. Don't you think?"

"Put a sock in it, Ciani, or that's the only pussy you'll be seeing for a long while."

Alan mimed her suggestion and muffled a few unrecognizable syllables.

After they traversed a makeshift bridge constructed of old wooden planks placed upon the bare earth, a large house came into view another hundred yards further up the path, which now plodded straight uphill. The stream they had forded ran down the hillside, paralleling the path alongside the house, and Alan looked behind him to see that it emptied into a large pond situated beyond the barn. The full moon shone on the water and cast deeper shadows of the trees and large boulders along their way.

Steps had been carved out of the hillside with little concern for aesthetics. Halfway up the path, he spied a four-by-four building with a crescent moon on its door. He looked to his wife for confirmation of his worst fears.

"No functioning indoor plumbing," she stated matter-of-factly. "They draw both drinking and bath water from the stream."

"Ah! How genteel!"

They mountaineered the remaining steps to a deck that wrapped itself around two contiguous sides of the home, taking advantage of a southern exposure and the view of the open terrain through which they had just come. Evelyn knocked at the door as Alan surveyed with suspicion the exterior of the hideaway residence. It was in need of repair, reflecting the strain of the extreme northwestern Pennsylvanian weather.

"Behave yourself!" she warned him.

Alan pantomimed the earlier sock-in-the-mouth gag. It drew an unsympathetic smile.

When the door opened, it framed a portly woman whose face was powdered to a ghostly pallor and highlighted with dark eye shadow and tar black lipstick. Jet black hair with lots of gray interspersed draped down to her waist front and back. She wore a short, plain black dress uncomplimentary to her spindly chicken legs, skinny as toothpicks at the calf with meaty thighs. A dead ringer, he thought, for the witch that occasionally showed up in old Bugs Bunny cartoons, sans the pointed hat, the vacuum cleaner she rode, and as yet no "Tee, hee, hee" cackle. Yet the most unique physical characteristic of this new acquaintance was the color of her eyes. They were a singular blue hue that were so captivating that the totality of her exterior appearance faded into background and Alan found himself drawn into their depths as if hypnotized.

"Linda, this is Alan. He's an ex-jock so don't expect much from him." That was about as flattering as his wife got. Alan had grown to realize he should not expect much of a eulogy from her when his time rolled around.

Their hostess spoke with a cultured British accent. "Well, just as long as he is good in bed and supports the arts, I'll overlook any crimes against good taste in another life. Hello, Alan. Please, come in."

To Alan's surprise, the interior of the home was spotlessly clean and tastefully decorated like pages out of Country Living Magazine. An assortment of throw rugs highlighted the polished light wood planked floors. Baskets of flowers and potted plants complimented the floral design wallpaper, dark English walnut-colored wainscoting, and matching floor and ceiling moldings.

"It's delightful to finally meet, Alan," Linda said brightly. "I've heard a great deal about you." Her voice was a pleasant one, words rolling off her lips like honey.

"Not from me, Alan," Evelyn informed him. "She reads rest room walls in town. Linda, I love this house more every time I visit. You have impeccable taste in interior design."

"Thank you, dear. Appearances are important, aren't they? And the home does reflect one's soul, isn't that true, Alan?"

"I think so. You've probably noticed that Evelyn has done our home in Twelfth Century Brothel."

Their genial host smiled. "I have hot water boiling for tea. Shall we go to the kitchen?"

Linda led them through the living room. The air was fragrant with the aroma of cinnamon and spices. Although sparse, the furniture was of an Early American motif. A variety of ornate metal table lamps of Tiffany glass fashionably adorned tops of oak wash stands and end tables. Tall tulip bulb floor lamps stood alongside the thick cushioned chairs and sofas. Beautifully sculptured wooden picture frames surrounded the numerous paintings that offered the only misplaced attention to interior design, being of the Cubist tradition with disjointed figures and actions, and lots of swollen-nippled breasts pointing in all directions.

The huge kitchen was spellbinding, highlighted by an ornate wood-burning oven, wall baskets, hanging utensils and cookware, glass canisters of spinach-colored pasta, and stained glass door cabinets. It was a forest of greenery, which in the daylight would mirror the verdant jungle outside the gigantic greenhouse windows, inviting in natural sunlight and offering a wondrous view. Despite the lack of running water, there was a large double washbasin sink with copper faucets, suggesting that if a plumber could ever locate the house the indoor plumbing problem might be solved.

Alan's fear of an unbearable evening began to evaporate.

"So where is Matthew, Linda?" Evelyn asked.

"Out walking in the woods. I'm surprised you didn't run into each other on the path."

"Matthew?"

"Matthew is Linda's roommate and longtime companion," Evelyn explained, exchanging a coy look with their hostess. The two women shared a giggle that reintroduced the Bugs Bunny cartoon crone into Alan's thoughts.

"Matthew and I have known each other for ages. We lived in an artist's commune in Greenwich Village before growing tired of the rat race and crime in the City. We wanted to get away from it all and so Matthew purchased this property a little over a year ago.

"So, we have another artist," Alan said feigning enthusiasm.

"He writes short stories and did very well freelancing before he burned himself out."

"I didn't burn myself out!" a gruff voice echoed behind them from the doorway. The tone was edged with hostility. "I just grew fed up with having to sell my soul to multimillion dollar conglomerates, posing as literary magazines, which didn't give a damn about whether I lived or died and only worshiped the almighty dollar." A heavily mustached man with an unnerving belligerent gaze made an entrance, craning his head and freakishly long neck like a swan in order to safely breach the threshold. At six feet, four inches tall and tipping the scales at no more than one hundred and forty pounds, a gaunt assemblage of bone and little flesh, Matthew Cartier cut a figure that would attract attention even without the pageantry of his outer trappings.

His large feet slapped heavily across the hardwood floors as Matthew sauntered toward them with an awkward camel-like gait. His black hair was cut Mohawk style on top with clean-shaven sides, allowing clearer view of a colorful assortment of earrings that ran the entire length of both ears. The back of his head was uncut and full, and the curly mane hung on his bony broad shoulders. Dark complexioned, the hawk-nosed man was a fashion disaster in multi-colored pleated pants, baggy at the thighs and tapered to an ankle collar, and a silky red Russian peasant shirt with yellow garters mid-arm. A tattooed neck peeked out from under his shirt collar. He wore combat boots that he had remembered to lace only half way, permitting the remaining twelve inches of shoelace to whip about wildly with his every step. He pushed his hair back off his shoulders pretentiously like a runway model, revealing unfurled condoms, the kind with reservoir tips, mounted on the shirt's epaulets.

Alan suppressed a smile and with arched eyebrows looked askance at his wife, who simply grinned and offered the newcomer a hug as a greeting. She then provided a formal introduction, which the beanpole and Alan cemented with a handshake. Up close, age showed in the wrinkles of Matthew's haggard face. His huge heavy-lidded eyes resembled walnuts. They appeared filled with pain, repressed anger, and the disappointment of a difficult life. His mere presence disturbed Alan at the deepest levels of consciousness.

"Nice rubbers, Matthew." Evelyn chuckled.

"One's body is a canvass for the soul's art," he said theatrically, his long fingers tracing the outline of his frame in a slow, unfolding ballet adagio. As quickly as it had mellowed, Matthew's face darkened again with anger. "God! I wore this outfit to town and people just stared at me! Literally, they just stared at me with hatred in their eyes. In New York, nobody would have even noticed. Here, they just stared." He looked to Alan. "Can you believe that?"

"Gee, no. I can't see any reason why somebody wearing condoms on their shoulders should attract any attention," he responded with exaggerated disbelief to a background of giggles from the ladies. How the hell had he let his wife Shanghai him to this insane asylum?

"What's wrong with these people?" Matthew scowled, pouting like a persecuted child. "I hate these hick farmers. They have no respect for the integrity of others. They should all be shot." With that, the lanky malcontent threw himself despondently into a big cushioned chair, his long spidery legs and giant combat boots cutting the room in half.

Then, in the wink of an eye, Matthew sprang to his feet again. With eyes wide with expression in complete contradiction to the preceding moment, he asked Evelyn whether she had brought with her the photographs she had promised. She had, pulled them from her purse and was immediately surrounded by Matthew and Linda at the table. Standing behind them, Alan made faces meant to convey to his spouse his unfavorable impression of their male host's mental health. Her eyes laughed at his antics but she managed a straight face.

"These are terrific!' Matthew gushed as he examined the photos with a keen interest and then laid each out on the round oak table, allowing him to view all the pictures in panorama.

The pursuing dialogue about colors, shapes, shadows, perspectives and comparisons demonstrated an understanding and appreciation of photographic art beyond Alan's comprehension or interest. "I've repeatedly told Evie that the nature portraits were beautiful...as good as any I've seen in books and magazines, and for years I've encouraged her to attempt to get them published." Nobody was listening so he added, "I sent a copy of the one with the two tulips to Hustler but never heard back from them. I don't have the technical expertise with which to evaluate the photos artistically, but ..."

"Evelyn, these are very professional, and publishable," Matthew proclaimed. "Don't you agree, Linda?"

Alan ignored the intrusion. "... I have always enjoyed intimate relations with barnyard animals."

His wife's smile showed her displeasure. "Without a doubt."

"Would you allow me to show these to a few people? We have friends in high places who share our fine appreciation of photographic talents."

Evelyn's excitement was tangible. "Sure! I've been considering doing something with these for some time but didn't know where to start."

The photographs were reexamined and rearranged in different orders on the table, then collected and placed back into the envelope from which they came.

"Let's retire to the dining room for supper. Shall we?" Linda suggested, leading the way.

Matthew followed with dishes and silverware, and dutifully went about preparing the table. Meanwhile, Linda turned on the stereo, inquiring if Alan has ever heard of some performer of whom he had never heard. She proceeded to play an album of bizarre noises that by comparison made Yoko Ono's whining sound like an Andy William's ballad.

"It's got a catchy beat that I could dance to, but I don't like the lyrics. I give it an eighty-six." Alan made a series of awkward dance movements. Evelyn and Linda smiled. Matthew frowned, seeming offended. Whatever festered in him needed lancing, Alan thought.

The musical discord provided the ambiance for the peculiar cuisine that Alan had fearfully anticipated. An endless assortment of political and social commentaries delivered with enmity by the taller of the hosts was also served with the meal. His discourse was made even less appealing by the unsettling way he stared right through Alan, making eye contact but never actually looking at him.

Linda tried to make light of Matthew's diatribes and with Evelyn's assistance was successful in bringing some merriment to the discourse. Unfortunately, he seemed impervious to all such attempts. Perseveration was the scarecrow's middle name and he'd start up all over again whenever the laughter subsided. He grew increasingly more hostile and frightening, until finally his ranting reached a fever pitch as he shared his feelings toward the Catholic Church and his attending parochial school.

"I had this one black-hearted nun, we called her Attila the Nun. She absolutely relished stomping up and down the aisles with her cat-o'-nine-tails, asking catechism questions and beating the living daylight out of anyone with a wrong answer or who stuttered. She was a vicious bitch, too ugly to be anything but a nun or a whore!" His hands had clenched into fists and he was battering his own thighs. "I would have enjoyed returning her favor by slowly torturing her to death. She probably experienced orgasm every time she whipped those nine leather straps across my backside," he said reenacting the beatings. "My ass would sting for days."

Alan agreed, having shared the uneasy experience of a Parochial School childhood. "Some of those nuns were pretty sadistic and seemed intent on nothing but beating our souls into shape. I think it might have been something in the holy water." He looked to Evelyn for acknowledgement of his clever quip, but received none, as she appeared far more interested in the food than in him. He took the wicked smile painted on her lips as an indication that at least she was listening. "I was elated when my parents opted to shift me over to public school. I never looked good in uniforms anyhow."

The irascible Matthew fumed. "Well, my parents thought that beatings built character and instilled discipline and humility. I went to a Catholic high school and then on to Loyola in Los Angeles. By comparison, the Jesuits were saints. Nobody could ever compare with those merciless nuns for employing torture."

Alan tried to make light of the matter. "You know what drove me crazy?"

"Oh! If you finally figured that out please do share, darling," his wife intruded.

"I meant about Catholic school. You know what drove me crazy? The way that every year they asked you the exact same catechism questions but each year also changed the answers. Remember? They'd ask 'Who made you?' In the first grade, 'God made me' was the proper response. In the second grade, 'God the Creator of heaven and earth made me' was the proper response. Then it was, 'God, the Supreme Being, Creator of heaven and earth whose only begotten Son, Jesus Christ, who was crucified and died for our sins made me.' If you ever forgot what grade you were in, look out! What a diabolical plan of indoctrination! Man, I sure as hell must have been one petrified little kid to have learned that stuff so well that it still rolls off my tongue today."

Matthew's voice trembled. "It was mind control. That's what it was. I could kill every one of …"

Linda rolled her eyes. "Oh Matthew. Get over it! Lighten up!" Turning to her guests she explained, "He has some horrible childhood memories. I wish he could just block them all out."

"Those sadistic nuns. I'd like to …"

"Matthew!" Linda interrupted sharply. "Here. Take this into the kitchen." She shoved the large kettle of nondescript all-natural soup into her inconsolable roommate's hands, then turned, rolled her eyes again and shook her head.

"I …" he began, but Linda cut him off by ramming the kettle harder into his chest and stared point blank into his eyes. Not quite under her breath she ordered, "Now!"

The sardonic Ichabod Crane cringed and did as ordered. Linda followed behind him, having collected the basket of herbal grain bread and a few teacups, still a smile on her face and shaking her head to indicate that she knew that her stork-like companion was acting childishly. "Please excuse his churlish behavior. He's like a big baby sometimes."

With his view to the kitchen unobstructed, Alan could see the backside of the barrel-chested hostess, who evidently had a few additional words of wisdom to share with Matthew. The demented peacock cowered from her, tucking his head into his shoulders and flinching at her every gesture like a puppy awaiting a smack with a rolled up newspaper. Linda pointed toward the door and her partner made haste in the direction of her gesture.

Evelyn, meanwhile, had set about gathering up the remaining dishes and silverware. She organized every last item on the table according to size and shape and transferred the piles into the kitchen. Together the two artists washed and dried dinnerware while filling the kitchen with laughter.

Left alone, Alan rose from the table and decided to busy himself by examining up close the artwork adorning the walls. On one, he counted ten breasts and only two eyes. Another had an extensive assortment of penises and scrotums in a variety of shapes, sizes, and levels of arousal. He pursed his lips and shrugged a befuddled sigh.

Following the trail of Cubist work from the dining room, he next entered a reading room. One wall was covered floor to ceiling with massive bookshelves. On another wall, ornately carved bookshelves surrounded a stone fireplace that had been sealed off. Standing on thick soapstone slabs in front of the original hearth was a Ben Franklin stove with the stone pipe vented through the ceiling. One of the remaining two walls gave background to a small sofa and two chairs each with their own oak end table supporting glass reading lamps. This wall also supported several additional canvasses that were even more offensive, having added what appeared to be a few animals and daggers leaking droplets of blood into the chromatic chaos.

The far end of the room was taken up almost entirely by two large oaken doors, but with enough wall space to display an additional painting on each side of the doorway. Both canvasses featured a malevolent goat's head with piercing crimson eyes that made Alan shudder. These drawings were masterfully painted in chiaroscuro, contrasting a myriad of shades from the red end of the color spectrum against the yellow and orange coloring of fleece and the beast's spiked horns. The paintings resembled the design engraved on the gold band of a red emerald ring he had observed on Linda's wedding finger.

Insinuating his head through the opening created by separating the massive wooden barrier, Alan discovered a chamber larger than all the other rooms he had already visited. His nostrils twitched at the lingering smell of incense and a familiar metallic scent to which he couldn't put a name. The room was void of furniture but housed the main cache of artwork. As he executed his first step into the cathedral of art, Evelyn beckoned him.

"All finished in here. Are you ready to hit the road, Al?"

Four hours past ready, he sprinted to her side even though that meant forsaking the opportunity to ogle more of Linda's creative efforts. They said their good-byes, accepting left over bland berry pie in a doggie bag from Linda and a damp handshake from her recalcitrant partner as parting gifts.

The full moon lighted the way back down the rough-honed stairs, and made for easy passage across the open field, over the wooden planked bridge, and around the cathouse. The hundred yards up the trail through the thick woods to the Pathfinder they were engulfed in a deep and unrelenting darkness that Alan feared might never end. He held his wife's hand and spoke little. When they closed the vehicle's door behind them and Evelyn started up the motor Alan signed relief.

"Well, you outdid yourself with this pair, honey."

"They're real interesting. I like them," she responded.

"Matthew is a major loon who shouldn't be walking around loose," he informed her, rolling his eyes and tilting his head to make his point.

"He's harmless, just a bit frustrated in trying to acclimate to his new surroundings."

"He's psychotic! Depressingly surly at the least."

"Depressingly surly! I see him as more like mysteriously broody."

He gave her a half-hearted smile and in his best television broadcasting voice said, "Matthew is depressingly surly. No. Matthew is mysteriously broody. Stop! You're both right. Matthew is both a depressingly surly and mysteriously broody psychotic. He's two," he clapped his hands twice mimicking the Doublemint Chewing Gum commercial, "that's right, two personalities in one."

That merited a chuckle. "You need to be a bit more understanding of others' universes."

"Yes, dear," he thought but didn't say aloud because it would have sounded too obviously condescending. Instead he nodded and asked, "Don't any of your friends eat pizza in their universe?"

Despite his outward offhandedness, his inner voice told him that these two spelled trouble.

Chapter 5

There was a noise outside the door. Samantha sat upright and moved forward in her chair. Tense, listening, she absently rotated the ring her grandmother had given her around her finger. Lately, the young LPN had begun to feel uneasy at night in the empty hospital. "Must be my imagination," she thought aloud, nervously sweeping her hair from across her forehead and shaking the long black tendrils off her shoulders.

She returned attention to massaging her patient's atrophying leg. Her slender fingers worked up the man's calf, around his knee, and across the thigh. DeLucci's limbs were waxy, holding any position in which they were placed.

"Oh! I finished reading another of your novels last night. It was terrifying. Where do you ever come up with your ideas?"

There was no response.

She hadn't really expected any, but the physicians she most respected favored a humanistic approach to treatment, and Samantha believed that even catatonic patients were listening.

"I envy your ability to make up such unusual characters and incredible stories. You have such a wonderful imagination."

DeLucci lay motionless and unresponsive.

She continued undeterred, all the while kneading her patient's thigh, encouraging the body to rejuvenate its flow of life-sustaining fluids to the dying limb.

"I understand they're making a movie of 'Yankee Run.' If it's half as scary as the book...oh boy! I couldn't sleep for a week after reading that one."

Nick DeLucci remained lifeless.

Keep plugging away Sam; he's in there somewhere.

"Oh! I also picked up the book of short stories you wrote under the Paganini pseudonym."

Her ears perked up again. This time she was certain she heard footsteps. Samantha held her breath and turned toward the door. As it opened, snakes of anxiety slithered up her back. Her palms dampened.

"Good evening, Samantha," Dr. Bralich said. "How are things going this evening?"

Wayne Alexander was close at Bralich's back. "Hi Sam." When she sighed relief, Alexander added, "I'm sorry. Did we frighten you?"

"Guess I've been a bit on edge lately. Good evening, Doctor, Mr. Alexander."

"Can I speak with you for a moment, Sam?" Alexander nodded toward the hallway.

She looked to Bralich's stoic expression and back again at Alexander. Something was wrong.

Seconds later, Bralich heard Samantha's muffled sobs in response to Alexander's bad news about Robert. Her grief was authentic, Bralich knew. Sam was a wonderfully gentle and loving young woman whose attractiveness merely reflected an internal radiance. That is why he had suggested to Robert Miller that Samantha be assigned as Nick DeLucci's private nurse.

Bralich looked down at the unusual little man in bed with ambivalent feelings of pity and revulsion. It had been Samantha who had called attention to DeLucci's singular nighttime activities. Bralich recalled how she had pulled Robert and him into the room late one evening several weeks ago.

"What is it, Sam?" Robert asked.

"I wanted you to see this. It starts about the same time every evening; just about ten."

"My word! That is some profound REM, isn't it?"

"Yes, and look at his hands." Samantha pulled back the bed sheets.

"Remarkable."

"I hadn't noticed any spasms before tonight, Dr. Miller. You had asked me to increase the massaging routine, so I had the covers pulled back. The hand movements commenced with the onset of rapid eye movement. Should I get the EEG machine so we can monitor this?"

"Good idea."

"Doctor, I know that this may sound silly, but you know what it looks like to me?"

"What Sam?"

"It looks like he's typing."

"Typing?" Robert looked toward Bralich with a questioning expression.

"Yes, like he's working on a book."

"Interesting observation, but I don't think it likely."

"Robert, the movements seem too controlled to be spasms. He is a writer and you told me yourself that this typewriter appears to be his connection to the real world."

Robert considered Bralich's words.

Sam added, "Maybe this will bring him back to us."

She had been correct about the typing. The next evening when the hand movements began, Bralich watched Robert situate the portable typewriter on a hospital meal stand above the patient's lap. DeLucci's hands went to the keyboard as if drawn by a magnet.

"Tony," Alexander said, sticking his head into the room. "I'm giving Sam the rest of the evening off and driving her home."

"Good idea."

Samantha reentered the room, tears trickling down her cheeks from her molasses colored eyes. She reached out for Bralich. "I'm sorry for your loss, Dr. Bralich."

"Thank you, Sam."

She kissed his cheek, gently hugging him.

"You're all right, Tony?" the administrator asked.

"I'll be fine."

"I can stay, Doctor, if you need me," Samantha added.

"Go home, Sam, and get a good night's sleep."

She took hold of the arm that Wayne Alexander offered and headed toward the door.

Bralich checked his watch; nine-forty. The theatrics would begin shortly. The antiquated Smith-Corona was next to the bed on a bedside stand with a large stack of perforated computer paper that Sam fed into the cartridge of the obsolete machine each evening. He positioned the stand over the patient's midsection. Separating previously typed sheets from the stack, he then arranged the perforated paper in a neat stack behind the typewriter so it would self-feed without jamming.

"What have you been up to, my little friend?" he asked aloud as he examined the nonsense pages. His mind wandered.

"This is very unusual, Tony."

"What is, Robert?"

"Well, the records indicate that he was abandoned and placed in a children's home in California."

"Yes?"

"It appears that he was transferred to an orphanage in New Jersey."

"Transferred? Do orphans get transferred? To other states?"

"I don't know for certain, but I think not. It does, however, create some interesting parallels with his writing."

"Oh?"

"Fantasies and projections, most likely, but ... "

"I don't believe you sound as certain as you once were," Tony Bralich said, leaning over his desk. *It looks like your trail starts in California."*

Tat-a-tat-a-tat-a-tat the typewriter clattered, startling Bralich to attention.

Only the inordinate amount of rapid eye movement behind DeLucci's large, walnut shaped eyelids matched the bustling activity of his stubby misshapen fingers as they pounded on the outmoded keyboard. The remainder of his anatomy was devoid of any animation. DeLucci's face was changeless, frozen in a grotesque mask of liquefied flesh that hung in such a manner that it appeared as if it would detach from his skull. It was a face that horrified most of the staff and, Bralich suspected, most everyone who had ever had the misfortune to witness it during this patient's forty plus years in an unkind world.

Tat-a-tat-a-tat-a-tat ding. A tiny hand clutched at the return lever and dragged the cartridge cylinder back to the left, sliding the machine along the surface of the bedside stand, yet barely skipping a beat. Tat-a-tat-a-tat-a-tat.

Rubbing the stubble on his chin, Bralich looked down at the fruits of the explosive activity; a nonsense grouping of letters. "What are you trying to tell us, Nick?"

It's as if he is working on a book. That's what Samantha had said.

The thought stopped Bralich. Robert had mentioned that DeLucci had been working on a new manuscript. He had carried the pages of his latest efforts along with his typewriter to each of his therapy sessions. Surely, these must be somewhere in Robert's office. Bralich hadn't read them, but Robert had, and uncovered within the unfinished manuscript pages clues that enabled Robert to track down DeLucci's mother.

"Are you completing Embodiment of Evil, Nick? Is that what you're doing?"

Tat-a-tat-a-tat-a-tat.

Bralich hurried down the empty corridors passed the nurses' station toward Miller's office.

"Good evening, Dr. Bralich." The nurse on duty called out.

"Evening," he responded without looking up.

Robert's office was across the hall from his own Spartan confines, and Bralich spent enough time there to find his way around with little effort. He sat down in the heavily cushioned chair at Robert's desk. A nine-by-twelve photo of Robert and Lois Miller occupied the center focal point on the desk. He reached for the photograph. She had been so beautiful, and her suicide devastated Robert. That had been about a year ago, at about the time that Nick DeLucci had first begun individual therapy sessions with Miller.

DeLucci's file was housed in the lower right desk drawer. Locating the thick folder, Bralich laid it open atop the desk. Inside were more of the perforated computer pages of gibberish that DeLucci had been typing every evening, but none of the original manuscript Bralich hoped to find. Could Robert have taken it with him? He fingered through the pages lost in his thoughts.

The grandfather clock in the corner sounded eleven o'clock. He had to teach a class in the morning. Alexander hadn't mentioned anything about funeral arrangements and whether the police would release Robert's remains to him or to the hospital since there were no living relatives to claim them. Maybe he would just sleep here in the hospital and talk to Wayne in the morning first thing before heading out to Columbia.

With tired eyes, he labored through the DeLucci's ramblings. Occasionally, a line or two of readable text jumped out at him.

... head bowed, he looked up from under his thickly furrowed brow, his

glare filled with an icy fury that propagated outwardly tentacles of terror that wrapped fear around Alan's brain, strangling his mind. Unremitting...

Then, five pages later:

The house on Walnut Avenue had burned down, but police forensics had determined that the remains found in it did not belong to Danny Cox...

The notion that he was overlooking the obvious cawed at Bralich's brain, but his aging body was losing a battle to fatigue. "Shift your frame of reference," his mind whispered as the last remnants of wakefulness evaporated and he slipped away into dreams of Robert Miller.

Chapter 6

Alan Ciani was disoriented. The last thing he remembered was laying down on the waterbed.

His breath misted in front of his eyes and floated ghost-like up to the dimly lit city streetlights. A cold night air vibrated with urgency. He had seen this place before, had shuddered with the same fearful anticipation he was now experiencing.

Harm lurked in the unfeeling and incoherent city that sprung up around him. Demons danced in the alleyways, and wickedness conspired in dark corners and dingy tenements. He could feel evil spirits hovering all around him in the discordant cacophony and ambient light of the unnatural metropolis. Perched atop the monolithic monuments, concrete gargoyles readied to pounce. His heart raced out of control.

Alan had always felt out of his element and secretly feared cities. He couldn't say why, but he felt hostage to those fears. He longed for silent skies salted by crystal stars.

His mind filled with the anticipation of dread as he plodded through the alley, his head turned to one side and collar up to fend off the cold. Every step brought on a rush of memories that gnawed at his brain like the gusty winds biting at his face. There were blank spaces in between blurred images. Nothing seemed to fit together. The body of Stevie Cox materialized, wiggling and squirming, fighting off death. Alan reached for his dying friend, then pulled back as eyes snapped open on what remained of Stevie's bloodied and mutilated face.

The corpse spat out unconnected sentences with machine gun rapidity. "The campfire on the river. You don't know what it's like to lose your little girl. He was the Devil," Stevie screamed, gurgling blood and phlegm. "Devil...devil...devil." The voice faded into distant echoes as the illusion evaporated like some kind of magic trick.

Alan shuddered with fear, but that emotion dissipated as quickly as his friend's specter had. He moved on, ever vigilant looking over his shoulder for whatever unseen horror stalked him.

"You had better be careful," a venomous munchkin voice spat at him mockingly from somewhere below his line of sight.

A twisted and bent creature on a wooden dolly sprang out from the nothingness of shadows, out of the dark and foreboding world that existed only in the darkest recesses of Alan's mind. "I'm dreaming," he thought.

Bulbous eyes protruding from a misshapen head looked up at him, locked in a threatening stare. The dwarf's face was a nightmarish mask frozen in a menacing grin. "You're lost, asshole," the little man snapped with certainty, "You had better go back. You shouldn't leave your woman alone."

Alan struggled for a breath as he considered the suggestion and its implications, but couldn't hold the thought.

As quickly as he had appeared, the creature turned and vanished into the night. "There are no answers here," the munchkin voice cackled from the darkness. "Go back!"

The sun catapulted into the night sky, nighttime erupting into day without warning. A decaying fortress pushed its way up through the barren earth and anchored itself to the ground with giant talons. An old man with a grizzled beard and penetrating eyes jabbed his finger at Alan.

In a voice sounding like a record played at the wrong speed, the old man roared, "T-h-e r-i-v-e-r!" A hint of burning flesh insinuated itself upon his senses.

Alan turned and ran. Gripped by terror, he labored every step. An unseen evil was close at his heels, ready to pounce on him, consume him, and inflict him with its malignancy. He pumped his arms and legs with all the exertion he could muster in order to out-distance the pestilence. His knees and head jolted, corresponding to the repetitive thud, thud, thud of feet striking the unpaved road.

A second wind rushed oxygen into his blood and lightened his steps. His urgency lessened. Up ahead above the tree line, he spotted the top of the big rock he recognized as the Indian God Rock. The massive boulder was adorned with ancient writing as well as graffiti that dated back to the late seventeenth century. According to his wife and local lore, it functioned as a make-out spot for over three hundred years.

Suddenly, the force of gravity amplified, exerting an enormous pressure that compacted his body into the ground. His second wind evaporated as quickly as it had materialized.

As Alan rounded the tree-lined curve, the gargoyle-faced dwarf reappeared at the base of the rock, ravenous hunger emanating from his eyes.

"You needn't feel all alone," a high-pitched disembodied voice informed him.

When another, more familiar, voice called out, "Hey, are you looking for me, paisan?" he froze in place. Silhouetted by the morning sun was Danny Cox, standing completely naked atop the massive boulder.

"Come to join us, Alan?"

At Danny's feet lay a woman, her hands bound in front of her. She too was naked except for a hood covering her head. Danny's foot was planted on her chest, pinning the woman's tanned body to the granite. She turned toward Alan. Her dark eyes and sensuous mouth were visible through the large circular openings cut into the hood's fabric. He could read the pleading in her eyes.

Danny Cox sneered, his handsome face suddenly wild and cruel, filled with a demonic lust. His hirsute and muscled chest heaved. "Do you know me?" he asked.

It took Alan to his limits to summon a response. "Yes," he muttered finally in response.

"Do you know me?" Danny asked again, punctuating every word with malicious intent.

Again Alan struggled to find his words. "Yes, I know you."

"You pathetic little man," he laughed; a laughter that grew increasingly more deafening and animal-like. It echoed across the wide river with such volume that out of necessity Alan cupped his hands over his ears to shut out the noise.

His surroundings morphed into a swirling vortex of phantasmagoria. Amidst the clamor and confusion, Danny pounced on the woman like a beast on fallen prey as the dwarf cackled in eerie delight, quivering with inhuman pleasure at the captive woman's whimpering.

Alan started toward the giant slab of stone to intercede but was stopped dead in his tracks as Danny turned toward him, his eyes narrowed into glowing red serpentine slits. Frozen in mid-step, Alan could do nothing but watch as Danny pried his captive's legs apart with his knees and forcefully entered the woman. Her screams served only to incite Danny to more violent action. He struck at her face and body with a clenched fist. Alan's stomach turned sour.

The victim now showed little resistance. With each passing second and a changing in their body alignment to a more participatory position, it became clear that what he was witnessing was not rape at all, but mere theatrics to engage him. His eyes remained riveted in the coupled partners' frenzied gyrations.

With the grace of well-rehearsed acrobats, they contorted into a new position, the woman total in her submission to Danny's domination. Alan felt himself aroused. His hand slid to his groin to discover himself erect. He felt ashamed,

Panting and howling returned his attention to the rock. Before his disbelieving eyes, Danny's lower torso metamorphosed into a physical form more appropriate with its current manner of bestial copulation. The woman stared at Alan and now appeared much closer spatially to him than she had been only moments ago. She smiled an affected and familiar grin that Alan knew was meant to inflict mental pain. He knew this woman!

"I am ready for the child," Danny bellowed.

It was at that instant that Alan first became cognizant of a child's fearful sobbing. He looked past Danny in the direction of the spasmodic yelps. Seated in a rusted cage, a young girl, hooded and bound by rope, choked on her tears.

"Please help me," she cried out in anguish and fear between gulps for breath.

"Bring the virgin to me," the unnatural creature that Danny had become commanded. His sexual partner obeyed.

The child's wailing accelerated to a hysterical shrieking pitch.

"You must choose," the dwarf instructed Alan.

Alan found himself tap dancing on the edge on hysteria. "Choose?"

The child was placed at Danny's feet, naked except for her bonds and the hood that covered her head.

At Alan's side the dwarf stood clutching a crescent shaped knife in his disfigured fist. "A sacrifice is required and it is your choice as to the lamb." A mischievous anger contorted his already hideous countenance. "Be a man for crissake!" he said in a tone saturated with contempt. The words came out in an airy hiss. "Choose or we choose for you!"

Alan was stunned to incapacity.

A sudden flashing of metal momentarily blinded him. There was a wet gasping sound followed by a thud similar to that made by a watermelon splattering on the ground. When Alan's sight cleared he saw that Danny's head had rolled down the rock and lay at his feet. A nauseating quiver filled Alan's stomach.

Another flash! There was a lot of blood. Danny's body crumpled into a pile of flesh, then slid down the face of the Indian God Rock as the monstrous dwarf brandished the knife above his head in a victory wave.

He knew that he would not escape this scene with his sanity intact.

"Dreams are the vehicles of portent," the diminutive troll hissed between gritted teeth, stroking the backs of his hands as if trying to wipe clean his blackened and rotting fingernails. The hatred in his eyes was so fierce that it skewered Alan.

To Alan's further disgust, the bloodied gremlin dug his twisted claw-like hand into the lifeless form that had once been Danny Cox and wrenched the heart from the carcass. It was as black as a lump of charcoal. "Evil rests in the heart of all men," he snickered, holding out the black mass to Alan and brandishing the look of someone savoring a delicacy. "Take heart, Pilgrim. Partake, for this is our body."

This could not be real. Gripped by hysteria, grasping for air, Alan turned to flee with the voiceprints of violence still ringing in his ears. His arm and legs flailed uncontrollably, unable to coordinate any movement that would permit him escape from these terrors. He screamed, uncertain that any sound escaped his lips.

"Wake up. Wake up, Alan!"

Alan screamed. His eyes snapped open.

"Are you all right?" his wife asked. Long tendrils of thick dark hair fell across her face.

"Nightmare," he panted. "I guess I'm having a nightmare."

"About what?" she queried, staring darkly at him.

"I don't know," he lied. It frightened him to think that the wickedness that permeated his nocturnal dreams even existed in his mind, and feared even more that putting such pornographic thoughts into words might somehow validate them. Although he recognized that one could not control their dreams, he felt both guilty and embarrassed for having them.

"You are an odd duck, you strange little man," she teased, but Alan heard the ever-present undercurrent of disdain in her voice. "You live in constant denial, can't tell the difference between dreams and reality, can you?"

"Tried reality once. It just didn't work for me," he retorted, sweaty and still shaking.

"Think you can fall back to sleep?"

The digital clock on the bedside end table told him that it was five-o-one. He was wide-awake, he realized. "No, I don't think so."

"Well, I'm exhausted, so if it's okay with you I'll try," she huffed rolling away from him and pulling the covers back over her shoulders. "Why don't you go watch TV or read a book to make your eyes tired. Preferably nothing scary."

Reluctantly, Alan got out of bed, fully aware that the act of standing meant acknowledging that he would be starting the new day.

What should have been the tranquility of the pre-dawn hours instantly transformed into an amusement park of hidden terrors. Floors creaked ominously. Elusive shadows scurried from corner to corner only to vanish when he confronted them. Beyond each window, camouflaged among the trees, demonic eyes watched his every move. His night terrors had come to define his waking reality. There were devils in his head.

A tiny voice of rationality struggled to be heard beneath the weight of mind-numbing fear. This paranoia was complete foolishness, he told himself, but he was a hostage to these misgivings. He expected Danny Cox and his companions to materialize right there in his home.

At the doorway to the upstairs bathroom, he cautiously reached around the corner seeking the light switch. Only after a shower of fluorescence offered safe passage could he dare enter. A bath of Epson salts might relax him, he thought, and as he acted on his impulse, caught sight of his own reflection in the mirror. Over the past few days when he saw his reflection the image that stared back at him looked like someone else. He looked ungodly.

He drew a bath. Water thundered from the spigot, exploding onto the surface of the porcelain tub. He tested the temperature with his foot and stepped into the tepid water. Steam quickly engulfed the room. Closing his eyes, he sank into the protective envelop of warms fluids and placed a warm washcloth over his face.

In his head, Alan recited the mantra he had memorized from a self-hypnosis tape he had purchased.

Breath deeply, slowly. Visualize each breath as it enters the nostrils and flows peacefully into the lungs. It circulates there, oxygen nourishing the body. Exhale all tension. Relax. My eyelids are heavy. All expression evaporates like mist from my face leaving it relaxed. My entire body is relaxed. Another deep breathe. Exhale. My mind is at rest, peaceful.

The slow drip from the tub's spigot intruded into Alan's consciousness, battling against his serenity. Each drop seemed to increase in volume, pounding a maddening rhythm inside his brain.

A droplet of perspiration trickled on to his lips and he twitched with agitation. He dabbed with annoyance at the succeeding globules with his tongue. They tasted coppery.

His nostrils filled with a metallic scent. He attempted to rub the odor from his senses but the intensity of the pungent scent only increased. Annoyed, he removed the washcloth from his face. His eyes widened with horror, realizing he lay submerged in a bath of blood. A knot tightened in his stomach.

He fought against his body's involuntary gagging response.

Without warning, his head plunged below the red liquid, a powerful hand pinching his nostrils shut while another pushed heavily upon his chest. There was no air. His lungs were bursting. He struggled but was helpless against the tremendous force being exerted upon him.

Somebody was screaming words he could not decipher.

"Wake up, you fool! Are you trying to drown yourself?" Evelyn scolded as she pulled him by the chin and hair above the water's surface. "You're damn lucky that I couldn't fall back to sleep and decided to check on you or you'd be dead meat!" She sighed a haughty breath. "Alan, what is going on with you?" Her voice was hard and unsympathetic.

Uncertainty held his tongue. For three consecutive evenings, his psyche had been prisoner to the identical torturous dream. Dread had been creeping into his life during the last few months but it wasn't until his trip to the West Coast that these malignant fears had begun to take shape. Now this trepidation had found expression through his dreams. Like a chain of dominoes set in motion with the felling of the first black rectangle, he felt helpless to stop it. The impenetrable wall he had constructed for to ward off the painful onslaught of horrid memories was crumbling.

Chapter 7

Bralich rubbed the sleep from his eyes, struggling to focus on whoever was accosting him from his slumber.

"Wake up, you crotchety old coot," Wayne Alexander commanded.

The psychiatrist scratched the back of his head and yawned. "What time is it?"

"Eight-fifteen."

As the last vestiges of grogginess fell away, Bralich shot up. "Jesus! I have a nine o'clock class."

"Not to worry, Big Guy. I've called you a cab." Alexander looked at his wristwatch. "It'll be here in ten minutes. If you can get your wretched bones in high gear, you'll make it to class with time to spare. Work all night again?"

"Just reading," he said gathering up the garbled DeLucci manuscript.

"Gibberish," the administrator snorted. "How are you feeling this morning? You okay?" he asked with concern.

"Don't pretend you give a rat's ass about how I feel. Don't you have pencils to sharpen or bed pans to count?" He was up, on his feet, and heading toward the sink to freshen up. He couldn't walk onto campus looking like a derelict.

"That must be psycho-babble for 'Fine, thank you, and how are you this glorious morning?' Well, I'm doing as well as can be expected given that one of my associates has just lost their life in a tragic car accident. Thanks for asking."

Bralich cupped water over his face and scalp, and smoothed the wild hairs in his beard. The mirror had grown increasingly uncomplimentary over the years. While he had become accustomed to the effects of aging on his body, he found it increasingly difficult to see his advancing years so severely sketched upon his face. No wonder Wayne's salutations were expressed in chronologically challenged terms that reinforced that Bralich should have retired years ago. Maybe he should have, but he needed to keep busy, have a routine. "Did you check up on Samantha this morning?" he asked drying his hands.

"She's very upset. I think maybe her feelings toward Robert extended beyond their professional association."

"You shouldn't waste your time thinking, Wayne. You'll only hurt yourself."

"Fuck you, you miserable curmudgeon."

"Not if you were the last disease-free sentient being on the planet," Bralich said grabbing the brown corduroy sports coat that had functioned as his pillow during the night. He hung it over one arm and tried to rub out the wrinkles with his hand as he went across the hall to his own office. Alexander was close behind.

"Tony, when the police called last night regarding Robert's accident, they informed me that they took his…remains to Lakewood Hospital to do a post mortem. Since he had no surviving family, I took the liberty of approving their arrangements."

"I'm family, damn it." he bellowed in knee-jerk reaction. He pulled back his emotions and stoically added, "Thank you, Wayne."

"I told them I'd call back this morning regarding cremation. You okay with that?"

"That would have been his choice."

"Okay. I'll tell them to go ahead and send a driver down to pick up the urn for you."

"I'd appreciate that," he said stuffing his briefcase and avoiding eye contact to hide his emotion. "Really, thanks." Closing his case, he headed for the elevator across from the nurses station with Alexander at his side.

Wayne put his hand on Bralich's shoulder. "Tony, what was Robert doing? Why was he pushing himself so hard these last few weeks."

He had asked Robert the same question although he knew the answer. Working on other things to avoid dealing with your own personal pain was a tactic he had often employed in his own life. Pressing the button to summon the elevator, he replied, with a half-truth, "Robert felt responsible."

Alexander took a step closer and lowered his voice. "His office is filled with books on Satanism and witchcraft, and literature on multiple personalities. Not exactly light reading. This is all related to DeLucci, isn't it?"

"I don't know." It wasn't the first bold-faced lie he had ever told Alexander and it wouldn't be the last. Even big-hearted bureaucrats should not be trusted unconditionally.

A ding chimed the elevator's arrival. When the door opened, Bralich stepped through and pressed the button for the main lobby. He conjured up his most insincere smile, "But when I do, you'll be the first kid on your block I'll tell. That's a promise, Boss."

The doors slid closed between them and the elevator jerked into motion.

A pang of guilt gnawed at Bralich. He had steered Robert toward exploring the implications of the occult in the DeLucci case.

"I've checked out these two books from the university library on your behalf, Robert. They're written by a therapist in New Jersey who has been treating multiple personalities."

"Surely you're not suggesting that DeLucci is a case of multiples."

"This second book, 'Satan's Foundlings,' you may find particularly interesting. It reviews case histories of multiples who reportedly were raised in Satanic covens."

"Jesus!"

"Have you made inquiries in California?"

"And New Jersey. Additional records are in the mail. Why multiples, Tony?"

"A hunch.

"The etiology?"

"Severe trauma, too powerful and threatening for a young child to withstand; repression and denial in their most extreme forms."

"Resulting in the fragmentation of the ego."

Bralich shrugged. "Read a few more of your patient's novels, too, Robert. Fiction isn't always completely contrived."

A few days later, Robert Miller had called him at home.

"I've read the books you gave me on multiples as well as a three more of the DeLucci novels. The parallels are astonishing. No matter how cleverly disguised in the plots, the satanic themes are too graphic to be pure imagination."

"I suspected as much, Robert. The fact that it was the hypnosis which triggered a complete withdrawal is what set me thinking in that direction."

"It's as if he was programmed not to allow certain memories to surface in their original context."

"Hmm, programmed! That's an interesting supposition."

"The question is, given his current condition, how can we de-program him in order to re-integrate his multiples if they exist?"

"Anything on the mother yet?"

"I'm still working on that."

"You obtained a list of other children who were transferred out of the Children's Home in Garden Grove. Correct?"

"Yes."

"It will be interesting to see what kind of adults these children have become. Can you find the time to follow up on some of the names?"

"I'll make time. There's one other thing, Tony. As I read his novels, something kept gnawing at me that I couldn't quite point my finger on, something subtle. It drove me crazy like an itch you can't scratch. It took me awhile to figure out but finally I got it."

Bralich cocked his head in anticipation of the explanation.

"It was so obvious once I could put words to it. All of his stories were out of time. There is no modern technology or even awareness of anything current. No cell phones or the Internet or any sort of devices with the exception of maybe names of automobiles that have become commonplace. His analogies and similes are rooted in the sixties and early seventies. All of Nick's characters are thirty years out of time. You know what finally allowed me to make the connection?"

Instantly it came to him. *"The Smith-Corona."*

"Yes, the Smith-Corona. He still works on a typewriter and carries that bulky, inefficient thing around instead of computer."

"His world is fixated in the past."

"I need to make a paradigm shift backwards if I'm going to help him," Robert said as if thinking aloud. *"Oh, there is another interesting pattern*

on which I picked up in his novels, Tony. The child characters in his novels are virtually all faceless. They have personalities and participate in engaging dialogue with the adult characters, but seldom are any physical descriptions of them provided. They're little more than stage props for the most part."

Bralich stepped out of the elevator and walked briskly to the cab pickup station outside the front door of the facility.

A cabby with wild frizzy red hair and wearing a military fatigue jacket was leaning out the window of a battered Yellow Cab. "You, Dr. Bralich?"

"Yes," he answered and got in. The enclosed confines of the vehicle amplified the unpleasant stench of the city.

"Columbia University. Psychology Building, right?"

"Yes, thank you. And I'm running late."

"I'll have you there in fifteen minutes…twenty at the outside," the cabby informed him confidently. He glanced at the side mirror and back over his shoulder, then punched the gas and slid through an infinitesimally narrow space between two oncoming trucks. "My old stomping grounds," the cabby said, oblivious to the bleating complaints registered by other drivers who didn't realize he was sharing his road with them

"Pardon me?" Bralich peeked at the cabby's license posted on the dashboard, "Mr. Albans."

"Tommy. Call me, Tommy. Everyone does. Columbia is my old stomping grounds. Got my BS there in Social Work. You teach?"

"Yes, I do."

"That's the direction I'm headed, too. Applying to a couple of graduate programs." He braked sharply in order to change lanes, again to the discontent of other sojourners on the New York roadway.

"It's a noble profession."

"That's what I once thought about social work. Man, was I ever naïve."

"Oh?"

"Pray to God you never find yourself trapped in the social services web. Shit…I got stories that would curdle your blood, Doc!"

The cabby pounded his horn and swerved to miss another cab. "Fuck you! You goddamn fucken idiot!" he yelled, sticking his head out the window and supporting his argument with a finger gesture. "Goddamn towel heads, should be riding camels." The back of his neck reddened, matching the color of his hair. "Social services are a sewer, an absolute dung heap."

As his driver continued his diatribe, memories danced across Bralich's mind.

Miller looked perplexed. "The Home in Garden Grove was shut down, Tony, allegedly some kind of scandal. The children were redistributed all over the map."

"The scandal...was it fiscal or human atrocity?"

"The latter from what I could find out. The facility records were sealed and there wasn't a single mention of any indiscretions in the local papers. However, I did find a talkative ex-employee who claims that sexual abuse was a problem."

"Isolated cases or ritualistic?"

"I couldn't tie my source to anything specific but ritualistic is a plausible guess. Everything was really hushed up and the whole matter seemed taboo. You would think that something so horrific would be front page news for months."

"Such atrocities have seen the light of day only in recent years. Pre-fifties and sixties were the Dark Ages as far as mental health facilities go. State institutions were notorious for employing socially functioning sociopaths and marginal schizoid personalities."

"That's a comforting thought."

The cab came to a jolting halt.

"Psychology Building. Made it in seventeen minutes and fifteen seconds," the cabby said looking at his watch, then at Bralich for validation.

"How much do I owe you, Tommy?" Bralich asked leaning over the front seat.

"That'll be forty dollars."

There was an open newspaper on the front seat. "What's this?" He fingered the section that had letters penciled in.

"Huh? Oh, you mean the Cryptoquote. I pride myself as being the fastest Cryptoquote solving hack in the city. Takes me a couple of minutes to solve regardless of how difficult they make 'em."

Bralich pulled the paper to his face, knitting his eyebrows across his forehead in concentration. "Paradigm shift!"

"What? Oh yeah, I never thought of it that way. I just look at the grouping of letters and try to find what might be the most common small words found in a quote. You know like 'I', 'a', 'the', 'that', 'he is', 'you are', etcetera. Once you can assign a few letters to the small words everything else falls into place."

"Very good, Tommy." He pulled three twenty-dollar bills from his wallet to pay for his fare, including a generous tip.

"Thanks, Doc."

"Good luck with graduate school," he said exiting the vehicle.

"You bet," the cabby said, checked traffic and sped away.

Bralich patted his briefcase to his chest, lost in thought, and hurried for class.

Chapter 8

Footsteps pounded across the ceiling from Vinnie's bedroom immediately above them. The ceiling vibrated with the hard drum background of Fleetwood Mac as his son harmonized with Stevie Nicks. Alan lay in bed waiting for the rest of the household to come to life.

Evelyn unfurled from her fetal position, stretched her arms and legs like a cat. A mouse-like screech, her version of "good morning," preceded a gentle pumping and grinding of her buttocks into Alan's groin. She turned her head toward him, opened her eyes with a smile and another screech, and pecked his cheek. "Good morning, Sunshine. Ew! You don't look much more rested today. I could go traveling with those saddlebags under your eyes. Are you getting sick?"

Years of marriage had taught Alan that her inquiry as to his health was merely a reflex, much like the way a sneeze elicits a "God bless you," even from an atheist.

Had he ever been in love with this woman, he pondered? The question warranted no thoughtful response. She had gotten pregnant and he couldn't overcome the guilt incubated by his Catholic upbringing. He stayed married and tried to keep things upbeat for the children.

Evelyn rolled out of bed and dropped to the floor to select clothing to wear from the dresser drawers upon which the waterbed rested.

At this juncture, Alan desperately needed to talk about his experience in California and the three nights of recurring terror he had undergone since. Before he could broach the subject, however, a car pulled up the drive outside their bedroom window, announcing itself with a fit of coughing and a loud backfire. A car door slammed, followed by the sound of heavy footsteps approaching the house.

Evelyn slipped a rugby shirt over her head and adroitly stepped into denims. She was into the hallway before the doorbell rang.

The gruff voice of Matthew Cartier echoed through the house, "Everybody up and at it?"

"What are you doing out and about so early?" Evelyn wanted to know.

"Linda and I are going on a hike."

"We thought you and Alan might care to join us," Linda's syrupy voice chimed in.

When Alan heard his wife exclaim, "Terrific!" he gritted his teeth, wording profanities under his breathe. Spending the day with these two freaks was more than he could stomach. Wasn't one evening sacrifice enough to maintain what passed for marital bliss in this relationship?

Evelyn beckoned her guests into the bedroom while she extended their invitation to the "slug in the bed." Within seconds, the voices had materialized into the personages of Evelyn, Matthew Cartier and Linda Windsor, all hovering above Alan as he lay in bed. He diplomatically greeted the visitors, hoping his lack of enthusiasm for their company didn't show.

It was apparent that Matthew hadn't listened to or understood the weather report which forecasted high seventies to low eighties temperatures. He was outfitted in a long black overcoat that reached to the tops of his unlatched rubber boots. A leather Elmer Fudd hunter's cap with the earflaps down and the chinstraps dangling crowned his unshaven face. He looked like an escaped mental patient, and if that were true it would not shock Alan in the least. He offered Alan a boisterous hello and reptilian smile, neither of which disguised the intensely hostile, untrusting look always present in his troubled eyes.

"Get dressed, husband dearest. We're going for a little hike."

"I can't. I'm still wiped out. Must be jet lag."

"Please do join us, Alan. We'd treasure your participation," Linda crooned in her Bizarro World couture; Margaret Thatcher on LSD. "We thought we might explore the Indian God Rock and then search for the lost Indian burial grounds that allegedly are a mile or so upstream." She stroked the back of her hands as she spoke. Her fingernails were again painted black, as were her lips, and the mere sight of them made him uneasy. Beneath her cordial expression a message waiting to be deciphered seemed to lay in waiting

"Come on, Alan," Evelyn demanded with her hiking boots in hand.

"I can't, Evie. I haven't slept in days. The exertion would kill me. You'd wind up carrying my carcass back with you."

The look in his wife's eyes told him that she would just leave his body where it fell for the scavengers to pick. "It's no wonder you can't sleep. You never get any exercise. What happened to the super-jock I married?" There was a trumpeting defiance in her voice and the feigned jesting was meant to sting.

When he shrugged, Evelyn crossed her arms over her chest, frowned and informed him, "Well, then, you're responsible for the children today. Enjoy."

"Maybe the girls would like to accompany us," Linda said.

"Oh, Jesus! They're not even out of bed yet."

Fifteen minutes later, the two artists and their stork-like, psychotic Sherpa left behind their farewells and were out the door. Alan watched from the window as they packed into a beat up burgundy Corvair. When the ignition switch summoned up only dry heaves, Matthew jumped out of the car cursing and began pushing the rusting scrap down the driveway. As the vehicle picked up momentum, he managed on the run to contort his lanky frame back inside and popped the clutch into gear, a technique that looked well practiced. The compact bucked once, hiccupped, and then started, vomiting a cloud of blue smoke. They chugged off down the road.

Alan sluggishly performed his morning rituals. He didn't find the bathroom mirror flattering. Evie was right; the huge bags under his somnolent eyes transformed his normally smooth olive complexion an unhealthy gray and made his Roman nose appear elephantine. When he finally made his way to the kitchen, he found the girls awake, dressed, and doing Julia Child impressions.

"Now you roll the dough into a little ball," Gabrielle, his sixteen-year-old was explaining in an exaggerated quivering falsetto, "and when your younger sister isn't paying careful attention, throw it at her!" The soft projectile hit Tia between her eyes, stuck momentarily, and then rolled down her cheek. Laughing, Gabby brushed her long blonde tendrils off her forehead with the back of her wrists. She was favored by her Neapolitan heritage, round and shapely, fleshy lips that would make her voluptuous as she grew into womanhood. Now, her hands and much of her face was powdered white with flour.

Tia looked more like her mother with the finely chiseled features of a model. She was more than pretty and, because of her beauty, Alan's other two children complained she was often given preferential treatment. Alan denied it, of course, although he knew it was the truth. Like Evelyn, brassy and green-eyed, Tia was never to be outdone. "Of course," she began, mimicking her sister's high-pitched impersonation, "there are many uses for common household flour. The most important is as hair coloring." She dumped a cup of the staple over Gabby's head and giggled.

Alan had grown accustomed to such antics and knew his daughters found as much enjoyment in destroying the kitchen as in the results of their culinary efforts. They shared in common the capacity to laugh easily and often, a quality he cherished in his girls. "I see that you girls are baking again. Other than a mess what are you making?"

The two Julia's chimed, "Cinnamon rolls!" and looking at each other with mischief, each stuffed an uncooked ball of dough into the other's mouth. Gabby chewed a few times, and then opened her mouth to reveal the half-eaten morsels. "Lookths gud, huh duhdee?"

"Save me a couple if any make it into the oven."

Bone-tied, he staggered out to the back deck and stared at the lake. Building the deck with a southeastern exposure had been the most useful improvement he had made to the home. He situated a lounge chair to take advantage of the sun's warming rays as it ascended above the treetops.

Stretched out in the chair, he watched sunbeams dance over the motionless waters. Two hikers, a young couple in bright-colored t-shirts and safari shorts, both with sweatshirts tied around their waist, emerged hand-in-hand from the towering conifers encircling the lake. Their shaggy black Newfoundland puppy slapped its oversized paws on the soft moss-covered ground, trying to keep pace with its companions without abandoning its playful pursuit of butterflies. The hikers waved and called out a greeting, which he returned. The Newfoundland looked up at the sound of Alan's voice and barked "hello." Alan smiled to himself and bade it a good day as well. The trio continued down the path until the thick woods swallowed them up again.

Tia poked her head out of the back door to report that the first batch of cinnamon rolls were ready and announce her sister's arrival with the goodies.

Alan selected the largest one off the tray and took a bite.

"Well?" Gabby asked awaiting the praise she richly deserved.

"Terrific! They're nice and gooey, just the way I like 'em."

The girls' faces swelled with pride.

"There's more coming," Tia added. She draped her arms over Alan's shoulders from behind him and kissed the top of his head. "Love you, Daddy."

"You too, Sweetie." Ensconced in the lounge, he stared up into the cloudless blue sky, savoring the moment, and the pastry.

His sleep-weary body ached and could manage only another large bite before sleep crept over him. Fitful dreams of his old high school buddies, Stevie and Danny Cox, and the fearful sobs of a little girl squirmed around in his brain.

Chapter 9

Bralich unconsciously straightened his tie and tugged at his shirtsleeve. "Can you do it, Jack?"

"Not if you keep interrupting me," Jack Widowmaker answered. "You're rather impatient for a psychotherapist, Tony. I thought you guys were supposed to be the paragon of internal serenity."

Bralich assumed his associate was cracking funny but he could never really tell for sure. Widowmaker appeared always to be at attention, both physically and interpersonally. He either lacked a sense of humor, Bralich thought, or the ability to make one evident. "Another stereotype bites the dust, I fear. By the way, I'm a psychiatrist."

Widowmaker showed no outward sign that the distinction meant anything of significance.

"I thought I had a pattern for a few lines, but it didn't hold up." Bralich had worked on deciphering the DeLucci manuscript during his first class while disgruntled students struggled with an unscheduled class assignment. He hoped that Widowmaker, a new addition to the university's Mathematics Department with twenty years of service as a cryptographer for Naval Intelligence, would have better luck with the task. Since the end of the Cold War and after every military action since then, the university flooded with retired armed services personnel. He wondered back then what long-term consequences this massive influx of authoritarian mindsets might affect on the intellectual environment. Time had given evidence to his worse scenarios. Much of the student body as well as the faculty had become mindless sheep, who not only lacked the intellectual acumen to question authority but also took extreme offense to those who did. Nonetheless, Widowmaker possessed a sharp mind and despite a few personality quirks and his military pedigree, Tony liked him.

The cryptographer combed the fingers of his right hand through his short-cropped hair. His left hand scribbled notes on the computer paper Bralich had given him. "Seems to be a random changing of code every couple of lines."

"How long ...?"

"Shhh. I can't think with you rambling on." His fingers tap-danced on his desktop and then moved up to the mathematician's high forehead. "Ha! Got it!" Widowmaker's eyes were tiny dots of coal in a large melon-shaped head that showed little expression. "A simple transposition of keyboard characters at apparently random intervals, but always at the end of a line."

Bralich followed the younger man's hand as Widowmaker pointed to check marks he had etched down the left side of the page that delineated the code changes.

"It shifts here...again here...and here...and here...probably here...here...here." Widowmaker turned back to his keyboard. "By moving the keyboard to the left or right, or up and down of standard position, you create a new alphabet, similar to the Enigma Code the Nazis employed during World War II. A move left, for example, changes the letter 's' to 'd', 'd' to 'f', 'f' to 'g', and so on. Each shift is a new transliteration."

Bralich reached into his briefcase. "I have a hundred pages of gibberish, Jack, and more of it coming. What kind of computer time are we looking at to unscramble all this? It's going to have to be billed as personal time. Will I have to mortgage my home to pay for it?"

A smile creased Widowmaker's face but it did little to change the serious expression permanently embossed there. "ASAP?"

Bralich cast a blank expression in Widowmaker's direction.

"Do you need this right away? As soon as possible?"

"Oh, yes, sooner would be better, but not immediately."

Widowmaker pushed away from the computer and stood up. "If you'll allow me to take these home this evening, I'll scan the pages into my personal computer. With all the shifts, I'll only be able to work on one line at a time, so it's going to take a while. If there's a pattern to the code changes, it'll speed up the process. Of course, I could just program the computer to decode every line separately and..." He rubbed his chin, lost in thought, and obviously thinking aloud.

Bralich looked at his watch. Time for his next class. Afterwards he wanted to go home for some much needed rest and freshen up before he had to get back to the hospital. A wave of exhaustion washed over him

"How about if I put what I can finish each day in your box, Tony?"

He clapped the taller man on the arm. "I'd really appreciate that, Jack. Thanks." He handed the retired Navy man all the pages he had rescued from Miller's office. "Bill me for the time."

"Forget it. We can have a few beers and barbecue spareribs some weekend," he said standing at attention.

"At your convenience and my pleasure. Sorry to rush off, Jack, but I'm going to be late for my next class if I don't get moving."

His graduate class in projective techniques was for doctoral students. It consisted of seven young men and two equally youthful women. These days everyone was young except for him. All nine doctoral candidates were experienced clinicians at the Master's level and preparing for their internship, a yearlong experience in a clinical setting required for licensure. They were a bright and enthusiastic group and Bralich enjoyed the hour-and-a-half he spent with them twice a week.

Bralich looked over the top of his glasses, balanced on the tip of his masculine nose. "We have a third Rorschach protocol due today. Is that correct ladies and gentlemen?"

Heads nodded in agreement.

"Please pass them around the circle to Ms. Rodriquez," he coaxed, pointing toward the thickly spectacled, Anita Rodriquez. She was one of the most capable students in the program and could be a movie siren most everyone agreed, if only she would lose the coke-bottle glasses. Nearly blind without them, she looked like someone lost in an LSD hallucination when she took them off.

Papers were shuffled across the room as instructed.

"I've got a real wacko here," Bill Brown, the only male in the room not supporting a full beard reminiscent of Freud, whispered to Anita.

Bralich's bushy eyebrows retreated up his forehead. "Wacko, Mr. Brown? I don't seem to recall that designation in the DSM."

"Are you sure, sir?"

The other students snickered.

"Relatively so. And where did you find this…wacko, Bill?"

"Rasputin's Cellar, Dr. B." The handsome young psychologist had earned a reputation for his weekend indulgences.

The class snickered again.

Bralich massaged the stubble atop his head. "Female, I presume."

His student licked his lips and fought back a smile. "Most definitely."

"Enticed the young lady with promises of perusing your inkblots, did you, Mr. Brown?"

More snickers.

As he thumbed through the profiles, he found the one submitted by Brown. "Did you get Bambi's last name?"

"Macbeth, sir. She had this weirdly intriguing habit of wringing her hands while delivering poignant soliloquies. Made me very nervous."

"Then you won't be seeing her again for ongoing therapy?"

"Highly unlikely, sir."

Anita Rodriquez tossed her dark hair off her shoulders. "Rumor has it that most can neither afford nor stomach more than one session at the Brown Clinic."

The rest of the class applauded.

"Sounds like we have a consensus, Mr. Brown."

Bill Brown was all smiles. "Insufficient and biased sample."

"Be that as it may, I am afraid we must abandon this interesting and enlightening banter and return our attention to our discussion of defense mechanisms and projective techniques. That is why they pay me the big bucks at this prestigious cathedral of higher learning."

The group laughed.

Bralich leaned back against his desk and folded his hands in front of his chest. "We have already noted that if the source of anxiety can be attributed to the external world rather than to the individual's own primitive impulses or to threats to one's conscience, one is likely to achieve greater relief from the anxious condition with therapeutic assistance. The mechanism by which neurotic or moral anxiety is converted into an objective fear is called, anybody?"

"Projection," the students chimed.

"This is just too simple." Bralich pointed a thick finger at Bill Brown. "And the reason this conversion is so easy?"

"The original source of both neurotic and moral anxiety is fear of punishment from external agents."

"Attaboy, Bill. Ms. Rodriquez, I contend that our Mr. Brown isn't just another pretty face."

"Thank you, sir," Bill Brown said, a look of cocked assurance painted on his face.

Bralich nodded an acknowledgement. "Anita, projection as a defense mechanism often serves dual purposes. Tell the rest of us what those might be."

She hoisted the bulky lenses further up the bridge of her nose. "It reduces anxiety by substituting a lesser danger for a greater, more threatening one, and additionally enables the projecting person to express fearful impulses under the guise of defending oneself against enemies."

"Exactly, Anita. Now try saying the same thing without all the psychobabble, as if you were explaining it to one of your clients."

"It's a heck of lot easier to blame everything on someone else. If the enemy is out there, I don't have to change, and whatever I do, no matter how irrational, is justified."

"I really like this lady," Bralich said, blowing a kiss to his prize pupil.

A studious expression had replaced Bill Brown's infectious smile. "How does this manifest itself when the external environment is in fact dangerous and threatening?" he wanted to know.

"Good question, Bill. Pretty much the same way. Only now the dangers are real, not imaginary.

"How would a therapist know this?"

"Another excellent question, Bill. In the world in which we live, it *is* more convenient to assume the client is the problem, isn't it?"

A few hours later, Bralich made his way anxiously up the walk to the brownstone that he had called his home for as long as he could remember. Under his arm he carried a large express mail envelope that he had just retrieved from the mailbox. The return address and handwriting told him that Robert Miller had sent the envelope. His heart beat like a kettledrum. Droplets of sweat materialized on his head and neck and chills snaked down his spine.

He fumbled for his keys, struggled to engage them in the door, finally opened it and rushed into his study. At his desk he ripped open the envelope. Inside were several audiocassette tapes, a brief note, and several chapters of DeLucci's manuscript. Stooped in concentration, his thumb and fingers cradling his bearded chin, he read what very well might have been Robert's last words to him.

Tony,

I've had the strangest feeling over the last few days that I'm being followed. Today, the feeling is stronger than ever. Hopefully, as you read this, we are both sitting in your office and laughing at my paranoia. But just to be safe, I'm mailing these tapes to you. Six are of my sessions with Nick DeLucci and the other is a summary of my recent discoveries. See you tomorrow.

Robert

The psychiatrist eyed the tapes warily, drumming his fingers on the desktop. The ticking clock on the wall filled the room with urgency. He pulled a pipe from his collection in the carousel that he still kept close at hand on his desk even though he had quit smoking years ago. It still felt comfortable in his hand. He tapped the pipe's bowl in his palm and ran it under his nose, sniffing at the lingering aroma of his once favorite tobacco.

With the stem anchored between his teeth, Bralich opened the top desk drawer and loaded the tape marked "Tony, listen" into the tape deck. He pressed the PLAY button. Robert Miller's voice reached out to him from beyond the grave.

"Sunday, October fourteenth, two thousand ten, two-thirty, p.m. Summary of conversation with Dr. William Zent of the Cranford Psychiatric Clinic and Union College in Cranford, New Jersey. Zent specializes in the treatment of multiple personalities; has authored several highly acclaimed works on the subject. The name of one of his clients, Lucius Sangre (yes, that Lucius Sangre) also appears on the list of orphans transferred out of the Garden Grove Children's Home in California. Facility shut down in 1965, allegedly as a result of staff sexual misconduct toward the indigent population.

Zent has numerous well-documented case histories of clients who developed multiple personalities in response to sexual abuse during early childhood at the hands of Satanist covens. Under hypnosis, clients revealed amazingly consistent stories: references to the breeding of children for the use in sexual orgies and human sacrifices, baptisms of blood, initiation rituals requiring the murder of infants, cannibalism, children living in cages, and for many, sexual intercourse with their parents. These themes are similar to those found in some of DeLucci's novels as well as the content of the nightmares that led him to seek out therapy with me.

Several of Zent's clients had been hypnotically programmed by coven members to block these memories from conscious thought. Deprogramming uncovered information suggesting a highly organized international network of covens. Reportedly, membership included attorneys, medical doctors, psychologists, social workers, high ranking military personnel and government officials who, through their prestigious positions in the community, protect and perpetuate the existence of these groups.

Another disturbing consistency in these histories is the practice of selective breeding among coven members in an attempt to recreate Satan on earth. Zent believes his clients' reports to be reality based. After meeting with him for nearly three hours, I find the man credible.

Oh! And get this, Tony. Zent teaches at Union College in Cranford, New Jersey. Cranford is the home of Alan Ciani, the protagonist in the novel that DeLucci was working on when he started our therapy sessions. I'm finding all sorts of coincidences like this, where one reality folds into another. It's must be more than serendipity and a lot more than outright spooky.

Tony, I think we have stumbled unto something very big. I believe the Garden Grove Children's Home may have been a link in a chain of breeding factories. The Bricktown Home For Boys and the Staten Island Safe House For Orphans may also be part of that same network.

I've tracked down the first nine names on our list of orphan transferees. Seven of the nine died before age six. Statistically that has to be a near impossibility. The causes of death don't show any pattern: pneumonia, congenital heart failure, allergic reaction to a bee sting, accident, etcetera. Perhaps the lack of a pattern is a pattern. Cover up, maybe?

You may recall that Sangre is serving five consecutive life sentences in Rahway State Prison with no option for parole. I've been given permission by Zent to speak with his client, hoping he will sign a release form so I can listen to tapes of Sangre's therapy sessions. The ninth person on our list owns an antique shop in Greenwich Village. Her name is Linda Windsor.

And dammit, Tony, there's a 1964 maroon Corvair about three cars behind me. Hopefully it's just my imagination, but I'd swear I've noticed the old junker a few times today. How the hell many burgundy Corvairs are still on the road?

I'm heading down to Lakewood to talk to DeLucci's mother. Just in case I'm not merely having a paranoid episode and truly am being followed, I am FedEx-ing this tape to you with the DeLucci tapes, which I have been afraid to let out of my sight. Enclosed also find a few chapters of DeLucci's Embodiment of Evil."

Click.

Chapter 10

As usual, Alan awoke exhausted. As he blinked the sleep from his eyes, apprehension snaked through his body like a horrible affliction. The sun had already traveled passed its zenith and was hidden behind the house. The air had chilled noticeably. Narrow silver rays trailed across the lake in marked contrast to the dark shadows cast over the waters by the monolith pines. It created the illusion of fathomless depths. Days were shortening, he realized. Before long the air would turn a bitter cold, the deciduous trees barren, and the skies assume a gray and gloomy ambiance.

Winter nurtured death.

Where had that thought originated?

It was well past dark when Evelyn and her odd hiking companions stumbled into the house drunk and loud, each vying for center stage to describe the joys of nature they witnessed. With an unopened wine bottle in each hand, his wife explained that Linda and Matthew fermented their own elderberry wine and had made a gift of these two bottles. "You should have come with us, you greasy little dago." She made being Italian sound like a birth defect. "We sunbathed naked atop the God Rock!"

The corners of Matthew's mouth twitched as if he wanted to smile but was incapable of such a gesture.

His three offspring glanced at each other with a twinkle that said, "Man, Mom is really messed up!"

Carrying Tupperware containers of unusual foodstuffs and herbs retrieved from her Cubist quarters in the woods, Linda informed Alan that she was providing the supper. He fought the urge to flee.

There was a rattling and clanging of pots and pans, and of dishes being tossed on the table, all of which added to the confusion and clamor of everyone speaking at the same time. The trio was not yet prepared to put a cork on their drinking. Matthew rummaged through the kitchen for a corkscrew and wine glasses and become upset when they weren't easily located. After only a minor emotional episode, he asked for assistance and Evelyn came to his rescue.

A glass of murky red liquid with floating residue was shoved into Alan's hand without an opportunity for him to refuse it. The kids added a cutting board of cheeses, salami, and crackers and a bottle of Dr. Pepper to the festivities. Tia snuggled in next to Linda, Gabby next to her mother. The ease with which his daughters established rapport and could communicate with adults delighted Alan, even if it was with these escapees from the Manson family. It struck him that Gabby could be abandoned on a deserted island and still attract a party. His son was more socially reserved, like Alan.

In spite of Evelyn's deficiencies in the culinary arts, Alan would have preferred her gruel to any scary salads or suspicious potage that Linda might concoct. "Shit! Bat wing broth again," he whispered to Vinnie.

Evelyn had on her drunken face, wide eyes and the most sensuous of smiles. "Ooh! This is delicious."

"Yes, this is wonderful," Gabby agreed.

Alan stared deep into his bowl, playing ostrich and hoping for invisibility. This ploy failed to escape his wife's scrutiny and she asked, "Do you like it, Alan?"

"Yes, dear."

Vinnie laughed his soup up through his nostrils and dropped his spoon into the bowl. That, too, caught Evelyn's attention.

"Are you okay, honey?"

"Sure, Mom. It just went down the wrong pipe." He attempted a convivial smile while coughing up the noxious liquid.

Alan leaned close to his son's ear. "Missed the drain pipe?" This elicited a gagging response from Vinnie.

Evelyn's smile widened.

"Male bonding, dear," Alan explained.

Vinnie supported his father. "Yeah, Dad's really been into the male bonding thing lately. Pats me on the butt every time I walk by and calls me 'sport'. It's actually a bit creepy. I mean, that is male bonding, right, and not repressed homosexual tension?"

Tia feigned concern. "Is Dad turning into a homo, Mom? Only kidding, Dad."

Linda hugged her. "You are so precious, dear," she said.

"Your father is much too deranged an individual to be accepted into the gay community."

A scowl erupted on Matthew's face. His eyes darkened into charcoal brochettes and he opened his mouth to protest, but Linda jabbed him in the ribs with her elbow.

"Evelyn, dear, your friends Roger and Mickey, are they gay?"

"Asexual, I suspect. Although I do remember there was a time they were convinced they were the Andrew Sisters."

"Please, I'm eating, Mom," Vinnie objected.

"There's nothing disgusting about homosexuality," Gabrielle informed her older sibling.

Alan stroked his chin. "Any enlightened words of wisdom regarding bestiality, Gabby?"

His wife fielded that one. "If done tastefully, what's the harm? Don't you agree, Linda?"

"Not on the first date, of course," Evelyn's friend piped. The two women exchanged discreet but knowing glances and nodded in agreement. Alan could not help but notice that the dialogue the women shared seemed always to be rife with double entendres and racy innuendo, and hinted at dodgery to which he was unawares.

His youngest daughter looked confused. "What's bestiality?"

"Sex with animals, dummy!" her older sister informed her.

Tia screwed up her face, "Yuck!" Then, with a smile she asked, "What's it called when Fluffy humps my furry slippers?"

"Stupid!" her mother answered.

Gabby sucked in her lips and feigned a shudder. "Revolting if you still wear them!"

Everyone at the table was in stitches. Linda got up and rescued the whistling teapot from the countertop stove. "Anybody up for my home brewed herbal tea?" The girls all raised their hands. Alan and Vinnie shook the heads "No." Matthew must not have been capable of making a decision for he made no attempt to communicate a preference. He remained grim-faced. His eyes retained their menace; the principal target of which Alan felt certain was he.

"I understand you are in your senior year, Vinnie," Linda said.

"That's right."

"How have your first few weeks of classes fared?"

Before Vinnie could respond, Matthew reminded everyone that he had hated school.

Linda stifled his conversation with a piercing look, eyes flashed with displeasure. To Evelyn she said, "Eighteen? Vinnie must be reaching his sexual peak."

The women giggled, causing Vinnie to blush profusely.

"Alan, dear," Evelyn said with a twinkle in her eyes, "when did you reach your sexual peak?"

"This afternoon while you were out hiking. Too bad you couldn't have been there."

Tia and Gabby chimed, "Ew!"

Vinnie snorted more of Linda's ambiguous ambrosia out his nose and blushed again.

The merriment apparently annoyed Matthew for he started to revisit the topic of sadistic nuns. Linda attempted to put an end to the discourse by delivering her partner a swift kick to the shin under the table. The message had not adequately been comprehended as he groaned but started up again. "Those sadistic nuns …"

This time his roommate squelched his comments with finality when Linda grabbed a knife from the cutting board and reached under the table with her free hand. "Shall we test my ability to perform circumcision in my current inebriated condition?"

Judging from Matthew's reaction, Alan concluded that not only had she made her point, but that she wasn't joking. The sullen stork had no option but to hold his tongue and sunk down into his seat.

What had initially brought this strange relationship into existence was beyond Alan's comprehension; no more so than why it still existed. What was in it for Linda he wondered. She undoubtedly was the alpha here. Perhaps she thrived on dominating the miscreant.

A large belch interrupted Evelyn's laughter and she followed up with ingenuous giggles.

Vinnie's face flashed disapproval, knitting his thick eyebrows above his deep-seated dark eyes. They lacked the warmth and sparkle so prevalent in his sisters' eyes, and combined with his angular facial features forged a brooding countenance whenever a smile was absent. Outwardly friendly, like his mother he maintained his emotional distance, never choosing to seek advice or counsel from Alan, withholding his intimacy as if a treasure to be coveted or an activity too fearful in which to engage. Alan didn't believe his son's emotions to be transitory or superficial, just guarded or underdeveloped.

"If you adults have sufficiently belabored all the bodily functions, might we move on to more elevated topics for discussion?"

His oldest sister lifted her nose skyward. "Tsk, tsk, you people are intellectual amoebae."

Insult showed on the boy's face, which he tried to conceal with a confident but serious tone. "What topic did you draw from the hat for this week's essay in Honors English, Gabby?" Vinnie favored the two-page essay format of his sister's eleventh grade Honors course to the quarterly term papers required of his senior class.

"Something about moral constructs, ethical principles, and the nature of good and evil. I didn't read it very carefully. I'll probably start working on it tomorrow in study hall."

"That's a rather heady topic for Backwater, USA," Linda said, hoisting her pencil-thin eyebrows up her pallid forehead.

She had directed her comment at Alan and her expressive blue eyes demanded acknowledgement. He felt obligated to reply. "Last week she had to write about the appropriateness of allowing a pet pig to sit at the dinner table, especially if at some future date it might be the dinner."

"No!" Vinnie objected, intent upon setting the record straight. "The Honors English classes are really good, and Mr. Boyette's assignments are always very cerebral."

Linda smiled her appreciation. "How will you attack the issue, Gabby?"

"I really haven't thought about it yet. I have too much biology homework to finish first."

Evelyn turned to her son, the family scholar. "How would you handle the topic, Vinnie?"

Gabby screwed her face into a snooty grimace. "Teacher's pet."

Vinnie cast an anemic smile in his sister's direction. "Well, I guess a primary purpose of ethical principles is to induce wrongdoers to acknowledge their behavior as immoral, incorrect and not repeat it. Maybe I'd throw in something about Socrates' view of justice as virtue, and discuss whether a person can be separated from one's actions. You know, like are people evil for doing something bad, and should they be punished if they acknowledge their wrongful behavior."

Quite the mouthful, Alan thought.

Evelyn expelled a soulful sigh and peacock proud said, "My children are so brilliant. Aren't they, Linda? No thanks to the dogmatic jock with the sagging face and saddlebags under his eyes," she added, pointing an accusatory finger at Alan.

He conjured up a burp from deep within his abdomen and offered his standard, "Duh, yes, dear."

Vinnie steered the conversation back on track, "Do you think that people can be inherently evil, Dad?"

Alan thought. "Yes, some people are evil. Whether because they are inherently so or consciously chose to be, the effect is the same and the world would be a much better place without them."

"My dear, Alan, that is irrational," Linda snapped, somewhat nettled by his remark. She brushed her stringy black hair from her face. "Blaming an individual means confusing a wrongful act with a sinful being. And just who is the ultimate authority on what is sinful?" Linda's British accent elevated everything she said beyond refute. "The Muslims hate the Jews; the Jews the Christians; the Christians the Catholics. Which of these moral authorities has the moral high ground when all of them have been killing off each of the other groups, claiming God to be on their side. If there is absolute evil, it seems to me it's this God that demands that everybody hate everybody else."

Alan hardened his tone. "Organized religion aside, everybody has the inalienable right to be wrong, and everybody makes mistakes. That's only human nature. However, somebody who breaks into a home, ties everyone up, rapes the women and children, and then blows the victims away, isn't making a mistake. Such a person lacks moral conscience and is inherently evil. The devil didn't make them do it. They chose to do evil." He had worked himself up at this point, felt heat rising up over his collar. "Or what about Satanists who breed children for human sacrifice and keep them in cages like animals? These are inherently evil people!" Where the hell had that thought come from?

Matthew's back stiffened, which drew Linda's sharp-eyed attention. She seized his arm before he could speak. His lips curled around his unvoiced objections.

"It makes people comfortable to attribute evilness to differing points of view. Such attributions are merely intellectual laziness. Assuming an adversary is evil underestimates that opponent and undermines the humanity of both sides. The pro-lifer who in God's name murders the demonic doctor who aborts fetuses is an evildoer rationalizing their evil acts by believing themselves righteous. The same holds true for most acts of war." Linda's smile made him uneasy. "As to whether one might be inherently evil, it seems to me that any such philosophical stance is actually making a case for evil with a capital 'E'. The belief that any individual personifies or is the embodiment of evil legitimizes the concept of the Devil or Satan, and subsequently the religious practice of worshiping such evil."

Alan shivered unexpectedly. His eyes wavered under the woman's ponderous gaze.

"Speaking of the Devil," his wife announced sprightly, "Halloween is right around the corner. As she got up from the table and sauntered over to a calendar on the wall next to the phone, the tension in the room slipped away. "It's on a Sunday this year. Let's do a party here on Saturday so people won't have to leave early because of work on Monday."

The conversation easily shifted to costume ideas and party arrangements, but the weight of Linda's watchful eyes on Alan never diminished. Her syrupy smile mocked him.

Wine flowed freely. The evening grew progressively more silly and the gathering more raucous. Uncharacteristically, Alan participated in the binge. He didn't care much for his wife's party lifestyle, and especially frowned upon her getting drunk with her friends in front of the kids and the way she bantered freely about her sexual exploits. However, the kids had grown up witnessing their mother's excesses, and as with most points of disagreement, Alan had given up long ago debating them with his wife. He told himself that given enough time a natural maturation would enfold and her behavior would get better; but that, too, was fatuous.

Sometime during the evening's activities, the children departed with hugs and kisses, and vanished into their respective bedrooms.

Drunkenness had made Alan sleepy, too, and judging by the thunderous buzzing in his head, a huge bumblebee from Jules Verne's Mysterious Island had been set loose in the home. When he warned the guests of the intruder, their bellowing laughter added to the cacophony. The smiling faces of Evelyn and her bizarre companions circled around his head in the throes of hysteria. He smiled numbly as he attempted to maintain his equilibrium in the vortex of a wildly swirling environment.

Evelyn shouldered their uneven trek to the bedroom, although Alan could not remember choosing to retire. As he attempted to let himself fall onto the waterbed, his wife kept him upright with two hands at his belt buckle.

"Wait," she commanded, reaching for his lips with hers. Her tongue probed his mouth while she unloosened his belt and unfastened his zipper. He reached up under her rugby jersey for her breasts and held on to them as she slid down to her knees.

Enraptured in the entanglement of arms and legs, the boundaries dividing reality and fantasy lost distinction. Alan experienced himself leaving his body to observe the sexual acrobatics from the ceiling, puzzling how he could be in two places at once. His wife writhed in ecstasy; her legs wrapped high around his back. Moaning with a pleasure he had never observed before, she clawed at his back and tugged at his long blonde her.

But I don't have blonde hair!

Alan placed a hand on what should have been his own shoulder and forcibly twisted the body to face him. Danny Cox smiled in greeting. His expression was one of unfeeling savagery, a stare as penetrating as a surgeon's scalpel.

A silent plea was the only objection Alan was capable of offering. The icy grip of terror strangled his brain.

Danny ignored it. He turned back to Evelyn and flipped her unto her stomach, mounting her from behind commanding her to scream with delight. Evelyn obeyed eagerly, all the while looking back over her shoulder at Alan as her long hair swayed back and forth across her sensuous face. A demonic laughter filled the room, fueling his dread.

When he awoke, it was still dark outside. He was wringing wet with sweat, his naked body draped over his wife.

"You're crushing me," she murmured, not quite awake. "Move over to your own side."

The bed spun like a dreidle. Closing his eyes only made fighting off nausea more difficult. There was an unrelenting throbbing in his skull, like something was chiseling its way out from the inside.

Chapter 11

Bralich's fingertips gently stroked the metallic surface of the urn that contained Robert Miller's ashes. Having arrived by courier only a half hour earlier, he had been unable to handle it until now. It was cold to the touch.

Throughout his entire lifetime, he wanted to believe, and at times desperately so, that human existence was more than an accident. Religion had failed him miserably and psychiatry, once hailed as the new religion hadn't fared much better. Despite all its self-righteous discourse espousing the holistic nature of the human experience, his science in actuality diminished the human consciousness to little more than a series of electrochemical synapse connections of the nervous system, and minimized human nature to the functioning of instincts, repressions, and conditioned behaviors. Beyond acknowledging the importance of man's search for meaning, little had been accomplished to probe the deeper universe of internal flows and dynamic unfoldings that bridged a universe of mind and matter. There was no real comfort to be attained, no sense of transcendence experienced with the passing of a loved one. Alone with these ashes and his science of deterministic laws of a linear reality, Bralich felt profoundly isolated.

Robert Miller's time on earth had been reduced to an inert pile of dust at the bottom of a crematoria vessel. That was more than he had salvaged from the ruin of his son, Anthony. Then he had only an empty casket and the American flag that the Air Force had presented him in compensation for the loss of his only child. He had refused delivery of the flag, which hadn't won him any friends among the other grieving parents and didn't diminish the onslaught of inane condolences unsupported by any rational explanations for his loss. Those came mostly from television talk shows on which former POWs recounted the horrors of captivity. Unlike now,

Bralich had cried when he had heard of the torture and insult to human dignity they were forced to endure. Caged like animals, striped down to nothing until only the real self remained, they clung in a final desperation to their resolve, not knowing whether it would truly matter.

Cages. These too were a common denominator in the DeLucci nightmare and novels. Perhaps, these enclosures represented the externalization of the human neglect that marinated the emptiness DeLucci felt from his abandonment.

Bralich played the audiotapes of DeLucci's initial five hypnosis sessions. On each tape, DeLucci's voice recounted his recurring nightmare in greater, more agonizing, detail. Each session ended abruptly when the patient's discomfort escalated to hysteria. Bralich knew session six would be different. It was during this sixth and final session that the little fellow had withdrawn into catatonic detachment.

As Bralich stared out into the blood red sunset, Miller's voice filled his study. His words were articulated with the rhythmic cadence of a metronome. "Find a comfortable, relaxed position and allow your eyes to close. Become aware of your breathing and allow your energy to calm down, relaxing yourself to a tranquil level. Be attuned to your body's metabolism and allow it also to become calm. Tune into your physical body and allow each muscle to completely relax."

Bralich thought of DeLucci's frozen face, a mask of horror. Had it responded to Robert's suggestions?

"Say to yourself: I feel wonderful. I feel happy."

DeLucci mumbled something to himself that Bralich could not quite discern.

"Focus on your breathing, Nick. Feel the coolness of each breathe coming in, being warmed in your throat and lungs. As you exhale that breath, relax. Feel the soothing warmth of every breath you exhale. Feel your shoulders slump in relaxation. Feel your arms relax, your torso relax, your breathing relax."

Whimper.

"You are alright, Nick," Miller said soothingly. "You feel wonderful and happy."

Another whimper.

"Are you are alright, Nick?"

"Okay," DeLucci responded with little conviction in his Munchkin voice.

"Take a deep breath, filling your lungs completely and holding that breathe a few seconds. As you exhale that breathe repeat inwardly to yourself, 'one: I feel comfortable and deeply relaxed.'"

Miller paused, allowing DeLucci to make the autosuggestion. DeLucci sucked in air, expelled it with a sputtering hiss.

"Take another deep breath, holding it a few seconds longer. Exhale this breath repeating to yourself, 'two: I feel fine and wonderful.'"

Bralich heard the cold crunching of leather, no doubt DeLucci shifting in his seat. Then there was a silence as Miller waited while his patient settled.

"And now, one more deep breathe, holding it just a little longer than the last. Exhale, repeating to yourself, 'three: I am relaxing deeper than ever before.'"

Another pause was interrupted by DeLucci's stilted sigh. This was not going well, Bralich thought.

"Now focus all your awareness on the bottom of your feet. Feel a warm tingling sensation enveloping your toes, insteps, and the balls of your feet. Imagine this warming sensation flowing up your legs like a calming, deeply penetrating wave of relaxation. Allow this relaxation to massage your legs, calves…"

The ensuing discourse was one with which Bralich was well acquainted. Robert would guide his patient on a peaceful trek through the human anatomy with repeated suggestions to relax, culminating with Miller counting down backwards from ten to one, proposing that with each count DeLucci's level of relaxation increase exponentially.

DeLucci snorted more than snored, his intermittent breaths exhaled in an explosive shutter that rattled and whistled across the deviated septum that separated his misshapen nasal passages. He suffered from apnea, a sleep disorder that interrupted his breathing when his body relaxed. It would hinder the level of comfort the little man achieved under hypnosis.

"Can you hear me, Nick? Are you okay?" Miller's voice inquired.

Muffled mumblings.

"It's okay to speak out loud, Nick."

DeLucci's voice: "I'm alright."

"Do you know where you are?"

"Your office."

"That's correct, Nick. We are in my office. You are safe here. Nothing and nobody can hurt you here. We are safe in my office."

"Never safe. They're always watching."

"Who is always watching, Nick?"

No response. Miller asked again. DeLucci let out a thin anguished sound.

This scenario played itself out in each of the previous five tapes to which Bralich had listened. No response would be forthcoming, he knew. Miller abandoned further probing. This line of questioning was a dead-end.

"As you tell me about your dream, Nick, you will remain calm and relaxed. You will feel only mild curiosity as you report every minute detail that you can recall about your dream."

The room filled with an unearthly quiet.

"We're in my office, Nick. It's safe to talk here because it's just you and me. You look forward to the opportunity to tell me about your dreams."

"Dreams."

"You are merely an observer, Nick. You see everything as clearly as if watching a movie. Tell me what you see."

"I'm on the edge of a volcano, looking down into the crater. No! It's a well. I can see mortared stone."

Silence.

"What happens next?"

"I am very close to the edge. I can fall in if I'm not very careful."

"You are very careful and safe, Nick."

"I'm dizzy, losing my balance. No! I'm falling."

A sense of panic fills Nick's voice. "The well is empty…and I feel terribly empty. I'm empty deep down inside me like I'm not only inside the well but I am the well!"

Bralich recognized DeLucci's comment as a new insight, a connective bridge between his internal and external realities.

The diminutive author continued. "My screams echo into the black space. They ricochet in my skull. It hurts."

Millers voice: "Your head doesn't hurt now, does it Nick? You are only an observer."

"I am an observer." His voice was flat.

"Continue, Nick."

"I see the bottom of the well. It's cracked. Everything slips through. Falling. I must try to slow my descent, cushion the impact…but all the noise in my head shakes my thoughts loose. They drop into the pit and seep through the cracks. They're gone forever. Forever."

There is a long silence. Robert is patient, not pushing DeLucci faster than he is willing to proceed on his own.

"I'm falling very fast now. The bottom of the well is coming up quickly. I cover my head with my arms but it doesn't matter because I slip right through the cracks…as if I am nothing." DeLucci snorts. "I'm in the cave."

"Tell me about the cave, Nick."

"Drawings on the walls."

"Describe the drawings."

"Hurtful."

"Tell me how they are hurtful, Nick. You are only an observer."

Panting, gasps for breaths that don't seem to draw any air.

"Shadows. Everywhere. They seem alive. They taunt me. I hear footsteps. They're coming for me now. I must run away, get away now, fast."

"Who is coming for you, Nick?"

Bralich cringed. Robert's probe was too direct. He allowed himself to get caught up in the moment. DeLucci needed to be calmed before proceeding.

"That was a long time ago," Nick said. "I was just a kid. I don't remember much of anything of my time there."

"Your time where, Nick?"

"A long time ago. Just a kid. Don't remember."

Another dead end.

"What happens next, Nick?"

There is silence. Robert asks the question a second time. More silence. "What happens next, Nick?" he asks a third time.

"I'm lost in the catacombs. The walls are lined with cages; cages filled with children. They wait there. Don't hurt me! Please don't hurt me."

"Why do the children want to hurt you, Nick?"

"Children can't hurt me. They're afraid of me. Most are just blank faces, hollow stares, not even blinking as I walk by."

They are in unfamiliar territory, Bralich knows.

"The children are afraid that you will hurt them?" Robert Miller's voice inquires.

"Yes."

Miller: "Tell me what makes you think the children believe you will hurt them."

"Because I ..."

A chilling cry enveloped the room. The abrupt silence that replaced it only heightened the palpable terror. Robert had lost DeLucci.

Chapter 12

The ax hovered above Alan's head, sinister and deadly like a cobra readying to strike. Then, in an explosion of energy, it came crashing down. The timber split neatly into halves and fell to either side of the large section of tree trunk he used as a cutting block as the honed blade lodged into the wood.

The preceding evening had once again been filled with somnambulistic gothic monstrosities and so Alan had awakened drained and bone-tired. His stomach churned with nausea; his mind addled. He might have lingered in bed had not the thought of inactivity exhausted him even more then the chores he needed to complete.

The day started off poorly. The Pathfinder had a flat tire and the kids had managed to miss their bus for the umpteenth time, requiring him to drive them the sixteen miles to their high school, forty-five minutes each way on the meandering mountain roads. When the phone went dead, he had no choice but to make a second trip into town since there weren't any homes nearby from which to call in a repair order and cell phone reception was nonexistent. On top of all that, the truckload of firewood that had been delivered would not split and store itself.

With the back of his hand he wiped away the salty droplets of sweat that ran down his forehead and across the bridge of his nose. He squinted to ward off the bright midday sun that glistened off the metal flashing above the garage on the far side of the horseshoe-shaped driveway. Heat radiated in waves off the asphalt drive, casting a dreamlike quality over the lush surroundings as two deer approached the pond across the road from out of the nearby woods. They gracefully bounded away when a car sped by on the tree-lined country road. Soon, winter would impose itself upon all the luxuriant growth and wet, frigid air would sweep down from Lake Erie and deposit lots of rain and snow from eternally gloomy skies. It wasn't unusual for temperatures to plummet without warning in the fall and remain below freezing through May, so Alan stockpiled lots of wood during the good weather. Keeping the wood-burning stoves fueled was essential to thwarting the lake effect dampness from eating tight through to his bones.

He inhaled the crisp afternoon air, savoring the fragrance of lilac and honeysuckle that embraced his senses. How peaceful this country existence, safely hidden from the rest of the world, he thought.

He shouldered the ax again, focusing on his target, and powered it downward through the wood. Two splintered segments tumbled to the ground, sending a terrified squirrel scampering for safety of the nearest big oak. The day passed so quickly that he barely noticed the sun go down and the outside lights come on until Evelyn called him in to supper.

Physically spent, the smell of cedar, pine and perspiration still clinging to him, Alan collapsed into is favorite chair nearest the wood-burner in front of the television, a plate of pieroggies smothered in butter, fried onions and peppers balanced on his lap. The rest of the family filed into the room behind him. Dinner plates rattled, kids teased each other, and cats scurried beneath the onslaught of raucous human invaders into their quiet family room sanctuary.

"Well that's because you're a space cadet. Maybe you ought to try reading a book once in a while," Vinnie proclaimed only half in jest.

Gabrielle's green eyes showed offense. "I read all the time!" she insisted.

"Taking a year to read the biography of Marilyn Monroe constitutes neither reading nor reading all the time. The College Boards are not likely to ask you who Marilyn Monroe slept with in June of '59!"

"Just mark 'all of the above' if they do, Gabby," Alan suggested over his shoulder, stifling his laughter to avoid choking on the pieroggies.

Vinnie: "Class act, Dad. Mom, bring the old man a bib."

"Don't pick on my Daddy," Tia advised her brother. "He was always good to us when we were kids and he still had control of his bodily functions." She giggled self-consciously. "I'm only kidding, Dad." Tia always apologized when teasing so you knew for sure when she was kidding and when to be offended. She had picked up the habit from her mother who almost without exception intended backhanded insults directed at Alan.

"Let's put on Seinfeld reruns."

No. Put on Entertainment Tonight," Gabby countered to her brother's suggestion.

Evelyn handed Alan a cold beer.

"Mom and I want to catch the news. It wouldn't hurt you kids to watch either. You all need to understand world affairs, too!"

"That's why I'm reading the Marilyn Monroe biography."

Evelyn switched to the news channel. Disappointed, Vinnie said, "It's the same stuff every day anyway. Why bother?"

Alan couldn't argue with that. He had used the exact same argument on his parents at Vinnie's age and expected that someday his grandchildren would be no less correct in employing the same logic. Listening to the petty political agendas propagated on the news sucked the joy out of life.

He had nearly succumbed to tiredness, pieroggies, and the monotonous droning of the local newscaster, when a story caught his attention. A Paula Zahn clone stood deadpanned serious amidst revolving beacons that flashed blood-colored shadows across police sedans and news vans. Officers escorted a parade of bohemian clad and manacled captives from a storefront into police cars. The detainees turned their faces away as they passed in front of the eyes of the camera.

"Tom, I'm standing outside Ye Olde Antique Shoppe in the picturesque middle class community of Cranford, New Jersey, where just moments ago a sting operation successfully netted several members of a major child pornography ring. Tonight's arrests mark the culmination of a yearlong collaborative effort between the FBI, State and local police agencies. Reportedly, the ring has been operating out of this quaint little shop nestled among the beautiful tree-lined streets of Cranford for nearly three decades, unbeknownst to the local citizenry and neighboring community merchants."

"Wow, Dad!" Vinnie began.

"Shh!"

To Alan's astonishment, a photograph of his childhood chum, Danny Cox, materialized above the newscaster's shoulder.

"According to knowledgeable sources, the big break in the case came when one of the shop's owners, Danny Cox, a lifelong resident of

Cranford, died during a fire of mysterious origin that burned Cox's personal residence to the ground. While the names of those arrested have not been released, reportedly, the two surviving shop owners are not included among those apprehended."

Evelyn said, "Alan, isn't that the friend you are always telling stories about?"

Alan shushed her too.

She turned to the children. "Your father's sordid past comes to light."

"That's not in the least bit amusing. Be quiet, I want to hear this."

"You know that guy, Dad?" all three children chimed simultaneously.

"Your father was probably featured in one of Danny's first short subject documentaries."

"Jesus Christ, that's hardly funny, Evelyn." The depths of her irresponsibility as a parent seemed fathomless. Did she ever stop to think how such comments might impact the children?

Since she never knew when enough was enough, Evelyn added, "Notice I didn't say biggest stars," and held up her thumb and forefinger to indicate a two-inch span.

The newscaster lifted one hand to her ear microphone and nodded. "We have the name of one of the other owners. He is apparently a Nicolo Paganini, alleged porn king who specializes in violent, hardcore child pornography. It is rumored that Paganini is also a major player in a network of Satanist covens believed allegedly to practice human sacrifice. No current photograph is available of Paganini, but we'll have more as information becomes available, Tom."

"Hey, Dad," Vinnie said. "That Nicolo Paganini character…bet it's a pseudonym."

Alan looked absently at his son.

Vinnie explained himself. "Paganini was an Italian violinist and composer, known as the Devil's Fiddler because it was believed that he had a pact with the Devil. I did a paper on him in Honor's History. He was considered the greatest violinist of all time and was sort of the rock star of his age. He had such extreme personal magnetism that he mesmerized his audiences. The portraits I saw of him resembled Mom's friend, Matthew."

Maybe a physical resemblance, he thought, but Alan had bowel movements with more personal magnetism than Matthew Cartier.

"Geez!" Gabby put in. "This family gets weirder by the minute."

Alan's heart pounded in his ears. His vision clouded.

"No wonder Dad has hair on his toes," Tia said. "Like he's some king of half human, half goat, Satanist porn star. And we always knew Grandma wasn't quite right." She giggled, covering her mouth with her hand.

"I'm surprised you're not acquainted with Paganini's work, Alan, since you think you know everything," Evelyn added. "It's electrifying. Vinnie wasn't Goethe's Faust inspired by the rumors of Paganini's spiritual covenant with the Devil?" She smiled as if contemplating a personal joke.

"Yep."

An involuntary trembling wiggled through Alan's body. Forty-plus years of living and still he continued to be shaken by the reality that little in life is what it appeared.

"Linda recently played me Paganini's 'Le Streghe.' For the uninformed," she said looking at Alan, "that translates to 'The Witches.' Speaking of which, did I mention that your mother called a couple of hours ago? And no, I have no interest in visiting her any time soon, thank you."

Alan's mind was some place else…with his old school chum, Danny Cox. A chill rippled through him and his hands and legs began to shake. The knife and fork rattled on his plate.

Aware that the room had gone silent, Alan zeroed his attention on Evelyn, whose expression was a hollow stare. He quieted his plate as best he could and asked, "Who called?"

"Your mother. You know, the mouth that bored."

"Did she say anything of importance?" Alan asked, realizing the folly of his question before he had finished the sentence.

"Doesn't she always? I listened a couple of second's worth of rambling, then left the phone unattended about five minutes. When I picked it up again, she was still going on about something. So I said 'um-hum,' as per your example, put down the phone for another five minutes, and got back just in time to say good-bye. She never noticed I wasn't on the other end of the line."

"You're a compassionate person."

"Your mother is a crazy old witch."

"See! Grandma's a witch. This whole family is straight out of a Stephen King novel," Gabrielle said.

"And your genes come from the low end of our genetic pool," Vinnie informed his sister, beaming.

Alan repressed his inclination to celebrate his son's cleverness and verbal acumen with a guarded smile, knowing Gabby would feel she was being bullied. "It's my parents' anniversary next week. We had better take a ride over to Jersey and visit this weekend."

"We all need new underwear anyway," Evelyn said sarcastically, which initiated a round of remarks from the rest of the family regarding the inevitability of Grandma making gifts of undergarments to all of them allegedly because all the stores were having sales and she felt she couldn't afford not to buy. His mother was probably the single largest buyer of underwear on the eastern seaboard. He still had unopened packages that she had sent him while he was away at college.

While his family exchanged underwear stories, Alan's thoughts returned to Danny Cox, the focal point of his recent bizarre dreams.

Until recent enlightenment to the contrary, Alan's perception of his childhood buddy had always been that he floated unencumbered along the river of life devoid of all complexities. Along the way, the best of everything seemed just to fall into his lap…the best jobs, the best girls, and the very best of times. It's as if he had been chosen for an easy life.

Danny's incredible good looks and apparent schoolboy innocence made him irresistible, and he was not above taking advantage of the throngs of females who showered him with attention and gifts for the privilege of being in his presence. He'd strolled with athletic confidence into any room and nonchalantly say; "Hi, I'm Danny." Hearts would flutter as his upcoming conquests swooned "Take me" with their eyes and Danny gladly accommodated their wishes. How wonderful it must have been to see the world through Danny's eyes; to see the love and acceptance in the eyes of all those who behold you.

Danny never said much. In all the years they hung out together, Alan couldn't remember him speaking more than two or three consecutive sentences. That seemed to tax the limit of his communication skills. Given his divine presence, he didn't need to speak to get what he wanted.

While the rest of their circle of friends compensated for less spectacular physical perfection by developing panache, Danny needed only to stand around, looking pretty.

Unlike Danny's younger brother, Stevie, there were no moral dilemmas for Danny. Such thoughts never appeared to enter his mind. Maybe God finds it amusing to place striking contrasts in close proximity, guffawing as they go unnoticed by most of humanity, unless there's a would-be writer, budding philosopher, or artsy movie director around to pick up on it.

There was no questioning that his chum had been a girl hound. However, Alan's recent discovery that not even his brother's wives, and maybe his own mother, were not off limits still seemed to him farfetched. If such a relationship truly existed, it caste new light as to why Stevie's wife had killed herself. Relationship was probably the wrong word since Danny had glided charmingly from day to day uncommitted to anyone but himself. That had been his tragic flaw; he just didn't know how to care about anybody but himself. It was a failing that hurt the people around him. Danny seemed unaffected by these consequences.

Right out of high school, Danny had used the money from a trust fund his father had willed him to purchase a little two-bedroom house on Walnut Avenue in Cranford. While Alan was spending the turbulent sixties in college, Danny was pulling in the big bucks working on the docks of Port Newark. A knee injury he had suffered in football during their senior year kept him safe from the Vietnam mess and only added to his charisma. It was an undisputed claim that Danny Cox could have been the greatest quarterback, or for that matter, the greatest athlete that Cranford High School had ever turned out. Maybe so, but Alan suspected that his friend's natural ability would have carried him only so far. Success demands commitment, discipline, and sacrifice. Danny wouldn't have been up to the task. Alan sensed that Danny knew this too, because whenever somebody recounted his unfortunate, short-lived athletic career, Danny would stare at the ground almost embarrassed. Then he'd raise his head supporting a Cheshire cat grin. Yeah, he knew it too. It made no difference to him, however. That smile would bring three or four star-struck young ladies to his side, touching and groping and ultimately sharing a piece of the legend.

He lived alone. Now and again, one of the guys might sleep off a party at Danny's place and he entertained an endless parade of women, but none had ever managed to gain live-in status. Not even Lois Early, and she was living proof that God existed and took part in our creation. The joke in high school was that Danny's dad would remind him as he was leaving on a date to get in early, and Danny would guarantee his old man that he'd get in Early that evening. He continued to do so even after Lois had married. It was common knowledge that when her husband went off on business trips Danny would drop in to relive old memories. Like Katie, Stevie's wife, Lois, too, had cashed in her chips. Not until just this moment had Alan realized that death seemed to follow Danny Cox, leaving him unscathed.

Despite, or maybe, because his mind whirled with crazy thoughts, Alan allowed himself to doze off. The television in the living room had been tuned into a local news expose program where the vapid host was exclaiming, "Satanism! Heavy metal rock! Is there a connection? Are our children being brainwashed and programmed to commit suicide…acts of violence…and even murder…through subliminal messages hidden within the lyrics of heavy metal music? Our focus today, on Pennsylvania On Guard."

Sometime during the evening Alan staggered semi-conscious to the bedroom. Evelyn threw covers over him and later crawled under the sheets herself, but he was too tired to do anything about it. The smell and taste of burning flesh and blood filled his dreams.

Chapter 13

The evening seemed strangely still as Tony Bralich stared out of his study window into a neon night that obscured all traces of the heavenly firmaments. His pulse throbbed in his temples, discordantly echoing the ticking of the grandfather clock across the room. The emotional undertow precipitated by the DeLucci tapes tugged at his psychological footing as the residue of DeLucci's anguish washed over him. He was not as resilient as he used to be. Currents of uneasiness rippled deep within him.

He had seen a lot of human damage over the years, had crawled around in dysfunctional minds for so long that he thought himself no longer capable of harboring any emotional vulnerability to the cruelties of the universe. Rarely did he allow himself to brood his own personal losses; his wife to cancer and depression, his son to Vietnam, and now Robert to…what? Fate? He had managed for the most part to adjust to each calamity, to sublimate his ghosts and fortify his heart against despair. However, this time his serenity fractured beneath the powerful imaged evoked by DeLucci's revelations. What previously he had only momentarily permitted himself to feel poured over him like a waterfall as he got caught up in reminiscences.

Vivid images of the torment he had experienced at the hands of his own father resurfaced and Bralich felt helpless to ward off the assault. The walls closed in around him like a giant vice. He now felt captive in the paralyzing grip of the nightmare that had defined him for much of his youth.

Even the harsh winters of eastern Pennsylvania were no match for the bitter cold storminess of Theodore Bralich. The twelve hours his father spent, seven days a week, in the coalmines outside Scranton blackened more than his physical body. When he returned each day from the bowels of hell, he carried within him assays from the netherworld that demanded expression. His father seemed to find recreation in inflicting punishment upon his family by pounding their sense of wellbeing into sand.

He was a short man, powerfully built with shoulders so broad and arms so immense that they made him look freakish. By itself, his physique unnerved most people. Yet, it was the fierceness of his persona that was the senior Bralich's most unsettling characteristic. A large-featured face, accentuated by chiseled cheekbones and a bushy black beard, projected a predatory aura. There were tombs in his eyes, and the intensity of his gaze served warning to any observer to be wary. He was possessed of an easily accessible primitive rage and anyone lacking the wisdom to avoid his ire quickly learned the extent of his brutality. He had beaten more than one unsuspecting victim to within an inch of their life. In a stoic era in which smiles were often an anomaly, Tony Bralich's most vivid memories of his father's face were of the hateful smile that marked his countenance during the unleashing of his limitless fury. His father's face rose up before him now. Residual fear knifed into Tony's heart, penetrating too deeply to dislodge.

From firsthand experience he was aware of what viciousness a parent was capable of leveling upon one's child, yet it still puzzled him how such evil was possible. He looked at his trembling hands as if he might find an answer in them and, to his surprise, found splattered tears that had coursed down his cheeks.

The image of his mother flickered across the picture screen of his mind.

Beauty had been beaten from Natalya Bralich's face long before Tony was born. She had retreated into the numbness afforded by a cocaine addiction that was easily nurtured in an era prior to the more stringent regulation of the drug in future generations. Narcotic stupor made impossible any generous doling out of affection to her only child. Tony Bralich held no remembrances of comfort and tenderness in a mother's arms or pillowy bosom, nor ever hearing a nurturing word that might buoy him against his father's physical and psychological assaults.

Left unattended and uncared for, he passed his earliest years in the soot-filled alleyways and anthracite slag piles of Scranton, praying each day that his father might not return from the mines. But he always did, and somehow each evening seemed worse that those it preceded. It was a childhood dominated by blind panic and a constant struggle to stay alive from day to day.

Ironically, it was upon the worst of all evenings, one on which the beating had reached new depths that Tony Bralich's life was saved. He had already spent ten seasons in Hell. Broken and choking on the phlegm and blood that gurgled in his throat, barely conscious, Tony had crawled out into the cobblestone street while his father returned to a merciless beating and rape of Tony's mother.

These memories were so sharp at this moment that Tony gasped painfully for breath, as if he was still being battered.

By the time his father had noticed his absence, a crowd had gathered around young Tony, police had been summoned and guns drawn. Natalya's lifeless body was plainly visible from the open doorway. As Theodore Bralich wildly charged from the house to retrieve his son, a hail of bullets riddled his hulking frame, dropping him to the ash covered cobblestone only inches from Tony's swollen and bloodied face.

When the audiotape of DeLucci's session groaned to be ejected from the recorder, Bralich looked up from his thoughts. The ashen reflection in the study window was queerly disturbing. His mouth was set in a straight grim line, lips compressed. Beads of sweat dampened his leathered forehead and plastered his shirt to the chair. Ice locked his joints. Even in the bone-crushing grasp of his own personal grief, he knew these tapes raised frightening possibilities and he was gripped by an urgent need to ensure DeLucci's safety. He was seized by the horrible certainty that the same evil that had stolen his own youth had visited itself upon DeLucci and left him slack as dead fish. This could not go unchallenged or unnamed.

During the instant in which his thoughts returned to outward action, Bralich's brief excursion into melancholy crested and metamorphosed into a powerful resolve. Long ago he recognized that everyone is damaged and few people really deserved the insults that life dished out. For those people without his inner strength and ability to find meaning in suffering, life was immeasurably harder to shoulder. He found it unfathomable to imagine how DeLucci's soul had managed to survive in the hideous shell in which it was housed.

He ejected the tape from the recorder.
There were arrangements to make before the evening grew too late.
He yanked the telephone from its cradle.

Chapter 14

By the time they reached the Delaware Water Gap, the kids were awake and attending to their mousse inundated mop-tops, which had been sculptured into asymmetrical peaks and valleys and illogical swirls and angles as a result of six hours of nesting in the back of the Pathfinder. Vinnie was the first to reopen lines of communication. "Can we stop at McDonalds and get something to eat?"

"We'll be at my parents' soon and you'll be force fed as usual. That is, of course, after we are put through the customary theatrics. 'Oh, my God! Oh, my God! They're here already.' Etcetera, etcetera. Want to bet?" The impersonation, on which Alan was well practiced and he thought quite superb, merited barely a chuckle from the kids and no reaction whatsoever from Evelyn. Later as they marched through the sliding doors into his parents' living room, it would earn a bigger laugh and amused conspiratorial glances.

"Oh, my God! Oh, my God!" Alan's mother exclaimed in her strong Jersey accent, cradling her round olive-complexioned face between her hands. "They're here already. I wasn't expecting you until later this evening. What time did you leave home this morning? I'm happy you're here, of course, but I'm not ready for you!" She allowed herself to be kissed on the cheek, and then pushed Alan aside as if his affections were a bother.

Alan was never quite sure how his mother really felt about him. He had grown up in an absence of personal intimacy and had become accustomed to not receiving it, which left him emotionally vulnerable. Affection bestowed upon a male child, he heard his mother once say, would make a boy weak and needy. Instead, he was showered with material gifts that had little to no value to him.

"Hi Grandma," the kids chimed, each presenting hugs and kisses.

Evelyn offered a disingenuous "Hi, Mom," and dutifully kissed the rotund Italian on the cheek; but it carried little affection. When it came to Alan's mother, she harbored within her dark feelings Alan found easy to comprehend. His wife had been orphaned at an early age and spent several years in an orphanage. She refused to discuss those years but Alan reasoned that somewhere within her secretive internal dynamics was a deep-rooted fear of being too close, for which he forgave her many affective deficiencies. Like his mother, emotionally Evelyn made no promises, not even empty ones. They were two peas in a pod.

"Are you hungry?" Grandma continued. "Grandpa is sleeping. Shall I wake him and tell him you are here?"

"How's Dad feeling?" Alan asked. His father had been bedridden for the last few years after suffering a heart attack and stroke. He required assistance with both eating and bathing.

Indifferent to his probing, his mother waddled into the kitchen, reciting the menu interspersed with her acute observations. She noted that Vinnie needed to put meat on his bones, Gabrielle was beginning to blossom into womanhood but needed to loose a few pounds, and hopefully Tia would be better behaved than last visit.

"And Alan, you look terrible. I'll never understand why you hadn't had the good sense to marry a nice Italian girl who would know how to look after you. Not that Evelyn isn't a wonderful wife and mother," she added as an afterthought in a feeble attempt to mask the insult.

The superficial smile ran away from Evelyn's face.

"Isn't nice Italian girl an oxymoron like jumbo shrimp? Despite their voluptuous beauty, most of the descendants of Caligula that I've known had a penchant for perfidy and a poisonous predisposition."

Vinnie chuckled. "Altogether an asinine attempt at alliteration, Alan."

"I have all kinds of Italian cold cuts and cheeses if you want to make sandwiches. There is rye bread and oh, my God, only a few rolls left. We have to go right out and buy more. Let's see, here's some homemade potato salad and left over chicken cacciatore. Shall I heat up the veal and peppers? They are really good. I bet you kids don't eat like this at home. Right? Tell me the truth. There is ice cream in the freezer for dessert and homemade chocolate chip cookies on the table. Alan, after you eat, you will have to drive me to the grocery store and then to the Bricktown Mall.

Do you need underwear or socks or anything? We're having lasagna for supper. Is that all right? And, Alan, I'll heat up some eggplant Parmesan for you too. I know it's your favorite and I spent all week cooking for you."

Menus, questions, critiques, and philosophical enlightenments were fired with machine gun rapidity, never leaving time for anyone to respond. Alan felt hollowed by his interactions with his mother. There was nothing in her eyes he could read. Animated in both action and speech, her most intimate thoughts, if such existed, were inscrutable. Had her incessant dispense of advice been well intentioned and not a double-edged sword, her company would be far more tolerable.

After finishing off a few sandwiches and digging into the ice cream and cookies, Alan's mother herded her grandchildren and Evelyn out the door and back into the car. Alan was not included in the decision to leave him behind but was appreciative for the opportunity. He would shower and look after his father should he awaken. The house felt empty, as it always did regardless of the number of bodies that filled its halls.

When Alan checked in on his father, he was awake, his frail body, pale and suffering from a variety of illness associated with his advanced years. The old man bore little resemblance to the powerful cigar-smoking longshoreman who had coached Alan's Little League baseball teams and had earned the respect of his fellow dockworkers for his fairness and as a tough customer whose good side was the only one to be on. He was a good man, Alan thought, who deserved far better than the three sons he had spawned.

His Dad struggled to return a greeting and initiate spontaneous conversation, but his mind and tongue were befuddled and sluggish from infirmity and the twenty different medications he was obliged to ingest every day to keep him alive. It was a painful sight for Alan to behold the once athletic, robust frame now so infirmed, and the certainty of death imminent. Alan felt a catch in his throat.

"Turn on the Mets game," the old man croaked.

Alan lay next to his father on the bed. "Season's over for them, Dad. They sucked again this year."

It took a long while and a great deal of effort to get all the words passed his lips but eventually they all came out. "They should trade Brickman. He's a cry baby, and a bum."

"They did, Dad. They pawned him off to Cincy, and then they shipped him to the Yankees, but he's retired now."

His father's memory was spotty and he held no recollection of the Brett Brickman soap opera...drugs, spousal abuse, IRS problems, suspensions, several times born again in Jesus, and then sinned some more, and finally cancer.

Alan watched his father sleep. He hoped that on this trip he would find the courage to tell his dad that he loved him, words that neither man was comfortable saying out loud. He recognized that if he failed to speak soon the words that were never spoken, the opportunity would be forever lost and forgiveness for all the pain he had caused his father over the years would be forever beyond his reach.

When it appeared that the retired longshoreman had dozed off for an extended nap, Alan rose and headed back to the living room.

"Alan ..."

"Yeah, Dad. What do you need?"

The old man paused for a moment, filling the void between them with his labored breaths. "Your friend ..." he groaned with effort.

Alan returned bedside and leaned nearer his father to better understand his words. "Which one, Dad?"

"You remember...good looking boy," he whispered in a raspy voice.

"Which one, Dad?"

"Danny, I think."

"Danny, Danny Cox?" Alan asked. The mention of his friend's name struck a frayed nerve and the flesh prickled on the nape of his neck.

His old man nodded. "Danny Cox," he confirmed.

"Yes, I remember Danny, Dad."

"Good looking boy," he stammered.

"Yes, he was."

"Best...in Cranford."

"Yeah, Dad. Everyone says he could have been the best athlete that Cranford high ever turned out."

His father weakly nodded his head on the pillow in a prolonged gesture of agreement, appearing to have forgotten what additional comments he might have wanted to make.

"Dreams."

"What?" Alan exclaimed, hanging on the old mans' next words.
"Dreams."

"You dream about Danny, Dad?"

His eyes closed and his breath became shallowed by sleep. Alan lingered at his side a few more moments, expecting him to rally and finish his thoughts. When he did not, Alan turned away and started out of the room again.

"Devil," his father said to his back.

Startled, Alan turned to face him once more. His eyes were still closed and he was obviously asleep. Had Alan imagined that word? Had his father said, "devil?"

"Dad? Are you awake?"

He wasn't. At least, not that Alan could tell.

His mother kept his high school yearbooks in a bookcase in the spare bedroom along with numerous photo albums, boxes of slides, and old sixteen-millimeter home movies that chronicled each of her offspring's non-meteoric rises to adulthood. Pulling the cache of old memories off the shelves, Alan maniacally searched through them, uncertain what he expected to find. He studied any photograph displaying one of the Cox boys. Nothing out of the ordinary presented itself. Every photo depicted the normalcy and banality of coming of age in suburbia America in the early sixties.

One album had been dedicated to sports and was filled not only with photographs but with news articles as well, describing Alan's Little League and football games, wrestling matches, and even a few clippings from his college rugby days. None of this held much interest for him; he wasn't looking to reminisce. Unfolding a full-page article found stuffed between two pages of colored glossies, he read the headline, "Baseball All-Stars Capture Tri-County Tournament Championship." The Citizen and Chronicle had devoted nearly half a page to a photo that captured Alan's father, who coached the team, standing proudly behind a three-foot tall trophy, and twenty jubilant pre-teens in two rows, the front row kneeling, with arms draped in comradeship across one another's shoulders. Hollywood smile and powerful physique far in advance of his peers, Danny Cox stood glove-in-hand on the right side of the photo. His right arm was wrapped around his younger brother, whose expression lacked the victorious exuberance so evident on all the other young boys. Stevie's left arm lay across Danny's shoulder but rather than completing a bond of unity, with his thumb and pinkie finger he formed devil horns behind Danny's head.

No…this was but a meaningless juvenile prank, signifying nothing, Alan told himself.

Alan continued pulling scrapbooks from the shelf until it stood empty. His indefinable need for answers unsatisfied, he rummaged through the drawers below. Nothing of consequence materialized on the right, but a drawer on the left held several envelops of photographs. He rapidly thumbed through them. There was a picture of his High School graduation, followed by one of Alan in front of a new '65 Corvair convertible with an old girlfriend. Several snapshots showed the guys returning from a white water rafting trip in Pennsylvania, looking haggard and worn but triumphant. That had occurred during the summer of their junior year in high school. A thought flittered across his mind concerning a second rafting trip but Alan couldn't catch hold of it.

Another photo depicted four indiscernible teenage entities coated head to toe in mud following a sandlot mud bowl football game that Alan recalled occurred during Thanksgiving break during freshman year of college. There were a handful of shots taken at Stevie Cox's wedding; one of Stevie drunk, smashing a piece of wedding cake into his bride's face, another of the newlyweds dancing, and, of course, one of Danny surrounded by an adoring female entourage.

It was the final snapshot in the stack that Alan found most interesting. It contained Alan and the Cox family at a picnic site and a frowning Stevie was once again making devil horns behind his brother's head. Mrs. Cox looked on with displeasure at her middle son's gesture. Stevie's new bride bore a look that Alan could only describe as uncomfortable. As he contemplated the significance of the photo, the floor creaked behind him and woke him from his musing.

"Oh, my God! Oh, my God! Look at this mess!" his mother exclaimed. "Put everything away exactly as you found it when you're finished. I can't be picking up after you any more. As a matter of fact, take those photos home with you. There's no room here in this small house. I'm starting supper. Come see what your kids bought. You know, I can't afford these little shopping excursions with your family. They need everything and it's not like the old days...I'm living on a limited budget now."

Although the food was always five-star, among the least warming memories of Alan's youth were the chaotic milieu of mealtime. Thoughts of Danny Cox provided a distraction that shielded him from the incessant and disjointed verbal bludgeoning being served with the meal.

"You are what you eat. That's why I always fed my boys the very best of everything even though it cost more and you boys never appreciated my sacrifice. We have spinach and broccoli. Everyone needs several cups of vegetables every day. Which do you want, Alan?"

"I don't care; whatever you have the most of."

With a stabbing glance and slicing tone she said, "I'll put both on the table and you can help yourself since it doesn't matter. I'm a dietary nurse, you know. Vegetables are very important."

All three kids looked askance at Alan. Usually, someone would remind his mother that she had been a dietary nurse during World War II, if at all, and that she probably shouldn't refer to herself as such any longer. Nobody bothered on this occasion. She never listened to what anybody had to say anyhow except when the need to argue for the sake of arguing arose. His mother's incessant babbling could have provided the disciple of Sigmund Freud with psychiatric journal material for a lifetime, he thought with ambivalent feelings of resentment and delight.

"Here's the lasagna," Grandma sang out. "I'd better dish it out so we don't have a big mess. How much do you want, Vinnie? One or two scoops?"

"Start me off with one, so I have room for ..."

Alan's mother dished out two large ladles of lasagna onto Vinnie's dish and followed with, "You can have more when you finish this."

Vinnie shot swift glances at his sisters.

"Tia, pass me your plate, honey. Lasagna is one of your favorites, I know."

"No, Grandma. I ..."

The old lady filled her dish and then looked attentively toward Gabby as if she might heed her forthcoming instructions.

"I'm a vegetarian now, Grandma. This isn't meat sauce, is it?" Gabrielle asked.

Grandma ignored her question and spooned lasagna onto Gabby's plate. The teenager stared darkly at the meatballs.

"Oh, my God! Oh, my God! I forgot all about the garlic bread. Evelyn, dear, you serve yourself." She waddled over to the oven, and wielding tongs retrieved the large loaf of bread wrapped in aluminum foil, placed the bread in a basket, and set it in the middle of the table as she sat down. "Vinnie, have you decided to which colleges you will be applying?"

"I thought that…"

"Princeton is not far from here, you know. You could visit us every weekend. Of course, we can't afford to feed you like this all the time. You eat like a horse. How come you're so skinny? Your Uncle Paul never put on weight when he was your age either and he ate all the time. But look at him now!" Without asking, she dished another large serving of the lasagna onto her grandson's plate.

Gabrielle laughed and then wrapped her arm around her plate to fend of an unneeded refill. When his mother couldn't get at Gabby's plate, she unloaded the ladle of lasagna onto Alan's. The kids chortled.

"Tia, I hope that you follow in your brother's footsteps in school. He's such a brilliant student. He'll get offered all kinds of scholarships. At least, he'd better because we can't help him financially. Not that we don't want to. How come we never see any of your report cards? Do you get all 'A's' too? You don't have to be as smart as Vinnie and Gabrielle. Pull your hair away from your face so Grandma can see your beautiful eyes. What grade will you be in this year, dear?"

Tia opened her mouth to respond.

"Your father was an excellent student, you know. I don't even know what degrees he has. What degree do you have, Alan?"

"I'm a Ph.D., Mom."

"But, he should have become a lawyer or a doctor like Mary and Joe Rizzzo's son. Jimmy has a terrific practice. He's a heart surgeon, ya' know, and last year he sent his parents to Europe for the summer. I know that my kids will never do that for me so I'm counting on my grandchildren. Okay, kids?"

"Sure, Grandma," they chimed, knowing she had such a fear of flying that they would never have to fulfill their promise.

"Eat as much as you like. I made plenty. I hoped Paulie and Frankie might drop by today," she said, referring to Alan's two younger brothers.

"I'm so disappointed that they didn't come. Of course, there really isn't enough room around the table for everyone. Why didn't they come, Alan? What did they have to do that was so important they couldn't bring their families over to see you?"

"We'll be here all weekend, Mom."

"Well, I just don't understand you people," Grandma continued. "You don't seem to have any sense of family. For some reason you don't seem to communicate …"

Vinnie leaned toward Tia and whispered in her ear, "Let's try a little communication exercise with Grandma." His expression was full of mischief and Tia's eyes sparkled at the suggestion.

"Gram, I've decided to pierce my nose and tongue while we're here. You know any good places around here for that?" Tia asked.

Evelyn eyed her offspring with amusement.

Grandma rambled on about the importance of interpersonal communication and her three offspring's deficiency in this arena.

"Grandma, what do you think about the piercing idea?"

"Leave room for dessert. I made ice cream pie," she replied.

The comedic opportunity too precious to pass by, the kids volunteered additional irrelevant questions in order to determine just how much foolishness they might dish out before their grandmother took notice. Vinnie gained permission to take the car, empty Grandma's purse, pee in the corner and have sexual intercourse with the cat, which had been dead for over a year. In addition to the piercings, Tia was promised an expanded Madonna-like wardrobe and a weekend alone with all the members of Metallica.

Not until Vinnie asked his grandmother for psychedelic condoms for dessert did she chuckle an acknowledging response, "I draw the line at buying your underwear. Get your own damn rubbers!" So much for the value of communication at the Ciani household.

When the doorbell rang, Alan's mother jumped up to answer it.

"Oh my God! Oh my God! Alan quick! Come see who's here."

Derrick Brown and Michael Mezzacapo walked into the dining room, both grinning ear-to-ear. Derrick was much skinnier than Alan remembered. Michael had lost most of his hair and had grown a mustache as a replacement. The three boys had been inseparable as kids. Seeing them again reminded Alan that he no longer had the luxury of true friends. Spurned as an outsider in backwater Pennsylvania, he was isolated by more than forest and miles from the security of male companionship that had both armed and protected him as a kid.

"Hey, Nude. How they hangin'?" Derrick asked, raising his heavily calloused hand for a high five. Alan stood, completed the ritual and embraced his taller friend. Michael extended a more reserved hand, befitting his professional stature. He had become a dentist and Alan's mother continually reported that she sent all her friends to him, although she herself went elsewhere. He, too, towered above Alan.

"Jeez, I was just looking at some old photos and thinking about you guys today. Derrick, I was remembering your disastrous date with Jackie Pendelton at the Beach Boys concert."

"Please, don't remind me!" He formed a cross with his arms in front of his face. "I just ran into Dr. Pain at the Mall," he said patting Michael's basketball belly, "and he told me your mom said you were coming to town, so I figured we oughta' drop by. Wow! Smells great in here!"

"Nude?" Vinnie asked with a glimmer in his eye. Evelyn and the girls exchanged glances and arched eyebrows.

"Sit down, boys," Alan's mother ordered. "What can I get you?" She proceeded to run through the list of items still available on the day's Ciani menu. She even offered to go shopping for whatever Alan's old friends wanted that wasn't currently in stock.

"No, nothing, really, Mrs. Ciani. My wife is waiting dinner on me," Michael said.

"Mine, too," Derrick added, flicking his fingers through the curly tendrils that hung at the nape of his neck. Gray was beginning to show on his temples. Alan thought he looked good, well, actually better than ever.

Each was immediately provided a dish of lasagna and told to sit.

"We have plenty so don't be shy. Derrick, you are too skinny."

"You guys remember Evelyn, don't you?" Alan asked. His friends nodded and said hello. "And this is Vinnie, Gabrielle, and Tia," he said, pointing to each according to their birth order.

"Here, you boys need garlic bread," his mother insisted as she placed a couple of pieces on each plate.

"Everybody knows that the place to go when you're hungry is to Ciani's," Derrick said to the entire table. "If we showed up in the middle of night, Mrs. C would get up and make us something to eat, whether we were hungry or not. God bless her," he laughed.

"Nude?" Vinnie repeated.

"Don't you share the highlights of your degenerate youth with the children?" Derrick asked.

"I try to restrict my stories to those that have a positive message," Alan explained.

"Yeah, Dad's big on messages," Gabrielle said, resting her chin on her hand.

"We have heard him referred to as the 'Animal' and 'Blackie' but we haven't been enlightened as to his being 'The Nude'," Vinnie said.

Evelyn cocked her head. "I suspect we're about to hear another story about your father's jaded and unsavory past."

"I think we can skip this story," Alan cut in, nodding in the direction of his mother to remind his friends she was still in the room. Unfortunately everyone disagreed and Derrick was bursting at the seams to spill the beans.

"There's ice cream pie for dessert," Alan's mother informed her guests. To Alan's relief she added, "Help yourselves. I have to go feed my husband."

After his guests inquired as to his dad's health, they systematically set about to destroy what little credibility Alan might have attained with his family.

"It was Christmas day, what '65 or '66?" Derrick started, his features animated.

"Anyone tell you that you have a New Jersey accent?" Alan interrupted.

"No fricken kidding. In case your college-educated, ivory tower peanut of a Dago brain hasn't figured it out, we're in fricken New Jersey. So it was '66, right?"

"1965," Alan chuckled. "It was just before my eighteenth birthday."

"Yeah," Derrick agreed, and turning to Alan's children continued. "And your Dad shows up at my house where my parents are throwing a huge party, and he's drunk as a skunk."

"Dad used to drink?" the kids exclaimed in unison.

"Hey, if you have to embarrass me, at least you can start at the beginning."

"Okay. You lay the groundwork, but I get to tell the story when you reach the part about what happened at my house."

Evelyn went to the refrigerator to get beers for their guests. Vinnie reached for one and got his hand smacked.

"It was Christmas Day, 1965, and I didn't want to spend the entire day with all the relatives, visiting one family after another, and winding up in front of a television while my parents shot the bull with the in-laws. Back then children were to be seen and not heard and we were seldom included in adult conversations. Besides, I wanted to spend some time with my friends on Christmas, and Derrick's folks were having a big party."

"And my cousin, Diana, was going to be there, and your Dad had the hots for her," Derrick said.

Evelyn interrupted, "I imagine that, even then, Alan found it tough getting laid." She flicked Alan a quick sideways glance.

Everybody chuckled and Alan felt a surge of warmth flush his face.

"No need to be embarrassed in front of us, Dad. We figured that you're probably not a virgin…and have known a long time that you're seriously warped," Gabrielle said.

"And delusional," Vinnie added.

"Your children are quite perceptive, Ciani," Derrick said.

Alan continued. "Anyway, I had managed to convince Grandma and Grandpa to let me drive alone in my Corvair so that I might leave early. There were eight stops before we finally settled in at Aunt Lee's for our traditional lasagna Christmas dinner. At each stopover, it was agreed that I was old enough to participate in a Yuletide toast. That usually meant homemade wine courtesy of one of my uncles. Eight glasses of wine were more than enough to wash away sobriety, but I mustered all the athletic prowess I could to demonstrate I could hold my liquor.

"In all my youthful wisdom, I had a third plate of lasagna even though the plate did seem a bit evasive and tried to escape from my fork. I was sure that nobody noticed, since everyone else had to be as drunk as I was and too self-absorbed to notice my condition. When the holiday meal was completed, I said my good-byes and headed to Cranford."

"Okay. My turn," Derrick said. "So your old man shows up at my place plastered."

"Don't forget to mention that he was wearing his favorite white corduroy suit," Michael added.

"Yeah right. He was very spiffy. And he plays at being polite and sober for my folks, although not very convincingly. Michael was already there, and so were Danny and Stevie Cox. Now Danny brought a bottle of rye whiskey with him, and the five of us goes upstairs and drain every last drop."

"Goes upstairs? Michael, did he say goes upstairs?" Alan chided in the thickest Jersey accent he could muster.

Derrick turned his head and shielded a silent, "Fuck you," from Alan's family.

"Oh, Alan. How could you have been so stupid?" Evelyn asked. "He seldom, if ever, drinks nowadays except for the occasional beer," she explained to the table of occupants.

Vinnie looked real impressed by Alan's accomplishments. "Yeah, Dad. Real brilliant."

"By nine o'clock the house was packed with my folk's friends, business associates, neighbors and relatives. The party was in full swing."

"Yeah, me and Derrick were wired, but our little paisan here was passed out on the floor upstairs." Michael snickered.

"Now, had your father only stayed passed out, Christmas 1965 would have been an unremarkable event. But I guess there was some bad chemistry between the lasagna, the wine, and the rye whiskey. The lasagna wanted out! The first of it he deposited on the carpet in my bedroom."

"Ew yuck!" the girls chimed in unison.

"That's not the worst of it," Michael noted. "We tried to get him to the bathroom and stick his head in the toilet. Unfortunately, Derrick and I dropped him a few times and he left a few puddles of vomit along the way."

"And then he couldn't find the goddamn—excuse my French—toilet anyway. Ruined all the new carpet that my father had laid down the day before the party."

"And his white corduroy suit," Michael added.

"Still, the evening would have remained unremarkable hadn't Danny proposed a plan. Creative thought just wasn't Danny's forte," Derrick said.

"Nor yours either," Alan felt obligated to contribute.

"Yo, it wasn't my fault. It was Danny's idea." He returned his attention to the kids, "… and I figured we had to sober the dumb Dago up and spare any further destruction to my living environment."

"Of course, I don't remember any of this," Alan said. "That means we must take this story on faith." With arched eyebrows and pursed lips he added, "Consider the source."

Derrick continued. "Danny's strategy was to get our retching companion out into the cold December air. But first we had to remove your father's vomit-soaked clothing because we couldn't walk him downstairs through my parents' party smelling to high hell."

"Does high hell and low hell smell differently, Mom?" Tia wanted to know.

"Go ask your grandmother. If anyone knows she will."

"So under Danny's leadership, Stevie, Derrick, and I disrobed our little paisan, which was near impossible since he could offer little assistance and every time we sat him up he fell over."

"I draped a long winter coat over Al's shoulders, and me and Stevie hoisted him up to his feet. Then, we attempted to guide him down the stairs undetected. Danny, who spent most of the evening putting the moves on Diana, Al's reason for showing up at my house to start with, provided a little push to overcome Al's inert body."

"They handled the first few step quite adroitly" Michael informed his audience, "the rest rather…quickly."

"Yeah, your Dad went tumbling down the steps like a bag of potatoes, but the coat never left my hands. It would have been difficult going unnoticed seated buck naked in the middle of my parents' guests, even if my sisters and cousin weren't shrieking hysterically on the stairwell."

Alan's children sat wide-eyed, mouths agape in astonishment. Evelyn shook her head feigning disbelief but Alan knew that her small, wicked mind cherished his moment of humiliation in front of his kids.

Michael said, "It was a rather noisy descent, as I remember it. It caught everybody's attention. And once it was obvious that Al survived the fall unharmed, a wave of laughter rolled over the partygoers, bringing observers in from the adjoining rooms."

"The next thing we know, Danny had my parents Instamatic camera and is encouraging everybody to pose with your old man in front of the

Christmas tree to preserve the moment for posterity. He had such a diabolical mind!

"Danny even pulled ornaments off the tree and hung them on your dad in order to add color to the Kodak moment. Women lined up for photo-ops with the new, drunk kid on the block. When the film ran out and the novelty wore off, we placed 'The Nude'," he punctuated the moniker by drawing quotation marks in the air with his fingers," in a lounge chair on the back porch. My folks still have the photos if you kids should ever want to see them."

"You do us proud, Dad. Would you prefer we just refer to you from now on as 'Nude?'" Vinnie asked.

"Wonderful story, Alan," Evelyn said feigning displeasure although her eyes glinted with a macabre amusement.

"Alan gave a small, self-conscious shrug. "For Crissake, I was just a dumb kid."

"We can vouch for that, huh, Michael?"

"Your father was a very dumb kid."

"A pretty messed up kid overwhelmed by events he couldn't control. Oh, the horror of it all!"

As the girls cleaned the table, Vinnie relocated to the television. Alan and his buddies continued their conversation. It didn't take long before they hit on the declining fortunes of Danny Cox.

Why Danny's house had been so neglected prior to the fire neither Derrick nor Michael was quite sure. The neighbors were extremely displeased with him. Neglecting to manicure the manor was akin to contracting leprosy in suburbia.

"His lawn always needed mowing and the paint on his house was beginning to peel."

Michael added that Danny committed the ultimate sacrilege of being the only Christian house on the block that hadn't put up holiday decorations. "Jesus, can you believe it...Danny and Stevie both dying so violently within weeks of each other? I wonder how their Mom is taking it? You know she lives not far from here."

Derrick's expressions turned somber. "We read in the papers that you were with Stevie when he cashed in his chips. What happened?"

Reliving the experience was not high among Alan's priorities. "It was really ugly. Stevie was a wreck and talking crazy. He just got up in the middle of our conversation, went into the bathroom, and blew his head off."

"Talking crazy, how?"

He shrugged his shoulders. "All kinds of weird stuff. Claimed that Danny was the devil."

"No shit," Michael Mezzacappo added. "My grandmother used to say the same thing about him all the time. She claimed that Danny had the evil eye, was evil to the core ever since we were just little kids."

"That would be the grandmother with the hairy mole on her cheek who lived on Lexington Avenue?" Alan queried.

"She the one who looked like the old gypsy woman that warned Lon Chaney that he had become the werewolf?"

"Reality check: Lon Caney did become the werewolf, you dumb shit. Considering everything that's surfaced recently, I'd say Gram might have been on to something."

"Is there any truth to the pornography charges?" Alan wanted to know.

"Who the hell knows," Derrick answered. "If there is, nobody that we know is talking. But over the last few years, Danny sure changed a lot. He really was getting spooky. Not just personality-wise, but physically too. Man, like he seemed to be aging at a frightening rate."

Michael nodded his agreement. "Gram said he was in league with the devil; all the time warned me to stay away from him. Hey, speaking of spooky, do you guys remember the story that Stevie told us one night on our whitewater trip?"

Derrick looked confused. "What story?"

"The Faustian, horned demon from Hell tale!" Michael answered.

Alan had only the faintest memory of some scary tale; Derrick claimed not to remember at all.

"Come on, how could you forget?" Michael replied in a disappointed tone. "It was our junior year in high school. We were sitting around the campfire having pretty much achieved our benchmark state of drunken unruliness and were philosophizing about the nature of the universe."

"One of our favorite activities during those years," Derrick reminisced and the others nodded in agreement. "I'd say we were pretty much responsible for saving the world."

"It's still here, isn't it?"

They raised their beers, tapped the three bottles together, and drank.

"The dialogue had shifted to unexplainable events, each of us sharing the strangest occurrences of our young lives and trying to scare the bejesus out of each other. Well, you know what a great storyteller Stevie was."

"Hell," Derrick interrupted. "Stevie was so totally full of shit that I never knew when his stories should be taken at face value."

"He embellished. It's considered an art form," Alan insisted.

"With all that's happened, maybe his story had its roots in reality," Michael postulated.

As Michael recounted the tale, vivid memories of Stevie's original telling around the campfire leaped into Alan's mind. Even as drunk as he had been that evening, Alan remembered how chills had run up his spine as Stevie acted out his narrative.

"Danny, Tommy and I shared a big bedroom upstairs when we were kids," Stevie explained. "One summer evening when Danny was about ten and I was nine, all three of us awoke suddenly in the middle of the night. I peeked out from under the covers and to my horror the Devil, himself, was looking down at me. His blazing red eyes shot daggers of fear right through me and I nearly shit myself as I dived back under the sheets. I'm certain that Tommy saw him too because we shared the same bed and the poor little guy actually peed the sheets.

"Hidden beneath the covers, I came to my senses and reasoned that I imagined the apparition. The moon was probably shining through the blinds, projecting a devil-like form on the wall and being groggy, my impressionable pre-adolescent mind conjured up something from one of my horror comic books. But hell, when I peeked out a second time, there was no mistaking that the damned thing was still there. The blinds were closed so no light was coming into the room. Once again I dived under the blankets for cover. I mean like I'm really scared stiff. Fear is a natural reaction, right? Trembling, I somehow summoned up the courage to call over to Danny in the next cage to find out if he was awake."

"Cage? You mean bed," Alan interrupted.

"Yeah, bed. I said bed."

"You said cage."

"Bed. Why the hell would I say cage. We didn't sleep in cages. I said bed. I called over to Danny in the next *bed*. 'Hey, Danny, you awake?' I whispered. 'Go back to sleep. There's nothing to worry about,' he answered, getting out of bed. I stayed hidden under the covers for what seemed an eternity and somehow, God knows how, managed to fall asleep. The three of us never discussed the incident afterward and I never asked Danny why he had gotten out of bed or what he did. But let me tell you, the door to our room never opened and Danny didn't come back to bed for a long time."

"Well, Danny. What did you do when you got up? Someone had asked.

Flashing his Robert Redford smile, Danny had responded, "Stevie just dreamed it all."

The star had spoken; the story was disregarded. Until now.

Alan wondered now if Stevie's childhood fantasy had set in motion a chain of events that ultimately ended in tragedy years later.

"I don't remember hearing that story before," Derrick said. "You just made it up so we wouldn't think your two hundred year old guinea grandma isn't loony tunes, right?"

"Alan remembers. Don't you paisan?" Michael's eyes crinkled into a smile, as he turned to Alan. Our buddy, here was probably roaming around in the woods looking for rodents to play hide the salami."

"If done tastefully, what's the harm?" Derrick played at taking offense. He looked at his watch. "Speaking of lower forms of life, my mother-in-law is visiting. If I don't get home soon for dinner, Ellen will have my hide."

"Me, too. Keep in touch, bro'," Michael said as he stood. "See you, Mrs. C," he yelled into the house.

"Bye, Mrs. Ciani," Derrick echoed.

Alan's Mom waddled put of the bedroom. "Oh, you're leaving so soon?" she said, sounding disappointed as Alan closed the door behind their guests. "Nice boys." To Evelyn she remarked, "Michael's a dentist, you know. I send all my friends to him. He's very good. Of course, I prefer to go to …"

"Mom, do you know where Danny and Stevie Cox's mother lives?"

She continued rambling on as if he hadn't said a word and vanished into the kitchen. When she reappeared she had the address and phone number written on a piece of paper.

"It's not three-quarters of a mile away." She couldn't help adding, "Ginny's a strange duck; never much interested in conversation or socializing. Dad and I sent her flowers in memory of the boys after seeing their obituaries in the newspaper. We haven't received a thank you note."

Still filled to the gills with the best homemade Italian food that could be found on the East Coast, Alan decided to take a leisurely stroll along the bay to aid digestion.

Evelyn declined his offer to accompany him. "If we both leave, your mother will claim we were trying to avoid her and tear into me whenever she can."

Evelyn cast a stony look that Alan knew meant don't you dare leave me here alone with your mother, but he ignored it and set out on his own.

Something gnawed at his brain. There had been a second rafting trip, he now felt certain. He had the uneasy feeling that something singularly horrific had occurred during that trip but whatever had happened was buried in the deepest recesses of his mind and he was unable to retrieve the memory.

The sun had already begun to melt into the horizon, casting an orange reflection over the velvety black water. His mind buzzed, rehearsing potential dialogue options, discarding them, and then re-scripting what he might say when he reached the home of Virginia Cox. When he finally arrived at his destination he was no less conflicted. He dawdled, alternated between starting toward the front door, retracing his tracks, and then stopping to clean imaginary dirt from under his fingernails. However, the vacillation between paying a visit and embarking upon the return leg of the hike was fatuous. He hadn't passed this way be accident. He needed to put his mind at ease and only Mrs. Cox could provide answers that would allow him to do so.

Alan's knock on the front door of the Cape cod dwelling summoned a silver-haired woman with a warm smile and dressed in the white uniform of a nurse. She asked who he was, then invited Alan in and pointed him toward the cathedral ceiling living room to wait while she readied her patient for a visitor. The wait was short.

When the nurse returned, Mrs. Cox was close at her arm. She guided the elderly lady to a rocking chair facing an expanse of tinted window overlooking the bay. Draping a peach colored afghan over the shoulders of her ward, the nurse bade Alan to settle in a nearby recliner and excused herself.

Time had worn heavily on the mother of his childhood chums, although, unlike Alan's father, the face and odor of death didn't pervade her presence. The fragile gray-haired woman bent with age but hadn't caved in under its assault. She was alert, coherent, and although from time to time appeared distracted, she did so only when it seemed to her advantage.

"Do you remember me, Mrs. Cox?"

"Of course I do. You're the oldest Ciani boy. How are your parents? I haven't seen them in ages."

"Mom is fine. My Dad isn't doing too well."

"I'm sorry to hear that. Sal was always a real gentleman…and quite a handsome man, I might add. He knew how to make a woman feel important."

"Thank you." Despite the numerous iterations he had rehearsed, Alan still hadn't any inkling as to how to begin probing for the information that prompted the visit. Mrs. Cox seemed appreciative of the opportunity to talk and so he let her, waiting for his cue to breach the subject of his sons' deaths.

"You remember my Tommy, don't you?"

"Um-hum."

"He still lives in New Jersey and is very happily married with five children! Can you imagine? They visit almost every weekend," she informed Alan. "The children are so cute, especially the girls. But spoiled, let me tell you. By their mother, of course."

"They must be a real joy," Alan said, still holding back.

"They are."

The conversation lapsed and Alan looked down at his hands while the old lady stared out the window.

"I'm sorry about Danny and Stevie," he finally blurted out.

The old woman ignored his expression of sympathy for the passing of her two elder sons. "Did you ever meet my granddaughter, Samantha?" she asked referring to Stevie's only child. "Sam stayed with me for a couple of months last year. She's a wonderful child. The most beautiful creature that ever graced this earth! And what an angelic singing voice she has!"

"I bet you enjoyed having her stay with you. Where is she now?" Alan asked but again the elderly woman fended off the intrusion by changing the subject. Her expression was unreadable.

"Do you have any children, Alan?" she asked.

"Yes, three. A boy and two girls."

He parried with another question about Stevie but his friend's mother showed little interest in her recently deceased son. Alan wrestled with the humanity and wisdom of pressing the old woman with unpleasant memories in order to satisfy his own morbid curiosity. He decided to give it one last shot by mentioning that he had been with Stevie during his last minutes. Should she choose to pursue the point, great; if not he'd let it slide and mind his own business. He'd suffer in silence and call it a day.

"Mrs. Cox, are you aware that I was with Stevie when he com…when he died?"

To Alan's surprise, Virginia Cox gasped, lifting her hand to her mouth. A frightened, haunted stare invaded her eyes and she tried to stand up. "What did he tell you?" she screamed. "What did the liar say?" she asked, her voice cracking as she attempted to rise but stumbled back into the rocker, thumping her skull on the uncushioned headrest. The rocker lurched to and fro in a couple of quick convulsions, and then settled into a less animated rhythm. Mrs. Cox rocketed her hands up to her ears as if to fend off any slander that Alan might hurl across the room at her.

"No! No! No! No!" she began chanting in harmony with the rocker's undulations.

The nurse returned at a run and hurried to the old lady's side, a questioning look on her face. "Ginnie! Ginnie are you all right? What's wrong?"

"No! No! No!" she raved on.

"It's okay, Ginnie," the nurse comforted, stroking gently at her ward's hair and face. She turned to Alan with an uncharitable eye, suggesting politely that he leave and would he mind showing himself out. As he did, Alan could hear the old lady trumpeting, "There is no devil. There is no devil. There is no devil."

"Of course not Ginnie," the nurse agreed.

Alan no longer could hold to that assertion with any confidence. Maybe no actual devil existed but something wicked and diabolic had taken hold in the lives of the family Cox.

He exited the home to find that nightfall had toppled onto the landscape. He grew rigid with tension. The sounds and shadows of night hurled themselves at him like daggers. In his new fledging dementia, he reacted in a superstitious pan. His quickened steps back to his parents' house evolved into a panicked run in which he repeatedly looked over his shoulder in search of some imaginary predator lurking in the night, waiting to pounce upon him. It remained unseen but its presence was unmistakable.

Alan's lungs choked on the heavy air permeated with the unseen beast's acrid breath. His chest ached in desperation. He could feel the creature's eyes on his back. He could hear its seductive song prying rationality and the willpower to resist from his mind. He was an empty vessel filling with terror.

When he finally reached the safe haven of his parent's home, Alan's body was lathered in sweat. Salted droplets of perspiration coursed down his forehead into his eyes and on to his lips. He was shaking.

Evelyn greeted him at the door. "What's wrong?" she asked.

"Nothing."

"You're shivering."

"It's getting cold out."

"You are a seriously disturbed individual," Evelyn noted. "I hate you for abandoning me to your mother's malicious intents."

Alan nodded in concession. Under his breath he muttered, "Maybe you deserve it," and behind her back flipped her the middle finger.

Mindful that the dreams of Danny Cox that now seemed to define his life would revisit him when he succumbed to his bodily need for rest, Alan tossed fitfully. It was dawn before he closed his eyes with any sense of security. In the ambiguous margins between a sleep-filled and wakeful state, the boundaries separating reality and somnambulistic fantasy obscured. The fragile weeping of the little girl echoed faintly in his mind, like an itch that couldn't be scratched. In the morning, again he awoke drawn and tired, already dreading the inevitability of another nightfall, as the house filled with the noises of busied activity.

His parents' anniversary celebration proved an unspectacular event. Occasional visitors, bearing congratulations and foodstuffs, and a reunion with his brothers and their families marked the event. The constant activity and clamor that engulfed the house for the weekend complemented the mind-numbing distraction offered by the television. Over-stimulation scrambled any attempt at focused thought, allowing little opportunity for concern, until nighttime again blanketed the day and imposed upon his mind a concession to irrational fears. As darkness deepened, whatever unseen power had been incubating its cancerous intentions within the shadows crossed into reality to terrorize him again. The previous evening's nocturnal pattern repeated itself.

Continued lack of rest did little to replenish him. Every joint in his body ached deeply, the fleshy areas in between had no feeling whatsoever, excepting for old athletic injures, which throbbed with a cold pain. A constant pounding between his eyes sent shock waves shooting across Alan's temples, down behind his ears, and around to the nape of his neck. His eyes burned from the inside out.

Disabled so, Vinnie and Evelyn tackled the driving when they bade farewell and headed home to Pennsylvania. His son embraced the opportunity; his wife resented it. A sunken-eyed wreck, Alan sat in a stupor like a heavily sedated psychiatric patient, fighting off the conflicting emotions that battled for his attention. He remembered little of the trip except that it was unbearably long and his forehead absorbed a great deal of punishment bouncing against the cold window upon which it rested. There seemed no shortage of potholes along Interstate 80 in Pennsylvania and no limit to his chauffeurs' ability in locating them. Focusing thought became increasingly difficult and he hadn't the energy to attempt anything beyond monosyllabic dialogue. If he had, he'd have reminded Vinnie that the dotted lines on the road were not merely suggestions, one was meant to drive in between them.

Chapter 15

Lucius Sangre swaggered into the grimly impersonal holding room in an orange body suit, his hands cuffed in front of him, ankles shackled. Considerably smaller than Bralich had pictured him, he was actually of diminutive stature. His steely eyes went straight to Bralich's and held them for a piercing instant before shifting away in disinterest. He fell into the chair on his side of the glass panel that separated the two men, and proceeded to smooth his thinning hair, using both hands since he was manacled at the wrists. When he finished grooming, he removed a pack of cigarettes from his pocket, knocked a cigarette out of the pack, and placed it between his lips. He looked toward the three guards that had accompanied him into the holding area. The largest of the three, a pock-scarred, pot-bellied man whose crimson nose foreshadowed liver failure, approached him, lit the smoke, and backed away.

Sangre turned to Bralich and exhaled a stream of smoke with a hiss. "Well, who the hell are you and what the fuck do you want?" he asked with a look that could kill. The cigarette acted as a punctuation mark.

Bralich observed that up close the killer's features were not nearly as sinister as the media had portrayed. Although a mural of tattoos slithered out from beneath his coveralls covering everything but his face, Sangre was not a physically unattractive man, but posturing him as such probably wouldn't have sold many newspapers or much airtime.

It had been several years since the demonic face of Lucius Sangre had monopolized the television screens and covers of national tabloids for several days. The carnage he had perpetrated on the unsuspecting populace of Trenton, New Jersey, rivaled the Manson murders.

Chances were that the Sangre slaughters would have remained front page and prime time for months to come had not then President Bush launched his massive offensive on Iraq that same week and given the media an anti-Christ in the Middle East to target.

Seated in a hard wooden chair in a room devoid of comfort, Bralich struggled to conceal his uneasiness. "My name is Dr. Anthony Bralich. I'm a psychiatrist and have come to get your permission to speak with Dr. Zent about you."

Sangre blew a smoke ring into the air and watched with amusement as it floated toward the glass that separated the two of them. Coiled in his seat, Sangre looked like a rattlesnake, readying to strike.

"How is ole' Dr. Billy? He doesn't much visit me any more." Sangre's dark eyes twinkled mischievously as a lecherous grim twisted his lips. The hairs bristled on Bralich's neck.

"I can't really say, Mr. Sangre. I've only but spoken to Dr. Zent on the telephone. I have brought with me, a …"

"Why?"

"Why? Why have I …?"

"Why the fuck do you want to discuss my case with Dr. Billy?"

The way Sangre said *my case,* almost in a sibilant whisper, wantonly cryptic, raised goose bumps on Bralich's arms. An icy stare hardened between the two men. "I have a client who …"

"Who?"

"I'm afraid I am not at liberty to disclose my client's name. Like Zent, I am bound by confidentiality, which is why I have come to request that you sign this form to release Dr. Zent from his oath of confidentiality so that we might …"

"Why the hell should I do that? What's it in for me, Ant-tony?"

"Not much really. I thought maybe you might be interested in helping a fellow orphan. Like you, my client spent a brief time at the Garden Grove Children's Home."

The shift was a subtle one, barely perceptible even to Bralich's trained eye. The muscles of Sangre's face slackened and washed of affect, metamorphosing into an inscrutable mask in a fashion that appeared to Bralich involuntary. His eyes dulled, became flat and inexpressive, and his head lolled lazily on his shoulders as if he was stoned. "That was a long time ago. I was just a kid. I really don't remember much of anything of my time there." Sangre chuckled and turned his attention to his cigarette.

Bralich wondered if he had imagined these abstruse changes. Sangre's words rang a familiar chord in Bralich's mind, but before another thought could congeal, Sangre had resumed his questioning.

"What do I have to do with your f'ing client, Ant-Tony?"

"I don't know that you have anything to do with my client. That's why I seek your permission to speak with Zent and listen to some of the tapes of your sessions."

Sangre rolled the cigarette onto his tongue as if performing a magical trick. It disappeared into his mouth, and then reappeared between his teeth. He tilted his head back and blew a cloud of smoke into the air. Looking down the bridge of his nose at Bralich, he asked almost indifferently: "And just how will Dr. Billy's tapes help your client?"

"I'm interested especially in your recollections of the time you spent at the Garden Grove Children's Home."

Again, Sangre shifted ever so slightly in his seat and Bralich watched as the outward appearances of spontaneity evaporated from the prisoner's face as if a cloud had briefly passed over it. "That was a long time ago. I was just a kid. I really don't remember much of anything of my time there." Sangre's cigarette regained its saliency.

I'll be a son of a bitch, Bralich thought, almost disbelieving what he observed. "Mr. Sangre, do you remember much about the Garden Grove Children's Home?" he asked expectantly.

"No. That was a long time ago. I was just a kid. I really don't remember much of anything of my time there." Sangre tossed the cigarette on the floor and pulverized it with his foot.

Bralich held the release form up to the glass so that Sangre could read it. "You'll be a sport then, and okay this?"

Sangre seemed confused, scanned the paper. "Like I said, it's all a fog. But it's no skin off my ass. Sure, I'll sign the fuckin' thing, sport, just to get you off my pimply back."

Bralich waved the paper at the guards. The big one came around the divider, accepted the form, and handed it to Sangre with a pen that Red Nose pulled from his pocket.

Sangre signed it and gave it back to the officer after feigning using it as a knife. "Now, I've had enough of this meaningless chit chat," he said, having lost all interest in his visitor. He started away, then turned to Bralich and said, "Happy hunting, Doc," with a wicked grin and mannerisms that Bralich recognized as Sangre's attempt at mimicking the acting of Jack Nicholson. He continued the impersonation, "Give my best to Dr. Billy and let him know that I hope to visit him and his family as soon as I can free up my social calendar."

"Jesus H. Christ!" Bralich mumbled to himself over and over again as he exited the Rahway State Prison with the waiver grasped firmly in his hand. "I have to talk to Zent...Dr. Billy...now!"

Chapter 16

"Are you in training for the Olympics?" Evelyn asked Alan with muted annoyance. "You were running in your sleep and whining again. We really need to get separate beds so that I can get some sleep! What were you dreaming about?"

"I don't remember," he lied. Marriage could be tough enough without throwing in crazy stuff, and Evelyn showed little interest in psychological gobbledygook, especially his. Although they had married out of necessity and not love, Alan still had hoped to be a good husband and make both their dreams come true, only to find that Evelyn had her own dreams and no interest in indulging his. They had different friends and led different, albeit interdependent lives. There was no room in Evelyn's fantasy world for a man who showed any sign of weakness. Her complete lack of empathy and compassion, required an infallible father substitute who could play to her perversely playful moods, feed her straight lines, and unconditionally attend to her affectual needs, while requiring absolutely nothing in return from her. Any breeches of their unspoken agreement by Alan were punished with cruel ridicule and public chastisement disguised as clever repartee. He tolerated the arrangement for the benefit of the children and looked forward to the day they all left the nest. He would follow not far behind.

"Well, it must have been a doosie of a dream. A couple of times, I kicked you, hoping you'd stop. But you just kept it up all night long."

Alan shrugged an apology and studied the carpet rather than face the familiar contempt residing in Evelyn's eyes.

"Well don't be surprised if you wake up one morning tied and gagged. I've considered that on numerous occasions."

"I could get into bondage," he toyed. "Shall I go buy anything special?"

Evelyn offered a dutiful chortle and gifted him an impish smile. It was the favor of this smile, saturated with sensuality, which had first attracted Alan to the petite, dark-haired artist in college and which, as much as anything else, kept him faithful for twenty years despite her failure to insulate him against the despair of emotional isolation.

Since they returned from New Jersey, the horrific mental images of Danny Cox being butchered continued night after night, steadily worsening during the week. And always, the trembling sobs of a little girl provided a backdrop for the gore. Residue from these nightmares clung to his soul, haunting his waking hours. The all-pervasive sense of evil was like a mist that clouded Alan's mind. He rubbed at the white pain that throbbed in his temples.

As if against her will, Evelyn reached for his hand as a demonstration of empathy. "Okay, Alan, tell me about your dreams. I'm listening."

So he did.

She listened and said nothing until he was finished. "Okay? Feel better now that you've purged?" Her face was cold and indifferent, without a hint of compassion. "Now get over yourself. You need go see somebody about your sleeping problem. You know, take a sleep test. I can't go on this way night after night."

"Maybe you should make a conscious effort to tire me out every evening." He slipped his hand under her t-shirt and cupped her breast. "I could stand a little exercise right now, as a matter of fact, if you have the time."

"I have the time but what are we going to do with the horses," they said in unison, mimicking one of their favorite Mae West lines. Alan rolled over on top of her.

"Mom! Where are my ice skates?" Tia yelled from the top of the stairs. "They're not in my closet."

"Did you check under every pile of dirty clothes, or just those piles closest to the door?" she yelled back.

Alan fell onto his back knowing the window of opportunity for sex had been slammed shut. His wife wasted little time in evacuating the waterbed and exited the bedroom with a large wicker clothesbasket in her arms. He grabbed the television remote in search of an alternative distraction.

"Mom!" Tia whined. "I can't find them and I wanted to polish them. Looks like we'll be skating before Thanksgiving this year."

"Clean out your closet. I guarantee you'll find them."

Tia met her at the bottom of the stairs.

"Here. Collect your dirty clothes and bring them down to the laundry room. All the dirty clothes!" she said sternly.

"There aren't any dirty clothes in my closet…just clean stuff I haven't had time to hang up yet."

"Tia! A pair of your jeans walked down to dinner yesterday by themselves, ate some macaroni and cheese, and walked back to your bedroom. And, while I'm on the subject, bring down any dirty dishes and glasses from your room too?"

"Mom! I'm trying to find my ice skates!"

"Alan! Tell your daughter to clean up her room. I'm tired of arguing with her. Alan! Alan! Earth calling Alan Ciani." Evelyn stomped into the bedroom. "Hey, Conan! I know you hear me calling you."

She stepped in between Alan and the television and folded her arms in front of her. Peyton Manning had just unloaded a bomb down field in an attempt to tie up the game for the Indianapolis Colts with less than two minutes remaining. He tried to view the game by swanning his neck around his wife. She reached back and slapped off the television.

"Your daughter's room is an absolute sty and she won't clean it up! Do something!"

"Hell, I don't want to go into her room. I might catch something fatal. Put the game back on; we're in the last two minutes."

"Make her clean up her room!"

"She's a teenager, she supposed to be a pathetic slob. Just as long as she keeps the door closed, who cares? She'll clean it up in a couple of years. Put the game back on."

"Alan!"

"Evie, have you forgotten the Augean Stables you called an apartment in college? You had a month's worth of dirty dishes in the sink, a year's worth of empty Coke cans, pizza boxes and wine bottles on the floor. Human feet never touched the carpet in your bedroom. Wasn't there also a group of vermin picketing outside against the unsanitary living conditions?"

"That's not true …" Evelyn smiled.

Alan cocked his head.

"Yeah, but ..."

"Don't 'yeah but' me young lady," Alan teased. "Lighten up on her."

He turned the television back on. "Let me watch the end of the ballgame."

Evelyn pushed him gently back into the chair and sat in his lap. She put her arms around his neck and shoulders. "I don't remember any vermin picketing my apartment."

"No, you dated most of the vermin, and then went back to their place."

"Your children, at the least your youngest one, is a total slob."

"Yeah, but she's got a pleasant personality and is fun to be with." Tia, small, dark and beautiful like her mother, also was not one to be put out by the demands of others.

Alan slipped a hand under Evelyn's shirt.

"You've had your thirty seconds ration of sexual frenzy for the day," she informed him.

"Yes, but ..."

"Don't 'yes but' me."

Alan hadn't noticed that Evelyn's friend, Linda, had come into the bedroom. "May I play too?" She had become a permanent fixture in the household. According to Evelyn, Matthew had gone off on some business, leaving Linda by herself. Evelyn didn't like her friend being alone and isolated in the woods without running water and somebody to cut firewood, and had asked Linda to stay with them until Matthew returned. Alan couldn't help but wonder what kind of business would tolerate Matthew's participation.

The two artists had become inseparable. Other than her horrific abuse of makeup and bizarre culinary tastes, she was pleasant company, with a quick wit and intelligence that fit well with the rest of the family's antics. His daughters seemed enchanted by Linda's company.

Often the two women disappeared for the day to take in garage sales or visit their arty friends, leaving Alan alone to perfect his craft as a couch potato. They would return, arms filled with packages of second-hand goodies or unusual foodstuffs and herbs retrieved from Linda's Cubist quarters in the woods. In exchange for her room and the luxury of a daily shower, Linda had assumed responsibility for preparing most of the evening meals, a task at which Evie had never shown much talent. Alan preferred the old cook in spite of her deficiencies and could easily have survived without the daily ration of scary salads and soups that Linda concocted.

"Ready for our walk?" Linda asked. "Alan, why don't you get dressed and join us?"

"I'll pass, thanks."

Appearing not the least disappointed by his refusal, Evelyn was quickly on her feet, heading toward the door, throwing a cautionary note into the air behind her. "There won't be many sunny days left before the cold weather is here to stay. Then you'll be trapped indoors for six months! Get dressed, you'll feel better."

"Please do join us," Linda said. "The fresh air will be good for you."

"Maybe next time," Alan heard himself say, not knowing why. "There are a couple of football games I'd like to watch," he tossed into the air as a rationale.

"Alan, you need to get up off your ass and do something! You can't just sit around the house and watch football the entire day!" Evelyn scolded.

"No, go ahead and enjoy yourselves," he said, although he had really meant to say, 'Okay, you're right. Give me a few minutes to get dressed.' There really was no excuse for his doing nothing, but human inertia becomes a habit easily maintained and difficult to overcome.

"We tried," Evelyn said.

Alan watched from the bedroom window as the twosome walked across the lawn, up the small grassy knoll, under two big oak trees, and past a flat clearing where several large tree trunk sections had been positioned in a circle around a fire pit. Ten yards past the pit, the girls stepped onto the path leading through the trees toward the stable, which was in poor repair and no longer in use. There, the path widened into a riding trail that disappeared deep into the forest. One could follow it across several acres to the edge of their property before the trail forked. One path cut a route along the perimeter of a neighbor's cleared farmlands and eventually down to the Allegheny River; the other circled downhill of the house and around the lake.

It was a beautiful hike virtually any time of the year—except during hunting season. Then it was a war zone! There were always plenty of deer in the area, attracted to the water, the nearby cornfields, and the camouflage of the woods. Spotting an occasional fox wasn't unusual and once or twice Alan and the kids had stumbled across a bear cub.

As he watched the nature-lovers disappear into the trees, Alan reconsidered their invitation. Evelyn was right. He shouldn't just sit around on his ass staring at the television. It was a beautiful day and a heavy early morning frost indicated that winter was close at hand. Alan retrieved a pair of jeans and a sweater from the cedar closet. He dressed, slipped into hiking boots, and went in to the bathroom. Better, he thought, to attend to his biological needs while he still had access to toilet paper. There was little glamour in wiping with dried leaves in the wild.

As he washed his hands, Alan caught his reflection in the mirror. Since returning from California, he seemed like someone else. His eyes were swollen from lack of sleep, his image that of a stranger, an unflattering caricature drawn by an insensitive satirist

He grabbed a windbreaker from the hallway closet on the way out the door and set out after his wife her rotund English companion.

The women had a twenty-five minute head start, but he estimated he could easily catch up to them in fifteen. Maybe sooner if Evie became distracted by wild flowering plants, which she loved to examine and smell, or by animal tracks, which she never could resist following. In the forest, Evelyn was in her element and assumed a personality akin to Daniel Boone or Ewell Gibbons.

Alan traversed the grassy knoll in long strides. Invigorated by the dazzling sunshine and clean country air, his skin tingled into alertness and his mind flooded with a feeling of wellbeing. He stepped up onto a section of tree trunk by the fire pit and looked out over his property with a sense of pride. Turning to take in the marvelous view from every direction a discomforting smell waft into his nostrils.

To his surprise, he noticed there were smoking embers in the pit. As he pondered who had burned what, and when, the frightening image of a human form consumed by fire rustled across the screen of his mind like a chilling breeze and then vanished. Vertigo forced him to his knees. He had no notion where such a gruesome image originated. He was certain, however, that somewhere lurking in the crevices of his brain was a memory too horrible to recall.

He was spared from further speculation when a mail truck pulled up to the box at the end of the drive and deposited the day's offerings from the outside world. When it drove away, Alan leaped off his perch and retrieved the mail, thumbed through it, and then stuffed it into his back pocket when as was most often the case he found nothing of interest.

As he turned back up the drive, Alan spied a car parked roadside a half-mile away where the lake bordered the road. Although an unusual place to abandon a vehicle, he didn't give it a second thought as he continued up the drive towards the woods.

The sylvan trail was slippery with fallen leaves, making the descent into a small gully tricky, and the ascent up the other side a comical farce. When the trail forked, Alan followed it towards the lake, knowing that Evelyn would most likely choose that route.

It would be another quarter mile before the women came into sight. The path emerged from the trees about fifty yards uphill of a small clearing along the shore of the lake. From his elevated position, Alan observed his wife and her friend, kneeling on the ground, in the company of a third person. Their voices carried up the hill to where he stood but were indiscernible at that distance. As he started down the steep path, slipping and sliding on the leaves, the girls looked up and spotted him. He waved a clumsy greeting.

Evelyn rose, wiped her sleeve across her face, and headed uphill towards him, chattering nonsense of which he could make no sense. Behind her, Alan could see Linda scattering leaves about with her foot as the third member of their party disappeared into the shadow of the trees. From a distance, the man looked like Matthew Cartier, although with the long trench coat and beret, it could have been anyone.

"Well, you took our advice and got dressed," Evie said with a smile. "Beautiful day, isn't it?"

"Sure is! What are you girls up to?"

"Just burying a dead baby."

"What? A baby?" Suddenly, the positive effect incurred by his excursion outdoors evaporated. Alan felt dizzy and disoriented.

"What are you talking about, Alan? I said we were just burying a dead animal."

His equilibrium stabilized. "Was that Matthew?" he asked, motioning with his head toward the tree.

"Matthew? No. Just somebody curious as to what we two strange women were doing on our hands and knees," she said, laughing sheepishly. "Matthew called yesterday. He'll be joining us for Halloween. Your head feeling better?"

"Well enough to venture out for a while."

"Good."

In the distance a car backfired, coughed, hissed and sped away.

"Well, Al, it's good to see you up and about," Linda remarked smiling as he approached her.

"So you are gravediggers now," Alan said, having regained his equilibrium.

"Excuse me?" Linda darted a quick glance at Evelyn.

"Evelyn said you were digging a grave for a dead animal you came across."

"Even squirrels deserve a decent burial," Evelyn interrupted, "Did you see any deer along the way, Alan? We did."

"A few." He looked past the women to the spot at which they had been kneeling. "What? No tombstone!" Alan said, eyeing the small burial mound.

They both chortled. Each grabbed one of his arms and directed him toward the remaining leg of the hike.

"So, Alan, Evelyn tells me that you have been suffering from nightmares."

"Did she? Have you also discussed how traumatized I was by potty training?"

"Have you ever had a professional analyze your dreams…and potty training memories?"

"Only Evelyn. She thinks that I'm acting out my passive-aggressiveness by interfering with her getting a good night's sleep."

"That sounds reasonable to me," Linda said.

"Evelyn also thinks that the cat has nightmares because it resents her use of the primate digit. It enables her to write checks and sign credit card vouchers. The cat feels cheated."

"Cats can be very jealous creatures," Evelyn said.

"The only one who resents you writing checks and using the credit cards is me. I suspect that cats dream of liver morsels and little else."

"And what do you dream of, Alan?" Linda asked. Her enchanting eyes narrowed.

"Carl Sagan naked," he answered. "And the contracting universe."

"Isn't the universe expanding?"

'How the hell should I know? Ask Carl Sagan, or Evelyn. They seem to have all the answers."

"I'm really interested. Tell me about your dreams, Alan."

"I usually can't remember them," Alan lied.

"That's not a good sign. It means you are repressing something. Are you repressing something, Alan?"

"If I was repressing something would I know what I was repressing? And if I knew what I was repressing, how could I be repressing it?"

"He hates his mother," Evelyn volunteered.

Alan flushed angrily. "I'm not repressing anything. You hate my mother."

"No shit!" The corner of her eyes crinkled in a confirming smile.

"Evelyn tells me you dreamed about a murder. Is that true?"

"Evelyn tells you a lot of personal stuff, and tells me very little."

"Alan's really sensitive about maintaining family secrets."

"Personal confidences, not secrets!" His voice filled with anger.

"I knew a Danny Cox in New York," Linda said. "I wonder if it could be the same one." Even without the thick makeup, Linda's face was an inscrutable mask.

Now Alan's interest piqued. "You did?" He asked and stared off into the woods to give the impression of being only moderately interested while he and pondered how much information to share.

"Handsome, muscular man. Blond, disarming smile, a real lady-killer. Used to come into our shop regularly."

"What shop?"

"Matthew and I owned a little antique shop in New York. Not terribly profitable, but it paid the bills."

"Isn't it a small world, Alan?" Evelyn asked.

In her eyes Alan saw something he could not define and a thought flitted across his mind too rapidly to catch hold of it.

"I was under the impression that Danny had a place of his own in Jersey. Why'd he visit your shop in New York?"

"We did business from time to time."

Alan had a sudden jarring thought. Danny's business activities were allegedly connected to pornography and Satanism. What business had he conducted with Linda and Matthew? "You still own that place?"

"Not anymore. We sold out to a nice older couple a little more than a year ago. That's when we decided to move here."

"And you actually knew Danny?"

"Only casually. As I remember, he was interested in one of our sales girls. And he was an old high school buddy of yours?"

"If it's the same Danny Cox."

"And he's dead?"

"My friend is, yes."

"If it's the same person, what a pity. He was the quintessential hunk."

"That sounds like Danny."

"And you dreamed about his death?"

"Sorta."

"Sorta, my ass!" Evelyn added mockingly.

"Do you have many dreams like that?"

"Like I said, I usually don't remember," Alan said dryly.

"You should listen to your dreams, Alan. They may be trying to tell you something important. It's said that dreams are the vehicles of portent."

"Yes, I've been told that."

"My husband is filled with big dreams, but no passion to pursue them," Evelyn volunteered.

"I've read that occultists believe that if the external physical body becomes inactive, as when we sleep, then the 'inner body' is awakened."

"Oh, really? I have an inner body, too? One isn't enough?"

"Then what, Linda?" Evelyn asked.

"When this happens, all the perceptive processes are transferred to an area of the mind which would normally be unconscious. But for all intensive purposes, it is like transferring one's perception into a living dream. You are no longer bound by the body and can travel at will. Sometimes, deeply buried fantasies awaken, and these will seem as normal reality."

What a crock of garbage, he thought, but instead asked, "Where'd you read that?"

"I'm not sure. I think it was the Occult Source Book by Drury and Tillett," Linda answered offhandedly.

Alan wondered if she didn't mean to convey much more than the face value of her statement.

"Evelyn, let's get our easels out and go paint down by the lake."

"Great idea. I've really been lax with my art of late."

The women chattered about garage sales and glass bottle collections as the trio plodded back towards the house. Alan attempted to shut off the static in his brain by listening to the sounds of his own footsteps and singing Beatle songs in his mind.

Chapter 17

Except for overflowing bookshelves and a poster of Albert Einstein with the reminder on it that today's problems could not be solved with the same minds that created them yesterday, the office that housed William Zent at Union College was nearly as austere as the holding cell in which Bralich had met with Sangre. Horizontal slices of daylight poured through old Venetian blinds that covered the solitary window. The desk was made of black metal that needed a paint job and a woman's touch.

Zent was as remarkable as his office was bland. His voice played so soft and melodic that Bralich instantly felt calmed in his presence. The absence of a pretentious air of self-importance so often found among fellow academics Bralich found refreshing. Zent was a small, athletically built man, who held himself with a quiet confidence. Despite his shoulder length gray curls, he looked considerably younger than his fifty-nine years. A thick gray mustache filled in his upper lip, but not enough to detract from a compassionate smile that inspired trust and projected a sincere humbleness that could not be feigned.

Calm, bespectacled blue eyes grabbed Bralich and held him as Zent serenely recounted how Sangre had raped and murdered an entire family in Trenton while other family members were forced to watch. Many of the particulars of the slaughter had not been a matter of public record. Justifiably so, Bralich thought, as he listened to the sordid details. Bralich blew out air over his upper lip and grimaced at the sour taste his host's narrative of mutilation left in his mouth.

Zent said that after testifying at Sangre's trial he terminated his practice in Princeton, surrendered his tenure at the prestigious university, and returned to Cranford, where he had spent his childhood. "I wanted to come home. Spend my silver years surrounded by the fond memories of my youth."

At Union College he was the paragon of scholarship among his less distinguished colleagues.

"You no longer maintain a private practice?" Bralich asked.

"I do volunteer work at the clinic in town and occasionally I'm referred clients through CFF."

"CFF?"

"The Citizen's Freedom Foundation. It's a loose confederation of small activist groups concerned with the problem of destructive cultism. My work with multiple personalities and interest in surviving victims of cults is well known. My sister died in Jonestown. I help when I can...in non coercive scenarios."

Bralich pushed his glasses onto the bridge of his nose, lowered his eyes as he expressed his sympathies, then asked: "What exactly do you mean by 'non coercive scenarios?"

"I don't advocate kidnapping cult members to save them from themselves. It's both illegal and unethical. I'm a strong proponent of free will, even when I abhor another's choices."

"But you are a deprogrammer?"

Zent leaned back in the swivel chair, which Bralich had decided was the most technologically advanced furnishing in the Spartan surroundings. His hands were folded against his chest, his chin rested on uplifted index fingers.

"No, I am not, Tony," he said with a calm air of Zen simplicity. "Deprogramming causes as many problems as it cures. It can be extremely detrimental to an unwilling subject. I've found that it often transforms the paranoia that accompanies mind bending into reasonable fear, worsening an individual's underlying psychological dysfunction. You see, Tony, while I do believe that the mind can be bent—that one's perceptions of reality, values, behavior, and self-image can be distorted and manipulated—I do not believe that the mind can be controlled."

Bralich pursed his lips. "I recognize that there is still considerable debate as to whether one can be induced to act against one's will, but isn't brainwashing, such as in the case of American prisoners of war during the Korean War, an accepted phenomenon?"

Zent smiled, extended his hands palms up on the desk. He looked saintly, Bralich thought. "The CIA has been searching for a method to create their own Manchurian Candidate for half a century. Yet with all their resources they still have not been successful in creating a mindless assassin. Thought reform techniques are well known and practiced, yes, of course. But forget the popular notion of an all-powerful, irresistible, magical method of achieving total control of human beings. Brainwashing is really just a metaphor for one person influencing another."

Bralich cocked his head and ran a hand over the stubble on his chin.

Zent continued. "Tony, I assume that like Robert Miller, you use hypnosis in your practice."

"I did early in my career. After I trained with Victor Frankl, my leanings took on a more existential bent."

Zent nodded approvingly. "Man's Search For Meaning...a monumental and undervalued contribution to the field of psychology. Frankl's experience in the Nazi death camps is a testimonial that an individual's self-image can never entirely be rooted out—no matter how rigorous the assault on one's identity—if one is secure in that identity and can find meaning in the world, regardless of its random cruelty."

Zent's understanding of the cornerstone of Bralich's psychology did little to dispel his confusion over his observations of Sangre's trance-like behavior in response to Bralich's questions. He leaned forward with his hands on his knees. "Help me make sense of Sangre," he said after relating his experience with the murderer at the prison. "My client reiterated Sangre's responses almost verbatim when questioned about his experiences at the orphanage."

"Groups define reality," Zent said matter-of-factly. His voice remained velvet, soothing. "They influence judgment and perception at the most basic level. And most people do what they are told to do, and believe what they are told to believe, without limitation of conscience, as long as they perceive the command comes from a legitimate source. Universally, humans readily abdicate responsibility for what they do...especially in situations in which they perceive they have no control. Agreed?"

"Agreed." Even in his non-directive therapy sessions, Tony observed that his clients seemed almost desperate for him to impose on them an absolute or totalistic belief system to provided structure to their faltering lives. He suspected that the human need for structure accounted, at least in part, for the worldwide epidemic of political and religious fundamentalism and the intellectual laziness to question the totalitarianism regimes that usurped personal freedoms under the guise of law and order, spreading democracy, or salvation.

"From your past experiences, Tony, what personal circumstances make people most susceptible to suggestion and influence of others?"

Bralich removed his glasses, cleaned the lenses with his handkerchief as he reflected. "Barring extreme coercive measures, persons who suffer from negative self-image are often acutely susceptible to peer pressure, as are those who have limited impulse control...hysterics or fearful and excitable persons."

"Yes, exactly. Addictive personalities...self-surrendering types...are prime targets. Preoccupation with the moment and an inability to plan for the future or to find meaning in one's life can be critical flaws. Such persons often make excellent hypnosis subjects."

Zent paused abruptly, became as inanimate as a statue, lost in his own thoughts. Bralich waited.

"We have also described children. Have we not, Doctor?" he finally added.

"Yes. Children, of course."

"In my work with multiples I have noted that the first of alternate personalities usually develop early in life, most often as an attempt to combat loneliness or insecurity, and not uncommonly in an environment of excessive parental punishment. Raised in an artificial atmosphere of seclusion, with an exaggerated sense of guilt, and threats of bodily harm, one not only learns to be obedient and reliant on the abusing adult, but to withdraw into fantasy."

"Dissociation," Bralich said absently. Unknown to Zent, he was remarkably close to describing Bralich's own youth. Tony had chosen, instead, to grow rather than allow the withered roots of his childhood to decay or perversely mutate.

Zent's voice maintained its soothing calm. "The tendency to fantasize from an early age, coupled with isolation and over-stimulation, can result in the induction of a trance state, which is really nothing more than a heightened perception focused on a simple stimulus—either external or internal."

"So Sangre's trance-like behavior was self-induced?" Bralich asked.

Zent nodded almost imperceptibly. "Remember that all hypnosis is essentially self-hypnosis. Typically, people are not pawns but partners...even in extreme thought-reform scenarios. Our Mr. Sangre may have been scripted to respond as he did to your questions about his time at the Garden Grove Children's Home, but it was a much to his advantage as to his programmers' to do so. People cannot be induced to act against their will."

If that were true, then how culpable was DeLucci? Bralich wondered. "Then you believe Sangre was a victim of thought reform, resulting from early childhood experiences in a satanic coven?"

"Yes. I'm certain Sangre was raised in a Satanic coven. And, similar to several clients I have treated over the years who had developed multiple personalities, Lucius Sangre was subject to extensive mind bending."

"So Sangre was brainwashed," Bralich said with a question in his voice.

"No." Zent's eyebrows rode up his forehead. "Sangre clearly knows the difference between right and wrong. He is a monster, not compelled to perform heinous acts, but finding total delight in doing so. It's his version of playing golf or sitting in front of a fire with a great book. He is the very embodiment of evil. Although in his defense Lucius Sangre was nurtured to be the despicable creature that he became. The literature suggests, and my experiences bare this out, that prolonged dissociation, let's say four to seven years, may result in permanent changes in brain function."

"But you do not believe he was programmed to commit the murders for which he was convicted?" Doubt tainted his voice.

"Have you read any of my articles about magnetocephalography in the neuroscience journals?"

"No, I haven't."

"As I'm sure you are well aware, it is now possible to measure electromagnetic brain activity. The human brain is plastic and changes all the time. Magnetocephalography shows us how the physical brain recomputes the meaning of its experiences. It appears that there are morality default settings for most people but not for sociopathic personalities like Sangre."

"So Sangre wasn't programmed to commit the murders for which he was convicted; he just lacks the innate programming that prevents him from committing such acts."

"Essentially, yes. He possesses such impulsive and fragmented psychodynamics that there was virtually no discernible electromagnetic brain activity when I queried him on issues of morality. There is ugliness in all of us, Tony. Hidden within every human are many antisocial desires, which we learn to sublimate into more socially acceptable behaviors through our upbringing. However, children raised in cults, in Sangre's case a satanic coven, are confronted with severely limited inputs. To reinforce group solidarity and denigrate individuality, cults control every aspect of a child's life. These poor kids are like rats in a laboratory. With such complete control, mind bending is little more than classical Pavlovian conditioning—ring a bell and they salivate. With Sangre's deficiency in neurological brain wiring, the task of mind bending is simplified. Aren't most children basically addictive personalities, weak-willed, with intense emotional lives that are now-oriented? Now annihilate the development of traditional societal constraints, the superego, and channel a child's psychic energies toward satisfying the most base of primal impulses ..."

"Then you've created a potential monster! You created Sangre!" Bralich felt shaken by his own words. Was all choice only an illusion, he wondered? Maybe, given the dynamics of our social existence, human life was preordained. Not necessarily cast in iron but malleable enough to reshape only if one forged a powerful self-identity. But what were the possibilities for those who could not? Even now, Bralich felt himself pulled as much as choosing to go where the DeLucci case was leading him. Pulled as if summoned by a powerful hypnotic command.

"You have treated others like Sangre?" Tony asked.

"I've worked with others who have survived childhoods similar to Sangre's, although no one else that has turned out quite as he did. They chose otherwise and often suffered for their choices."

Zent reiterated what he had shared with Robert Miller about the existence of a highly organized international network of satanic covens thriving under the protection afforded by their politically powerful and socially prestigious memberships. Such covens, he said, used thought reform technologies and selective breeding, hoping to spawn Satan on earth. Bralich believed him. Lucius Sangre was damned close.

He listened intently as Zent explained the intricacies of thought reform methodologies, pulled a notepad from his coat pocket and took copious notes. "How have you been successful in undoing the effects? If you don't deprogram, what do you do?" Should DeLucci ever return from his psychological exile, Bralich wanted to know how he might help the little fellow.

"Tony, would you mind accompanying me to the cafeteria? I'm a Type II diabetic and haven't eaten since breakfast. My blood sugar is low and I'm feeling weak."

As they traversed the fluorescent-lighted hallways lined with notices of symposia, graduate school information, and posted test scores on yellow computer paper, Zent continued. "Deprogrammers believe the identity of a subject must be stripped down to nothing, much in the way the military handles new recruits. They strive to eliminate independent or critical thought and throw victims off balance emotionally to induce cathartic reactions. When their victims reach a breaking point, they take advantage of the subject's vulnerability and reshape their reality. This can only be achieved in total social seclusion."

"It sounds to me," Bralich said, "like deprogrammers use the same techniques as cult programmers."

"Exactly. The ends justify the means, they claim."

"And your approach?" Bralich asked as they exited the building and strolled across a brick courtyard where student smokers attended to their addictions.

"Isolating the individual from controlling cult influences is, of course, essential. However, I believe that you must heighten their perception of the immediate surroundings and people...increase their satisfaction in the daily living experience. With the help of friends and family, we strive to win their attention and support through affection and empathy...aimed at restoring personal dignity. The underlying problem is one of self-esteem, so my charge is to help them re-create or discover a positive self-image. I inundate them with affection, attention, and entertainment, not more physical and emotional abuse. I adopt only a conversational, non-authoritarian approach and continuously demonstrate my confidence and interest in them."

They entered the student union building. Two young men held the large glass doors open for them. One greeted Zent, who stopped momentarily to ask how the student fared on his Graduate Record Examination.

"I aced it," the boy replied. "Got a 720 Verbal and 730 Math score."

"Very nice, John. Let me know if you need a recommendation. I might be able to come up with a compliment or two," Zent said.

Inside the student union, the walls vibrated from the din in the cafeteria. A gaggle of giggling teenage girls chimed, "Hello, Dr. Zent." He smiled a greeting, then picked up where he left off with Bralich.

"Of course in most instances, a subject has little faculty to communicate outside of the script of cult doctrine, at least, initially. I've found the most successful strategy is not to debate the merits of one's beliefs with the subject, but to remain, instead, scrupulously neutral while expressing unconditional support. Redirect attention away from all possible cues that might trigger post-hypnotic suggestion. Never, and I repeat, never engage in discussions about philosophy, religion, or politics, nor morality rhetoric. Ask only questions they cannot answer on the basis of cult-formatted programming. In a nurturing environment, it becomes increasingly more difficult to deny that love and affection are preferable to the self-denigrating lifestyles of cult existence."

In the cafeteria line, Zent grabbed a banana, an orange, and a small salad. That explained his lean and healthy physical appearance. Tony opted for a large piece of triple chocolate cake.

"How will I know DeLucci's cues?" Bralich asked.

Zent pealed his orange. "Unless you are familiar with the specific cult, you won't. It will be trial and error for the most part. Sometimes, it will be obvious, like what you witnessed with Sangre and with Robert's client. Other times, you won't know that you triggered something. Keep an audio, and if possible, a video record to which you can go back and analyze. Review it every chance you get to check for some slight alteration in body language or intonation you may have missed that suggests some internal shifting of gears."

Tony pawed at his cake.

Zent tossed another orange slice in his mouth and sucked at the juice. "Be forewarned that a single word, sight or sound can trigger a cult member's imagination, and almost literally transplant them to a place that the sensation conjures up. This is worsened if the person is also severely psychotic, which is not uncommon. There are no coincidences for psychotics. In their reality everything has a symbolic meaning."

"Like Manson believing the Beatles' song, Helter Skelter, was a revelation about the final race war that Manson was fated to start?"

"Exactly. And the magnitude of the responses you might trigger depends upon how deeply the subject believes in the fantasy."

DeLucci apparently was so rooted in his fantasy that when Robert had pushed, Nick broke. Bralich asked Zent how to best avoid a reoccurrence should DeLucci find his way back to reality.

"Establishing a routine of physical relaxation is very important. Don't employ any meditative techniques that might allow your client to fall back into cult-programmed chanting or other repetitive ritual. Use relaxation techniques that heighten personal and physical awareness rather than dim it. Be prepared, also, that all shocks to one's sense of identity and security may elicit a wide range of emotional responses. Initially expect denial and withdrawal. This usually is succeeded by anger, depression, and only if you persevere, acceptance as a sense of identity finally reemerges. Each of these states must be worked through at the individual's own pace. There is no formula. Don't push."

Chapter 18

Alan's father had often told him that one finds truth in the oddest of places. The night of the Halloween party, Alan's home was certainly the oddest of places. That being so, he anticipated truth would be found in abundance.

Evelyn's life had been a magnet for weirdoes, perverts, and mankind's most unique, eccentric, and totally off-the-wall personalities. Alan surmised that every such individual within a fifty-mile radius had been invited or attracted to the party. Artists were drawn in by the numbers, as were poets and members of the local theater group who played at being teachers, insurance salesmen, and travel agents in order to support their thespian craft. All were either gay, bisexual, asexual, trans-sexual, overly sexual, or in a transition between one or more of these alternative lifestyles. Most didn't need to assemble costumes; their day-to-day apparel was sufficiently bizarre. That, of course, didn't stop anyone from accessorizing for this occasion.

Fairly represented among Evelyn and Alan's guests were back-to-nature farmers who supported themselves with homespun arts and crafts, herbal concoctions, and archaic wilderness survival skills and trades learned through the Mother Earth News. The women were typically large and podgy, many tipping the scales in the two to three hundred pound range. Most were friendly and openly flirtatious. When not discussing food, they chatted about who was sleeping with whom or cheating on whom in this rural Pennsylvania community where the intricate web of marriages and divorces was so complex that an outsider like Alan required a play bill to follow the action. The men were usually strongly built but gone to seed, toothless or nearly so, balding, and reluctant to abandon their Pittsburgh Steelers, Pittsburgh Pirates, Caterpillar tractor or U.S Marine Corps rimmed caps even for a Halloween party. Therefore, they came attired as football players, baseball players, construction workers, and military personnel. Although many were Evelyn's high school classmates, most looked twenty years older than her, and weren't much into verbalizations beyond "Nope", "Yep", and "Shi-i-it!", and for the truly loquacious "Aw shi-i-it!" Alan was fairly certain that at least two of the party attendees had received elocution lessons from Goofy, the cartoon companion of Mickey Mouse.

Unfortunately for Alan, his local friends, few as they were, never showed for Evelyn's parties. They were most often ex-jocks and golfing buddies who couldn't handle the zoo fest. Most were also homophobes, or at least, not supportive of men who showered together without first playing ball.

When Matthew Cartier arrived, Alan sensed that the evening was destined to slide deeper into the depths of degradation, if not outright hurl itself over a precipice to disaster. Matthew's expression was as sour as ever. Turbulent emotion always seemed just beneath the surface of his too-thin, swarthy skin. Spidery and sulky, even at a party, he appeared to be perpetually on the verge of a violent schizophrenic episode.

Matthew came dressed as an exhibitionist; donning a navy cap, blue pea coat, and bell-bottom pants, his hands hidden in the coat pockets. As he entered the party, the gangly man spread open the pea coat, allowing onlookers to observe that he was shirtless, that the front panel of his pants was unbuttoned, and that he wasn't wearing any underwear. Throughout the evening, Alan could hear Matthew's caustic voice resonating above the din. "Have I showed you my costume?" he asked everyone at least half a dozen times. On each such occasion, in his mind Alan saw the twisted smile on Matthew's lips and the anthracite black eyes that never lost their brooding ambiance and menacing quality, issuing unspoken threats.

Cartier's fleshy companion, Linda, who as best as Alan could tell, actually functioned as his caretaker, was costumed as a streetwalker. This required only wearing less makeup than usual. She was very convincing. Alan overheard more than one partygoer remark that they found it miraculous that a halter top could hold up her cantaloupe-sized breasts. They swayed like bass drums in a marching band as she walked. Upon arriving at the party, she sought out Evelyn and never drifted far from her side throughout the evening.

Evelyn was decked out as Betty Boop and her on-mark impersonation of the cartoon vamp kept people in stitches all night. She had little difficulty in crooning seductive melodies and provocative discourse a la Betty Boop upon request. The silky form-fitting black dress she wore showed off her spectacular physique, attracting a good deal of attention from most of the men-gay or not-and some of the women as well. At moments such as this, Alan had little difficulty in remembering what had first attracted him to his wife.

After a great deal of contemplation—a pitcher of margaritas worth—and upon Evelyn's insistence, Alan had settled on being Conan the Couch Potato for the evening. His weaponry included a television remote control in a dagger sheath, and a long stick of salami for a sword. A cutting board and bag of potato chips were dangled from his thick leather belt, and he carried a pillow across his shoulder as a pack. The role didn't demand much of a stretch on his part either.

The rest of the entourage included a standard assortment of priests, devils, cowboys, soldiers, nurses, clowns, football players, and weird artists with bizarre haircuts, who came as their favorite weird artists with bizarre haircuts. Many of the men were in drag, ballerinas being popular. Alan supposed that for some, Halloween was an event to which they most excitedly looked forward.

Everybody brought a dish, and Alan was especially thankful for those guests who were too lazy to create something special and had stopped at the grocery store on route to the party. As it was, he spent a good deal of the evening avoiding Evelyn and Linda, who, whenever they saw him, stuck a cracker in a pate or some other God-ugly tasty, and crammed it into his mouth.

"Isn't this delicious?"

He relied on his standard, "Yes, dear," response.

He snacked only on the foodstuffs he recognized, circulating among the menagerie, catching fragments of conversations and cautiously avoiding being lassoed into any, or being cornered by perverts acting independently or as a team. Alice had fit in more in Wonderland than he did at one of Evelyn's gatherings.

He overheard a particularly effeminate man with a boy's face say: "The human condition can improve only after human beings have acquired enough virtue to atone for their past sins of greed and corruption." The speaker was dressed as a monk and fidgeted nervously with his rosary beads. Three of the four persons surrounding the man nodded their heads in agreement while stuffing their mouths with potato chips and dip.

"It's not the nature of man, but the nature of society that is corrupt," the ballerina with the hairy back and mustache countered. "Man is good," he explained while fondling the friar's crucifix. The onlookers again shook their heads in agreement and washed down the chips with wine.

In another corner, a maid of gargantuan proportion scolded a hardhat construction worker about his inhumane attempts at house-training their new puppy. "The only thing you'll teach that dog is that he'll get the hell beat out of him every time he's around you! You damned fool!"

"Aw, shi-i-it, Mary," the hard hat responded.

The theatre group isolated itself in the dining room engaging in hackneyed discussions and high cultured issues from their perceived elevated perspectives.

"I prefer roles which require me to stretch," said the big-framed, heavyset man dressed as a Roman Centurion, who always played the Roman Centurion, knight, soldier, policeman, or similar role that required his deep voice. Nobody else in the group had a range below soprano. "Man's reach should exceed his grasp. What else is heaven for?" he continued theatrically. "Alan, you must know who said that," he said when Alan stopped briefly to listen in.

"Those are lyrics from an Elvis Presley song," Alan answered straight-faced.

"No, really?"

"Absolutely."

"You sure?"

"Yes. Little sister don't you walk out that door. Man's reach should exceed his grasp. What else is heaven for?" Alan hummed what might be mistaken for a tune only to failing ears, and the drunk Centurion nodded his head to the beat.

"Elvis Presley, huh?"

"Powerful lyrics, man!" Alan insisted, straining not to laugh as the last scintilla of doubt evaporated from the centurion's face.

"Beat that!"

"He was the King, Centurion," Alan added and extended a Roman salute, clutching fist to breast.

The Centurion drew his sword and returned the salute. "Marcus Aurelius, at your service, my liege," he bellowed. He repeated that line with only moderate alteration in every local civic stage production Alan had been forced to attend, allowing the thespian to "stretch." His performances had not lost their saliency for Alan and he wistfully recalled "Chief Constable O'Toole at your service, my lady."

"Sir Gwen, at your service, your majesty."

"James West, at your service, Mr. President."

Everyone appeared to be enjoying him or herself or itself and was engrossed in their own brand of stimulating conversation. When Alan's teenage offspring, Vinnie and Gabrielle, returned from their party at about 1:00 a.m., the crowed still hadn't thinned out. Tia, the youngest child, was home all evening and had invited two friends over to keep her company. Occasionally the three giggling teenybopper wanna-be's circulated through the guests, tasting different dishes and sneaking a sip of wine or beer when they thought nobody was watching.

By 2:30, there were a lot of drunk and loud people trying to out-shout louder and drunker people. Evelyn was inviting a handful of departing guests to spend the night rather than drive home intoxicated.

"Noooo. I'mmm perfuckly find, Evil-ine," one friend explained. He was bent over at the waist, dangling like a puppet on strings while frantically searching his pockets for the keys he already held in his hands.

A glass shattered to the floor near the piano.

The young woman dressed as a nurse screamed, "Leave me alone!" She pulled her arm from a red devil's grip, and staggered away, leaning on the wall for support. "I want out! Do you understand?"

"Not here, Judy! This isn't the time or place!" the devil said as he glanced around, trying to look composed but too nervous to pull it off.

"The hell it ain't!" said the nurse, her voice thick with anger. Alan now recognized her as the high school art teacher. The devil was her husband, Tom Wesley, a local real estate agent whose archaic wardrobe of polyester was unequaled anywhere on the globe. "I don't want anything more to do with you and your sicko Satanist friends! I'm not going tomorrow night and you can't force me!"

The party grew instantly silent. Tom Wesley forced an unconvincing laugh and pointed to his devil costume.

"Judy's really drunk," he said awkwardly.

"You are all sick!" Judy Wesley screamed, then miscalculated the stability of a card table to support her weight. The table collapsed, and she and the platters of raw vegetables and bowls of dip cascaded to the floor.

Alan rushed over to her aid. "Are you okay?" he asked, kneeling at her side.

"He's a devil, ya know," Judy whispered, pointing at her husband her eyes glazed from inebriation.

Alan looked up at her husband wearing the ridiculous red body suit and devil's cowl, who regarded him with suspicion. The man forced another laugh and reached for his wife. She recoiled.

"Don't touch me! None of you touch me ever again!"

"Let me help you up, Judy," Alan said and held out one hand while placing the other under her arm. She hesitated briefly, looking up at the assembled group now surrounding her.

"Look at them!" she whispered into her ear. "Can't you see what they are?"

Alan lifted his head to a sea of expressionless faces. The woman's cryptic warning had transformed the gathering of ridiculous artists and loonies into an ominous coterie. The scene was so surrealistic that the entire evening suddenly seemed a staged production. For who, he wondered?

Linda and Matthew broke through the ring of onlookers. "What's happening, Alan?" Linda asked. Judy Wesley tensed in Alan's arms and gasped. Her reaction set his spine tingling.

"Just a little mishap," he said instinctively rather than in response to the question.

"Oh, my! What a mess," Linda commented, looking about at the spilled dip with blue eyes expressionless and calm. "Matthew, help Alan get Judy off the floor."

The miscreant exhibitionist came forward. He looked down at the fallen teacher with undisguised coolness.

Again, Judy's grip tightened on Alan's arm, her nails digging into his skin. "They want your daughter," she whispered into Alan's ear.

"Tom, come take care of your wife," Linda commanded. The sharpness in her voice was so out of character that Alan snapped his head around expecting to find that someone else had spoken. Linda smiled at him. She had the look of a vulture.

Their eyes locked for an instant and during that brief moment, her long thick black hair, peppered with gray, framed the face of a dreadful old hag. Alan blinked. The old hag vanished and the original Linda in her hooker's costume reappeared.

Judy was on her feet, resisting her husband's attempt to usher her through the crowd. Perspiration stood out on Tom Wesley's face. "I'm sorry," he said to nobody in particular.

"Is everything okay?" Evelyn asked as she craned he head over Linda's shoulder. "Crazy Judy drunk again?" Evelyn laughed. "What is it this time, flying saucers and little green men, or were the plants talking to her again?' Snickers and chuckles emanated from the group.

Evelyn grabbed Alan's arm and in her best Betty Boop voice said, "Hey, Sweetie, wanna dance? Ew, what strong arms you have!" The few remaining onlookers laughed and moved off. The tension dissipated but Alan couldn't dispel the feeling that something might be truly amiss.

Alan looked back over his shoulder at Linda. Her eyes followed Evelyn and him across the room. She looked at him strangely. He found her smile disturbing. Matthew had come to her side and leaned over to speak directly into the portly streetwalker's ear. His steely eyes shifted focus from Linda to Evelyn and Alan, and then back again to his companion. Hatred flowed like a river from Matthew Cartier, and washed over Alan.

"What's with the Wesley's?" Alan asked his wife.

"I'm not sure whether she comes by her schizophrenia naturally or is helping it along with cocaine."

"And she's teaching our kids at the high school?"

"Teachers are human, too, darling" she said as if that was an acceptable excuse.

"She made some nonsensical remark about someone wanting one of our daughters."

Evelyn leaned close to his ear. "Judy was raped as a child. Can't have children of her own. It damaged her."

Within an hour the house had emptied. Evelyn said good-bye to the last guests, Linda and Matthew, and encouraged them to be extra careful in driving home. A heavy snow was falling. "The road will by icy. The first snow is always a wet one," she said, closing the door.

Evelyn rubbed her hands over her bare arms. "You better stoke up the woodburner, I'll go warm up the bed." She shot Conan an impish smile and reached for his crotch. "Ew," Betty Boop exclaimed.

Chapter 19

The waiter arrived with Bralich's scotch. Jefferson Thorne had ordered a double martini, dirty with extra olives. With three rounds under his belt, Thorne had become more talkative and less guarded in his choice of words, but his inflated sense of self-importance remained intact.

"I've represented Mr. DeLucci for the last two years," Thorne informed Bralich. "Mr. Underland personally hand picked me for the assignment when Rollin Moers, DeLucci's previous agent, retired."

Bralich removed his glasses, polished them under the table with the tablecloth. "Isn't that a little unusual for an author not to select his own representation?"

"Yes, it is unusual. However, the most important authors require the full attention of their agents. If I'm doing my job correctly, there isn't time to handle more than one client."

Bullshit, he thought. Throne hadn't even been to visit DeLucci at the hospital. With Nick's success he'd be much in demand, could have any agent he'd chosen.

"And, of course, Mr. DeLucci relies heavily on my abilities to edit his work. Believe me, that requires a great deal of effort. While Nick is strong on plot and character development, his technical skills...well, let's just say they need professional polishing."

Thorne had the look and mannerisms of a prissy prep school graduate with Ivy League credentials. Bralich suspected the only authentic attention he squandered was on his hair and wardrobe. His cherub face hadn't lost its baby fat, and alabaster skin and soft hands suggested that he was not much of an outdoorsman, nor ever done an honest day's work. He was probably the underachieving offspring of a Fortune 100 executive hired by Underland as a personal favor.

"Besides, Mr. DeLucci has little interest in the business side of publishing. He writes because it's his life," the self-opinionated cherub informed him as he guzzled his fourth drink.

"What do you mean?"

"As you can well imagine, Dr. Bralich, Mr. DeLucci hasn't much of a social life," he snickered. "If it wasn't for a lifetime of psychotherapy, he'd have little interaction with anyone, other than myself."

"Nick was seeing another therapist prior to Robert Miller?" he asked. Nick DeLucci had sought out Robert Miller for therapy about a year ago alleging that to be his first such intervention experience.

Thorne toyed with the olives in his new martini. "Yes, that's my understanding...that he had been in and out of therapy for twenty years...since the time he first started writing. But I really have little first-hand knowledge about Mr. DeLucci prior to Underland recruiting me."

"Do you know why?"

"Well, I hate to brag," the doughboy said with a smile that accentuated the rolls of fat beneath his chin, "but I had quite an impressive collegiate record at Dartmouth." Spying the waiter, Thorne signaled for another double martini.

"Yes, I'm sure you did," Bralich interjected, "But I meant why Nick DeLucci was in and out of therapy. We have no record of previous treatment."

Thorne shrugged. "Just between you and me, I've heard talk that he suffered from delusions, believed the stories he was writing were real, not fabrications."

Bralich asked, "Is that what he told you?"

"Well, no. Our relationship is strictly professional. He sends me his manuscripts to edit and I take care of all the publishing concerns. It was obvious to me, however, that he needed professional help for his personal problems." After gulping down a big swallow of the newly arrived martini, Thorne added, "Mr. DeLucci doesn't talk to anyone. He's a frightened little fellow who shies away from social situations. Then, of course, half the time he...well, you know, slips off...and is unapproachable anyhow."

Bralich couldn't believe what he heard. "He's been catatonic before?"

"Er...I don't know that for certain," Thorne stammered with a spark of recognition in his eyes that said he realized that he was breaking confidences. A rivulet of sweat rolled down his pallid forehead and he hurriedly brushed it away with the back of his hand. He looked at his watch and downed the last of his martini. By the look of him, it scorched his throat.

"Oh, my, look at the time. I hate to rush off like this, but I do have another appointment."

When he started to get up, Bralich reached across the table and grabbed his arm. "How do you know Nick has been hospitalized before?" he said, locking his eyes on Thorne.

Sweat dampened the younger man's forehead. "I think I…overheard someone talking about it." He jerked his arm, but Bralich held fast.

"Where?"

Thorne half stood and tried to back away from Bralich's grip, but with little success. Looking around the room embarrassed, he sat again. "I don't know. Nobody talks about DeLucci's personal life at Underland. It's taboo."

"Then where did you hear about his prior psychotherapy?" Bralich tightened his grip. Thorne's eyes skittered about the dining room, then returned to Bralich. "From Underland," he murmured, wincing. "I overheard the old man himself say it to someone on the phone."

When Bralich released him, Thorne stood up and straightened his suit. Bralich watched him with suspicion as he hurried toward the door. Something inside him was winding tighter and tighter, and Bralich feared that that something might snap.

Dark forces surrounded Nick DeLucci, and it was drawing him in. Just like it had captivated all of Robert Miller's attention.

Back at the hospital, his evening group session concluded, Bralich looked in on DeLucci. The gentle warble of Samantha's voice as she sang to her ward provided the only personal touch to the hospital suite. There were no flowers or sympathy cards. Jefferson Thorne and the Underland Enterprises apparently felt little obligation to demonstrate concern for their cash cow. The stack of machines that monitored his brain activity and other vital signs made the room look like a science laboratory.

"Knock, knock. Anybody home?"

Samantha said, "Good evening, Doctor Bralich. Come to pay a call on our famous guest. Look who's here to visit, Nick."

No response.

"I figure that Nick may want to write me into one of his books when he comes back to us, so I better stay close at hand. I'm a good character study, don't you think?" Bralich inquired as he examined DeLucci.

"Without a doubt, Doctor." When Wayne Alexander lumbered into the room and playfully jabbed Bralich in the ribs, she added, "Not that everybody around here would agree with me."

Bralich laughed.

"Where have you been hiding, Tony?" Alexander asked. He nodded toward DeLucci. "How's he doing?"

"His right leg continues to atrophy. Let's increase the daily passive exercises and massages, Sam."

"I'd be happy to spend a little more time with him each day, Dr. B."

Alexander said, "You're an angel, Sam. But a beautiful young lady like you needs to have a life. I find it unfathomable that someone hasn't scarped you up yet."

"I guess I just haven't found the right man," she said as she twirled the ring containing a large ruby around her finger. "I've always felt I should save myself for somebody special."

"Indeed, you should."

The good-natured administrator leaned over closer to the vacant Nick DeLucci and whispered, "You are missing a treasure, Little Buddy. Sam's smile drives every male on staff wild. If I had her all to myself the way you do, I'd …"

Samantha feigned insult. "Letch! I guess I should start believing some of the interesting literature I've been reading in the nurse's rest rooms."

"Unfounded rumors to be ignored, Samantha." Alexander collected the string of perforated computer paper, shaking his head as he scanned the nonsense. "You have time to talk, Tony?"

Bralich raised the patient's eyelids and shined a light into the lifeless globes. No change.

"Keep up the good work, Samantha," Bralich said, snatching DeLucci's latest pages from Wayne Alexander who was at his back as he exited the room.

"Is everything okay, Tony?" Alexander wanted to know.

"Yes."

"You sure?"

That merited no response. Bralich tossed the administrator a passing glance and proceeded toward his office.

"What are you up to? Where have you been?"

"I do have a life outside of this hospital."

"Oh! Since when, Tony?" Alexander snagged the crook of Bralich's elbow and pulled him to a halt. "I don't have to worry about you, do I? You're not going to let yourself get totally absorbed with this DeLucci thing the way ..."

"What do you want, Wayne?"

"Alexander asked, "Who is Linda Windsor?"

"I haven't the foggiest."

"If I were to tell you she no longer owns an antique shop in the City and her current whereabouts are unknown, would that mean anything to you?"

"Not a thing."

Alexander's mountainous frame hovered over him.

"If I were to tell you, she is a very wicked woman, suspected of being a trafficker in child pornography, would that have some significance?"

Bralich tightened his lips in annoyance. "What's with the riddles? What the hell are you getting at?"

The tension dissipated from Alexander's face. He clapped his arm around Tony's shoulder. "Sorry, it's just that I don't want you getting mixed up with anything that puts you in danger."

"What's this all about?"

"Got a call...well, actually Robert got a call today from a cop friend. It seems that Robert had an Officer Morrell poking around for the whereabouts of a Linda Windsor who shares some history with our little friend, Nick DeLucci."

"How so?"

"Same orphanage, I think he said."

Bralich feigned disinterest. "Humph"

Chapter 20

Alan awoke at noon. He was alone in bed. Looking out the window he could see that snow had fallen throughout the evening, leaving about a foot on the ground. The lowest branches of the larger pines bowed and the smaller trees he had planed last spring bent in half under the weight of the wet snow. The skies looked unfriendly, and his suspicions that the weather threatened to drop an additional accumulation were confirmed when he grabbed the remote control, tuned in the sports network, and a weather warning flashed across the screen.

"Alan, if you are finished messing up the bed with your acrobatics, get your ass up and help me make it," Evelyn said, entering the bedroom.

"Good morning to you too, dear."

"We're running low on firewood, so if you don't want us all to freeze, you had better bring in some more. Linda just called me from town and needs a ride home. I'm just going to stay at her place for the afternoon and then this evening we're going out with some of the girls."

"In this weather! What's to do on a Sunday evening?" he said, tossing back the sheets and rolling out of the waterbed.

She avoided his eyes. "Just girl stuff. Come on, tuck in that corner."

"Now that Linda has Matthew back, I was hoping we could spend more time together."

"We're together all day long."

"No, we're not. You've spent most all week with Linda. And when you're home, you are doing other things, laundry, cleaning, avoiding me. We need to talk," Alan said.

"Talk about what? Pull harder, get that wrinkle out," she said pointing at the sheets.

"Just talk."

"We are just talking. And tonight I want to just talk with Linda and the girls.

"And what do you and Linda and the girls just talk about?"

"Girl stuff."

"We're becoming strangers."

"You're becoming stranger. Not me. Straighten those pillows. God, you're helpless."

"I've got some real concerns about Linda and Matthew," he finally blurted out, frustrated.

She avoided meeting his eyes. "Why, because they're not boring and mundane like your friends?"

"Because ..."

"You've become a real stick in the mud, Alan, a spectator in your own life. If you want to sit around all day and watch football, fine! But I'm going out to have fun with my friends."

"Stay home with me today."

"I can't. Linda is stuck in town. We'll talk tomorrow. Shovel the drive so that I can get back in when I come home in the morning. Better get Vinnie to help you before he goes out so you don't throw out your back. I think Leslie is planning to come get him around two. Some of the kids are going tubing. He'll want a shower and time to primp. I'm taking Tia to visit Rachel. She's planning to spend the night and said she'll get a ride home in the morning so we won't have to pick her up."

Evelyn ran an extended arm and open palm across the covers, then came around the bed and pecked Alan's cheek. Seconds later, she and Tia were headed out the door.

Alan heard his daughter say, "Oh yuck! On the National Geographic program they just showed this black widow spider eating her husband after having sex! Why do they do that?"

"Because they don't smoke, dear," Evelyn answered.

Then they were gone.

Alan was left with most of the shoveling and the unpleasant thought that he would spend Monday repeating the task or unable to walk and soaking in Epsom salts. Another large storm front was coming off Lake Erie and was expected to drop an additional eight to twelve inches during the evening.

Cold and disgruntled, he peeled off his boots, and hung his scarf, gloves, cap and jacket over the hallway heat register to dry off. The smell

161

of hot chocolate wafted from the kitchen. He followed the aroma to find Gabrielle at the stove.

"Figured you might need warming up," she said passing a hot mug over the counter.

"Thanks, I really appreciate it." Alan took the cup in both hands and sipped.

"Did Mom tell you about your phone messages before she went out?"

"No. She was in a bit of a hurry. Who called?"

Gabby showed him a piece of scratch paper covered with art doodles, a shopping list, and a week's worth of penned messages. "Your funny friend that we met in New Jersey," she said. Derrick Brown (201) 676-9615 was scrolled along the left margin of the page. "He seemed pretty interested in talking to you, but Mom said I shouldn't wake you up."

"What time did he call?"

"He called a couple of times, I think. I talked to him around nine this morning. You want me to make some more hot chocolate? If not, I need to head upstairs to do homework."

"I'm good, thanks."

Alan sipped again at the cocoa, then picked up the kitchen phone, leaned his elbows on the countertop, and dialed. Derek answered on the first ring.

A gust of wind slapped at the kitchen windows, rattling them in the frames. Snowflakes swirled across the yard and against the panes. The real storm was coming.

"Derrick? This is Alan. What's up?"

"Got some news I thought might interest you...about Danny."

"What's that?"

"Remember Bones MacPhearson? Skinny geek. He played freshmen football. Big mouth, no talent, no balls."

"Sure."

"He's a Cranford cop now. I run into him pretty regularly because his boys play hockey, like my Bobby. Anyway, they were down from Cranford skating against our team last Thursday night at the Bricktown Rink and Bones and me got to talking."

"So what about Danny?"

"The cops now believe that it wasn't Danny's body that was found. Officially, the cadaver has been reclassified a John Doe. Bones said the thinking is now along the lines of murder. Danny's the obvious suspect."

"How could they make such a mistake? Danny's obituary has already appeared in the newspapers."

"Administrative error, I guess. Dental and fingerprint records were lost or something."

The furnace kicked on with a loud bang. Alan raised his head to look after the noise and bumped it hard on the kitchen cabinets.

"Damn!"

"Alan?"

"Bumped my head," he said trying to rub away the pain. "So where the hell is Danny?"

"In hiding, I imagine," Derrick said.

"Any ideas circulating as to where?"

"None. At least none that Bones would share with me."

"Anything else the discreet Officer MacPhearson let slip?"

"You didn't hear this from me, okay?"

"Yeah, sure. What didn't I hear?"

"There's a record of an arrest on charges of child molestation and statutory rape. Two years ago, some rich bitch in the City filed charges that Danny had bedded her two girls, one sixteen, the other only eleven. Charges were dropped."

"My God!"

"Things aren't looking too good for the superstar. Bones said that the connection with that Paganini guy, the child porn king, is getting stronger."

"My God!" Alan said again.

"No shit!" The line remained vacant for a few seconds, then Derrick added. "Hey, look, I got to go pick up my girls. Just thought you'd want to hear the latest. Take it easy."

"You too, Big D. Take care of yourself, okay."

"I will. Come visit next time you're out this way."

"Count on it. Hey! They ever disclose who the third partner in Danny's antique shop was?"

"Yeah. It was in the Citizen and Chronicle. Hold on a sec."

Alan could hear him flipping through the newspaper.

"Here it is. Linda. Linda Windsor. Bones said something about her having dropped out of sight."

A cold gust of air passed through him, crystallizing an icy fear in the pit of his stomach. His heart pounded against his chest, his ears popped as if decompressing during landing on the shuttle flight he often took from Pittsburgh. The kitchen clouded gray around him.

"I'll catch up with you again soon."

"Goodbye," he mumbled in return, his thought processes muddled. His friend's voice disappeared, leaving a monotonous humming in its stead. Alan's hands trembled as he returned the receiver to its cradle.

No sooner had he hung up the phone than it rang again. He grabbed for the phone and screamed, "Hello."

"Is this Alan?" a faintly familiar woman's voice inquired.

"Yes, it is." He waited for the woman to continue but the line stayed empty. He broke the silence. "Who is this?"

"This is Alan Ciani?" the woman asked again, her tone stilted.

"Yes, this is Alan Ciani. Who is this?"

The woman hesitated again before answering. "Alan, this is Judy Wesley. I was at your party last night."

The crazy lady, he thought. "Yes, I remember." He had more important things to do than spend time on the phone with her.

"Look, I'm at the truck stop on Route 8." Her voice lowered to almost a whisper. "I'm catching a bus out of here. I just thought you ought to know that they have your daughter."

He tried to remain calm and rational but his head was spinning. "What are you talking about? Who has my daughter?"

"I told you last night," she whispered. "Tom's sicko friends. Linda and Matthew."

Alan froze. Judy had been rigid with fear at the party. He had willingly dismissed he trepidation because Evelyn said she was a cokehead. Now, suddenly his throat was parched and he was sweating.

"Did you hear what I said? They have your daughter." There was an unmistaken urgency in her hushed tone.

"That isn't possible. Tia is visiting a friend."

"Suit yourself. Check on her if you care at all for her safety. But I'm telling you that your wife turned over your daughter to that group of maniacs."

Fireworks exploded in his head. Not possible, this is insane, he thought. Evelyn couldn't. Wouldn't. He forced a question. "Why would she do such a thing?"

"Tonight begins the New Year for them"

His voice cracked. "What would anyone want with my daughter?" But he knew the answer to his question before the words were out of his mouth.

"Surely you've seen the movies or read the horror novels. The crazies who revel in darkness look to this evening as an excuse for excess."

"But …"

"My bus is here, I have to go. I thought you ought to know, that's all." She hung up.

"Damn her!" echoed over and over again in his head to the detriment of any more productive thoughts. "She's at Rachel's house," his inner voice reminded him. Rachel who? "Rachel, Rachel, Rachel" he said aloud, rapping the countertop with his knuckles. "What the hell is her last name?" What kind of a father was he, not to be more intimately involved in his children's lives; not to know their friends' names?

There's a telephone list on the refrigerator, he remembered.

Rachel Witkowski. That was it. He dialed, tried to calm himself while he listened to the phone ringing at the other end of the line. Somebody picked up.

"Hello, this is Alan Ciani. I was wondering if my daughter Tia has already arrived at your home?" he asked as soon as the connection was made.

"Oh, hello. This is Rachel's mom. No. Rachel said your wife called earlier and canceled for this evening. But let me check."

Alan heard the woman calling after her daughter, then some muffled dialogue. When she was back on the line, she confirmed that Tia had changed her plans.

He rang up Evie's cell phone. "Come on pick up. Pick up, you soulless bitch!" he pleaded but to no avail. Sometimes connections were difficult to achieve in the mountainous terrain.

Alan's heart felt as if it had been ripped from his chest. He had no idea what to do. Call the police? Maybe they could go after her, but he suspected they wouldn't. Imagine what they would think when he told them his daughter had been kidnapped by a coven of Satanists…with their mother's permission. For certain they'd peg him a crackpot. And they sure as hell weren't going to send anyone out in this weather to investigate a crank call. Unless, of course, they decided he wasn't just a crackpot but a psychotic. Pennsylvania had a seventy-two hour involuntary commitment law that permitted incarceration for psychiatric evaluation of persons who might be dangerous to themselves or others. He didn't need that. Besides, he was an outsider, a non-entity in Deliverance country.

Unable to come up with any other option, he called anyway.

"She's with her mother?" the policeman asked after Alan had provided an abridged version of the facts.

"Yes, she was, but …"

"And they've been gone for a couple of hours?"

"Yes, but I just got a call from Judy Wesley. She teaches at the high school …"

"Yes, Tom's wife," the policeman said, making no attempt to disguise his sarcasm. "Look, Mr. Ciani. Evelyn and I went to high school together. She's a nice lady and I'm sure that the two of you can work out whatever problems you're having. The police don't get involved in domestic affairs."

"This isn't a domestic dispute. My daughter's life is in danger."

"I'm sure she'll be all right with her mom. And even if we got involved, legally we really can't do anything unless your daughter has been gone for at least twenty-four hours. I'm sure you're over-reacting."

Alan hung up. Whatever had to be done, he would be alone in doing it.

It was Halloween—All Hallows Eve. Judy was right, he had read enough fiction and seen enough movies to realize that it was a night in which crazies turned nightmares into reality. For the psychologically deranged, Halloween was a celebration to mark the beginning of the season of cold, darkness, and decay. Vile scenes of unrestrained orgies and human sacrifice flickered across his mind. Somewhere perceived as a secluded and safe haven, the pawns of evil would be acting out their worst intentions. Linda and Matthew's hideaway! That's where they would take Tia.

"Dear God, protect my little girl," Alan heard himself say. He hadn't had any faith in God for a very long time. What little faith he had was in him self, and a commitment to constructive action.

Who the hell was he kidding? When he wasn't on the road for work, he spent most of his time either on the golf course or at home sitting idly in front of the television, watching the world go round. He had abdicated his role of parent to Evelyn, justifying to himself that a good father didn't act like a dictator, instead gave his family the opportunity to make their own mistakes and learn from them without his interference.

That was only half the truth. He avoided confrontation; afraid to allow any expression to the cruel and vengeful parts of his psyche for fear that it would carry him away at the first smell of blood. Controlling his demons extolled a cost, had destroyed the essence of his manhood. It was as if some beast had devoured him from within, sucking the marrow from his bones, leaving him little more than a prop in his family's dynamics.

He was going to seriously have to reevaluate his life when this mess was over. But now it was time to get his ass in gear.

You won't be able to live with yourself if you don't act right now!

Chapter 21

Bralich walked the halls of Columbia, oblivious to the hustle and bustle surrounding him. Between classes he had read the latest transcriptions of the DeLucci manuscript that Widowmaker had deciphered and left in his call box. Astounded by the autobiographical references and disturbing plot, Bralich played the coincidences against each other, hoping to find some key to discern fact from fiction. Without the Rosetta Stone, divine intervention or revelations coming directly from DeLucci, he could do little more than speculate.

For what reason had DeLucci chose to name one of the antagonists in his latest novel after fellow orphan, Linda Windsor? No wonder Robert had become obsessed with pursuing DeLucci's past. Bralich hoped the police detective with whom Robert had been working might cast some light on the Linda Windsor connection. He called Officer Morrell of the Roselle Park Police, and left a message. As yet, he hadn't heard back from him.

He made a copy of the deciphered manuscript that Widowmaker provided and distributed a few pages to each of the graduate students in his projective techniques class with instructions to score the writing as if it were a sample of a Thematic Apperception Test protocol. The TAT was a series of pictures about which respondents were asked to develop a story, and invariably projected their own psychodynamics on to the persons in the pictures, revealing their own fears, anxieties, and desires by attributing them to someone else. After all, Bralich reasoned, isn't that what an author does—projecting their inner imagings onto the blank page, embellishing characters that are composites of one's self and significant others in one's life?

Jack Widowmaker grabbed Bralich's shoulder from behind. "Hello, Tony. How are your classes going?"

"Hi, Jack. Good, thanks."

"You check your box yet? I made considerably more progress than expected decoding the papers you gave me."

"Yes, thanks. I really appreciate your efforts, Jack. If I owe you anything ..."

"I thought we settled that already. Actually, I'm enjoying it. Hope you don't mind, but I took the liberty of reading while my computer was busy deciphering. Very interesting."

"Knock yourself out."

Students hastened by en route to their next class. Bralich waited for a break in the traffic. When it came, he crossed the hall to his office. Widowmaker was close behind.

"Hey, Tony," Jack said. "Can I ask you something?"

"Sure."

He leaned in close to Bralich's. "By any chance am I deciphering a DeLucci novel?"

Bralich's success as a therapist depended upon his ability to remain nonplused in virtually any situation, but he was unprepared for Widowmaker's comment and certain his body language betrayed his surprise. He quickly regained composure. "What makes you ask?"

"I've read all DeLucci's novels. This is very similar." He emphasized the "very."

"I would have never taken you for a horror aficionado, Jack."

Widowmaker smiled his pleasure. "This is DeLucci, then? I thought so."

Bralich had wrestled earlier with the confidentiality issue, finally concluding that the novel did not constitute personal confidence since it was intended for public consumption. "Yes, this is a DeLucci novel. Tell me, how did you arrive at that conclusion from what you'd read?"

Bralich entered his office, planted his briefcase on the credenza, and sat behind the desk. Widowmaker, accustomed to military protocol, waited at the door for the invitation to enter and take the other chair in the room. When Bralich nodded toward the seat, Widowmaker thanked him and sat down. His back was as straight as a board. Bralich wondered if the man ever allowed himself to slouch, physically or otherwise.

"I love DeLucci's stuff, and figured this had to be either DeLucci or somebody copying his style."

Bralich nodded.

"The central theme in almost all of his work is that there is a deeper reality laying beyond the world of appearances. Nothing is quite what it seems in the real world. His protagonists constantly struggle to differentiate between conflicting realities."

So is DeLucci's therapist, Bralich thought. "What about the satanic theme?"

"That shows up often in DeLucci books," Widowmaker answered. "Most of his protagonists have both a good and an evil side; each of them a devil, as well as an angel. We all suffer our inner demons. I suspect he's a big fan of sociobiology. Takes it a step or two beyond what is generally accepted."

Bralich leaned back in the swivel chair, arms folded across his chest, holding his chin in one hand. He didn't know what to make of Widowmaker' s newly found loquaciousness. Bralich knew little of sociobiology, although he was well schooled in the nature versus nurture debate that had long pervaded his own discipline. "Nature versus nurture," he said.

Furrows appeared on Widowmaker's square forehead. "Yes, according to the tenets of sociobiology, it is possible that some choices we make are genetically programmed. Even though we have free will, we are predisposed toward certain behaviors and make predetermined choices unknowingly. Doesn't violence as a solution to disagreements seem to be woven into the very fabric of human nature? I imagine this is the underlying assumption in Satanists' belief that through selective breeding they can recreate Satan on Earth."

"What can you tell me about that?"

Widowmaker's face took on a more relaxed air of confidence. He appeared pleased by the invitation to continue. "Since repeated choices can become genetically engrained, it is possible to pass along dysfunctional behaviors. In biblical terms, that is in fact an eternal damnation. Of course, I imagine that in their own perverted way, Satanists believe that eternal damnation is what everyone else gets from choosing the wrong set of standards."

Bralich nodded in agreement.

"Actually, did you know that there is no mention of endless physical torment in the original Old Testament. Furthermore, if you examine the

Gnostic gospels such as those unearthed at Nag Hammundi, which were excluded from the New Testament for political reasons, you'd discover that Jesus talked more of enlightenment and illusion than of sin and repentance."

"I was unaware that you were a religious scholar, as well, Jack. You're full of surprises."

"I was a seminary student at Loyola. Chose the military over the priesthood. Actually, the two vocations have much in common, just different uniforms." Widowmaker's smile seemed more a reflex than affectation. "Did you know that the New Testament word for sin was 'hamartia' from the sport of archery, meaning 'missing the mark.' If you equate the tenets of sociobiology to that of eternal grace, by missing the mark, one passes sins from generation to generation genetically. So, the sins of the father are truly upon the head of his son. Some religions focus on karma, others on original sin or reincarnation. It's all the same thing."

Bralich hoped to avoid embranglement in religious debate, intended to steer the conversation back into themes less dogmatic, back to DeLucci's manuscript. Widowmaker didn't allow that to happen, he enthusiastically continued his course.

"What if the process of spiritual deterioration is accelerating because mankind is recessively breeding? The gene for righteousness might be more recessive than dominant because altruism is usually rewarded with a shortened life. Heroes and martyrs die young. Criminals, cowards, exploiters of the masses, such as sleazy politicians, live to a ripe old age and reproduce prolifically. And now we have cloning?"

"You're a geneticist too?"

"No, but I stayed in a Holiday Inn Express once," he chimed, mimicking the popular television commercial without cracking a smile.

Without a couple of pitchers of beer under his belt, listening to Widowmaker's curliwurly philosophy held little fascination. Mankind has been in its last days ever since the first loonies took to the streets to preach. Bralich didn't buy into a horned beast rising up from the pits of Hell, nor anticipate Rosemary's Baby popping out anywhere but in Hollywood, although he had to concede that the greater humankind's gains in knowledge, the less capable we proved ourselves in handling it.

Widowmaker continued. "People think evil is an event or persona so spectacular that one cannot help but recognize it for what it is—an Adolf

Hitler, Charles Manson, or demonic possession like in *The Exorcist*. Satan doesn't need to rise from the pits of Hell in Technicolor and cinemascope. Evil is hatred and greed, and the intolerance and self-righteousness that shapes and perverts the actions of every man. It is the sexual indiscretions of spouses; the disregard for the integrity of our children; the brow beating of our students; the humiliation of our employees; the adolescent, juvenile rebelliousness and antisocial behavior that we Americans pass off as rugged individualism; or blind acceptance to corrupting laws like the Patriot Act. These are the true essence of Evil."

These were not the words that Bralich expected to her from a retired military person and he couldn't agree more with them. However, he chose not to respond and sat motionless, providing a blank expression that was the hallmark of every good therapist.

Widowmaker's face erupted into a smile, this one sincere. "There I go again." He laughed. "The life of a celibate is often laden with mental and verbal masturbation. A cathartic release, isn't that what your Freud would call it?"

Bralich's displeasure eased. "You've never married, Jack?"

He shook his head. "First I was married to God, then the Army…and now to mathematics." Widowmaker pointed to the framed photograph on the desk. "This your wife?"

"Yes."

A warming swell of memories flooded across Bralich's mind. He never understood what she had seen in him, and missed her beyond measure. When Mary died, it left an emptiness that nothing could ever fill. She had been a highly affectionate woman, nurturing and patient. The sole child of a wealthy industrialist, she had been raised in the lap of luxury, yet was possessed of an unwavering social conscience and labored ceaselessly in charitable and humanitarian activities. Now, as he was counting down to the end of his years, alone, with only his work for companionship, he wondered what miracle had brought them together and what else Fate had preordained.

Widowmaker rose from his chair. "I'll look forward to the next installment," he said and then showed himself the door.

Life is full of little surprises, he thought. He might actually grow to like Jack Widowmaker.

Chapter 22

Evelyn had the Pathfinder. That meant Alan need venture out into the storm in the BMW, which was unsuited to the mountainous terrain in the snow. He grabbed a baseball bat from the downstairs closet and tightened his grip around its neck. It felt good in his hands.

"It's a little cold for batting practice, Dad," Gabby said from the stairwell.

"Guess so," he answered, trying to camouflage his distress. His heart was pounding so hard that is was nearly unbearable. "I've got to go out. You can fend for yourself while I'm gone?"

"The phone is for you."

"I don't have time right now," but then he had seconds thoughts. Who is it?"

"Got me. Some guy, wouldn't give a name but says it's important."

"I'll take it in my office."

Alan put down the bat and wrapped his arms around his daughter. "Don't let anybody in the house while I'm gone, especially Linda or Matthew...or any of Mom's other friends. No matter what they say or tell you. As a matter of fact, lock all the doors when I leave and don't answer regardless of who comes calling. Do you understand?"

"What's wrong, Dad? You're scaring me!"

"Just do what I say!" he snapped back and slipped through the double doors into the study.

"Yes. Hello."

There was no answer.

"Hello. Hello, is anybody there?"

He could hear somebody breathing on the other end of the line. A prank call?

"Hello," he said one more time. "I don't have time for this bullshit. Fuck you."

Then, sobbing. "Daddy?"

"Tia?"

"They're going to hurt me," her faltering voice said. A monotone droning told him that the connection was broken.

"Tia! Tia!"

Alan was defenseless against his fears.

He bolted from the study, grabbed his hat and coat, and raced out the door. Gusts of wind-blasted snow slammed into him. He bulled his neck against the storm and battled his way across the driveway to the garage.

The bluster tore the side door of the garage from his grasp, sending it crashing against the outside wall. Alan ignored the shattering of glass pane, and abandoned the freewheeling gate to the elements. Entering the garage, he smacked the automatic garage door opener button on the wall. He fumbled for the car keys in his pocket as he folded into the Beamer but they slipped through his numbed fingers and fell to the floor mat. Retrieving them, he inserted them into the ignition, started the car, rammed the automatic into reverse, and stomped on the gas pedal.

The car shot out of the garage, but skidded as soon as its wheels made contact with the slippery driveway. Alan slammed the brake pedal into the floor, but that only made things worse. The car slid sideways in a crab-like motion off the driveway onto the snow-covered lawn, jolting to a stop as the front-end passenger's side struck one of the pines that lined the circular drive. The sound of crunching metal and cracking glass was disheartening.

There was no time to inspect the damage. Again, Alan floored the gas pedal. The BMW fishtailed across the lawn; eventually finding pavement again, then proceeded down the driveway and out into the street. He sped downhill, his hold on the road precarious.

A coal truck ignored the stop sign where the frontage road intersected with Route 322. When Alan instinctively swerved out of its path, the wheels lost all traction and the car went into a spin.

Turn into the slide, he told himself, gritting his teeth. Doing so seemed to have little effect in gaining control over the vehicle. It spun around three or four times and slithered off the roadway and came to a complete stop.

In an inconsolable rage he pounded his foot to the floor. The back wheels whirred fiercely but failed to dislodge the car from the snow.

"Dammit!" he screamed, slamming his fist into the padded steering wheel.

When he got out of the car to evaluate the situation, Alan found one of the rear wheels was hung up several inches above the ground. His mind raced in circles of unproductive chatter as he stomped around his disabled vehicle cursing out loud. He had taken off half-cocked, without his cell phone, and now was stranded unless somebody came by who would give him a hand. It would do no good to return home on foot where no alternative means of transportation awaited him or to head out down the sparsely populated 322. The golden rule of highway safety was to remain with the vehicle and await assistance. Frustrated, scared and overwhelmed by his hopeless circumstances, he got back into the car, turned the hazard lights on, and waited. Near tears, he rested his forehead on the steering wheel and found additional lapses of foresight over which to berate himself; leaving the house without gloves, the baseball bat, a clear picture in his mind as to how to get to Linda's house, or a good plan regarding what to do when he got there. His daughter needed him now, and he could do nothing. He was a lousy father, protector, and human being.

"Damn you, Evelyn!"

Twenty minutes passed at a snails pace and the formulation of any constructive plan was obstructed by iterative rehearsals of admonition of his wife. More than a few times over the years he had wanted to punch in her face, which she richly deserved for a plethora of reasons. Not the least of these were the innumerable personal and career decisions based solely on her needs and irrespective of his. He had sacrificed friends and his interests and had even relocated so she could live near her crazy family. And now this betrayal.

Alan had grown up believing in the romantic myth that there must be a perfect someone for everyone; someone who would love him no matter what. Early on he discovered that simply wasn't true and stashed his heart in a place where nobody could ever find it. He had settled for Evelyn he thought bitterly. Even as his ire lathered into frenzy, he was cognizant that when the moment arrived, he would turn his hatred inward rather than acting on it. As a high school and college athlete, sports provided him a vent for his adolescent rage. Yet, he had come to fear the physical harm he was capable of inflicting on others. There was a vicious beast inside him that he could not let loose on the world. Keeping this brutality corralled, as much as anything Evelyn said or did to him, was the primary cause of the psychological gelding that lefty him spiritually gutted.

Finally, a carload of testosterone-laden teenagers pulled off the road and offered assistance. He suspected they were disappointed that he wasn't a stranded member of the opposite sex, but they helped anyway. There was little question that they had imbibed a few beers and were searching for adventure. One sat on the back right corner of the car to weigh down the suspended wheel while his friends pushed and Alan revved the engine. After a few tries, the car dislodged. As the boys patted themselves on the back, Alan slipped their leader a twenty without not much more than a thank you and rushed off.

Back on the road, he was anxious to make up for lost time, yet reconciled to proceed more cautiously. The windshield wipers thumped a funereal beat that amplified his urgency. He loosened his fierce grip on the steering wheel. He couldn't be of much assistance to Tia if he never made it to Linda's place.

Was it possible that Evelyn, too, required his assistance, he wondered? Could she really willingly have turned over her own child to such people? He wanted now to believe she wouldn't, but could find no solace in making such an assumption. Her psychological make-up had always been suspect. She made no attempt to hide the insanity that infested her family tree, merely downplayed its seriousness, turned the lunatics that comprised her conjugal family into colorful and comedic characters. Her own penchant for associating with the perverted and deranged was, from her point of reference, a commitment to embracing diversity. She had a capacity for sin, a propensity for wickedness, and a history of betrayal committed without compunction or guilt. Yes, she could do this thing.

When darkness fell, it covered the landscape like a blanket, eliciting in Alan a feeling of claustrophobia within the close quarters of his car. Any hope of rescuing his daughter was evaporating. In the dark, all the back roads looked the same. It was often difficult to find the roadway let alone pick out landmarks, and Alan seldom felt certain that he had chosen the correct turns. On a couple of occasions when it became obvious that he was on the wrong road, he executed impossible u-turns and backtracked.

Rivulets of perspiration ran down his face and neck. Smothered by his fears, he plodded on for more than two hours as the storm hammered the night. His eyes became agonized slits as he strained to set a course through the blinding snowfall.

"I'm coming, hold on," he repeated over and over in his head like a mantra, but by now it had lost any conviction. He focused his physical senses on the precarious task of driving.

Finally, he reached the long incline that he recognized as the last leg of the trip to Linda's and Matthew's seclude domicile. The steel bands that tightened across his chest, constricting his breathing, loosened. Fresh tire tracks in the snow let him know he was on the right path.

The Beamer strained against the steep hill. Although the road was unplowed, the heavy woods that surrounded the roadway had sheltered it, preventing much of an accumulation of snow. He crested the hill and began the rigorous descent, gingerly pumping the brakes, trying to keep the car under control as it snaked a tenuous course down the winding mountain passage. In spite of his best efforts, the vehicle picked up speed. The devil fools with the best-laid plans, he thought.

The road vanished without warning. Even if Alan had time to react to the sharp turn, there was nothing he could have done because the tires had caught in a rut and continued straight ahead. Every muscle in his body tensed, went rigid in anticipation of an impending collision that never occurred with the giant oak and evergreen environs. Instead, a small gully beyond the first row of trees swallowed the car, bringing it to a sudden jarring halt. The impact pitched him hard against the door and the side of his head slammed into the window before bouncing him in the opposite direction. A searing pain ripped through this skull and bolts of pain flashed down his spine. He instinctively folded his arms around his head. Something exploded into his left side with a whooshing sound, and pinned his shoulder and arm to his seat. The car tilted to its surroundings, rolled on to its right side, and settled with a final thump. Everything became still.

Alan clung desperately to consciousness but a velvety blackness soon engulfed him.

In a dream, a younger version of him lay semi-conscious by a campfire. As his eyes fluttered opened and closed, he could make out the blurred images of river rafts pulled up on a bank. There was a great deal of confusion. Screaming voices surrounding him as large unlaced combat boots passed before his eyes kicking up dirt and wildly whipping the untied shoelaces across his face. Out of his line of sight a scuffle ensued and he struggled to raise himself from the cold earth.

An interminable amount of time passed, and Alan was not certain if he had passed out or just closed his eyes against the pain that blossomed in his skull. He reached to the throbbing at his temple with his free arm as a biting wind whistled through the car. His hand drew away sticky and wet, but no thought registered as to the significance of the sensation.

His eyes adjusted to the inky darkness that enveloped him. An inflated air bag obscured most of Alan's view as he looked up at the driver-side door. Blinking in pain, he mindlessly grabbed the steering wheel with his right hand, freed his pinned left arm, and then fumbled for the seatbelt release. His head was spinning at a frenetic pace and he had difficulty making sense of how to unleash himself. When he was finally un-tethered, his feet planted firmly on solid ground beneath what had been the passenger-side window, Alan climbed over the airbag, forced the door upward, and pulled himself free of the car and into the cold night.

Disoriented and confused, he stumbled aimlessly among the trees. A sense of urgency he could not quite place gnawed at his mind.

By the time he staggered back to the roadway, his dizziness dissipated. He dabbed at the pain in his head. The wound had crusted over in the cold, he realized. He wondered how long had he been unconscious. Then he remembered the quest he had undertaken. Tia! Was he already too late?

Headlights approached from uphill. Excited, he started to call out for assistance then was struck with the realization that anybody traveling this road tonight was most likely not a friend. Alan ducked behind a big tree and waited for a white pickup truck and its passengers to go by. When it was out of sight, he tucked his hands, already stinging from the cold, into his pockets and took off in a slow jog after it. Pain jarred his bones and the pull of gravity seemed inordinately strong. He felt very, very alone.

Chapter 23

Tat-a-tat-a-tat-a-tat-ding.

Samantha made a point of saying nothing while Nick DeLucci typed. If his unusual nocturnal behavior was more than a mindless release of physical energy, if he was truly creating, she did not want to distract him. So every evening when DeLucci's lifeless body mysteriously erupted into activity she attended to housecleaning and administrative responsibilities. She took some time to exercise and massage her patient's atrophying leg, then sat down and read.

She surveyed the perforated computer sheets that rolled out of DeLucci's Smith-Corona. From time to time she came across an intelligible sentence or two but had retreated from her expectations that she would ever find much more than that. Someone had once told her that if you put a thousand monkeys in a room with typewriters, eventually they would turn out a Shakespearean tragedy.

The fluorescent lights overhead hummed along with DeLucci's discordant pounding of the keys. Tearing along the most recent perforated seam to exit the ancient typewriter cartridge, the words on the paper jumped out at her. "Oh, my God!" she mumbled to herself. She no longer stared at an incomprehensible and jumbled composite of vowels and consonants, but at a clean text.

She read.

Alan expelled breaths staccato like a woman in labor and his arms burned from exhaustion by the time he reached the turnoff to the house. He halted behind the family Pathfinder. The white pickup he'd seen earlier and few other vehicles, including a police car, were parked nearby on the side of the road. He located the path that Evelyn had led him down weeks earlier, and had just stepped onto it when blinding beams of light appeared around the last curve, just yards from where he stood. Scrambling into the trees for cover, he heard the slamming of car doors and faint voices descending towards him. He stood motionless, trying not to breathe but fearing his gasps drowned even the galling winds.

The newcomers disappeared down the path. If people were still arriving, maybe Tia was still all right.

He moved cautiously among the trees, gauging his proximity to the path by the voices of those who had the luxury of adhering to it, and hoping he was far enough from the trail to remain undetected by passersby. The air turned a wetter, more bitter cold as the wind kicked up above the treetops. The storm was coming in faster, urging him to proceed with greater haste toward the house.

He plodded with little efficiency through the snow, as fast as was safe in the dark. However, what nightfall and the trees didn't obscure, the blanket of snow did. The terrain unreadable, he lost his footing in a deep pocket of snow. His leg twisted when his foot hit solid ground, and he felt a lightning bolt of pain across the top interior of this knee. If there were nothing left of him when he reached the house, of what value would he be to Tia? The jaws of panic clenched around the thunderous pounding in his heart.

Ignore the pain, Alan told himself, reminiscent of his days playing college rugby with broken bones and battered body. He only needed to rediscover that place where the physical pain was not allowed to hamper performance.

The thick woods sheltered him from the gusting storm, but when Alan broke through the trees into the open area between the old barn and the house on the hill, he was full face into a howling wind. Amber lights shimmered from the dwelling's frost-rimmed windows. He pulled his coat tighter against the weather and scrambled in the direction of the makeshift bridge that crossed over the creek, dragging his injured leg. Not only was there no protection from the weather in the clearing, but he also needed to increase his pace if he hoped to avoid being spotted from the large kitchen greenhouse windows.

Alan searched the untreated windows for movement, saw none, and was about to make a feeble dash toward the hill when a light probed through the darkness from behind him. He forced down the smothering alarm in his chest. Scanning the shadowy landscape for cover, he spotted a large outcropping of rock about twenty feet off to his right and hobbled toward it.

The pain in his leg was unbearable. When he reached the rocks, he dropped to the ground, and pressed his back against the granite. Voices trailed off up the hill, and disappeared amidst the churning winds. The cold was numbing. He massaged his knee. When his fingers located the tender area above the kneecap, he pounded the snowy ground with his frozen fist, "Damn!" he groaned through gritted teeth. As if in response, the winds howled liked anguished animals.

He still was uncertain what to do when, and if, he ever reached the house. All along, Alan had hoped that some sort of plan would mystically pop into his head, but thus far one still hadn't.

His misted breath hung in the air. If he didn't want to freeze to death, he needed to start moving. He poked his head out from behind the boulders to survey the area again. Two yellow eyes hung suspended a foot off the ground only a few feet away. He muffled a startled gasp.

A cat! Too stupid to come in out of the storm, he thought, as it stood motionless regarding him with menace.

He pushed himself up off the frigid earth with his back braced against the stone, and then took a pain-laden step. The cat hissed a disapproving warning, halting Alan in his tracks. A low groan rumbled from deep within its throat as the feline held its ground. Alan ventured another step, circling around to the cat's right. It again made its displeasure known with a moan that rivaled the winds.

Cold stung Alan's face. The burning in his hands had transformed into a numbing ache. He kicked the cat out of his path.

Another set of glowing eyes approached from his left, followed by another, and still another. Within seconds, a sea of four-legged pests surrounded him, mewing with malcontent. Attempts to frighten them off with quick movements and by flailing his arms were unsuccessful. Alan plodded toward the house through the horde as the cats taunted him, scurrying in between his feet and hissing when he got too close.

By the time he reached the steps, what little reserve of energy he had left was completely used up. Under any other set of circumstances, he would have surrendered to his body's demands and collapsed into a stupor. No such option was open to him so he leaned into the hillside and shadows, and clawed his way up the wooden slats, doing his best to ignore his tormentors. When one slapped at his face with its paw, Alan retaliated with an elbow. It shrieked and backed off a few feet. Another scratched at Alan's hand and he pushed it away too. The kitty posse tightened the circle around him, and appeared to get braver, he thought, the closer Alan got to the house.

The wooden stairs creaked beneath his plodding feet. "Okay. I'm here. What the hell do I do now? What's the plan? What's the goddamn plan?" he asked himself.

Although the old door's glass-paned windows were nearly frosted over, he could still see all the way through to the kitchen. There was no sign of activity and no Tia. There had to be at least a dozen people inside, but nobody appeared to be in the front section of the house so he slid through the door, still fending off the aggressive cats.

A line of coats hung on the coat rack next to the doorway, and more were draped over the furniture. There were a lot more than twelve guests this evening.

Alan slipped quietly through the living room and into the kitchen. It was well lit, and thankfully, unoccupied. His shadow floated ahead of him. Half way across the polished wooden floors, he heard the outer door to the house open and the voices of several more arriving guests. There would be no place to hide in the dining room, so he hastened on tiptoes to a closed door in the kitchen. It opened to a long stairwell lit at the bottom by a dim bulb.

The rankest of odors wafted up the stairwell. Uric acid. The hairs on the back of Alan's neck and arms stood on end, eliciting undefined fears reminiscent of a long forgotten past. For reasons he could not identify, he simply couldn't move. It was as if he was merely a presence within a dream within another dream with no locomotive skill.

He stood as if a statue for an indeterminate length of time until loud voices headed in his direction dissolved his inertia and the instinct to flee involuntarily activated his muscles.

A large Siamese cat bounded into the kitchen ahead of the latest arrivals. Alan ducked into the cellar door, closing it behind him. He scampered down the steps like a wounded animal, wincing with pain, his knee unable to execute the stairs easily. At the bottom, he held on to the railing and allowed his momentum and centrifugal force to propel him around and underneath the stairs. He slid in between the support pillars. The pungent ammonia stench of urine and something else he recognized but could not name wafted into his nostrils. He leaned back into what he anticipated was a wall. Metal clattered at his back and the brittle cold outline of steel mesh pressed against him. He quieted the clanking cage with his hands.

The kitchen above filled with voices, footsteps resounded overhead. The cellar door opened.

"What is it, Magenta?" he heard Linda ask. "There's nothing you'd be interested in down there, you silly cat." The light flicked off and the door slammed closed.

In the all-consuming darkness, the stink of urine overwhelmed him, eating through his senses like acid. Alan wrinkled is nose at the tang and let out a stale breath.

Damp chill from the snowstorm outside penetrated into the cinder block basement, and his teeth began clattering uncontrollably.

The air vibrated with malignancy. For what seemed an eternity, he stood in total darkness, rigid with tension. A thawing sting appeared in his fisted hands as he waited for the conversation above to dissipate. The need to remain silent was nerve shredding

Shadows pulsed as if they were living creatures in the sea of divining darkness. In the oppressive emptiness, once again fear stalked into Alan's mind, slashing at his courage with razor sharp claws. A phantasmagoria of unsettling images rose to the surface of his consciousness leaping across his mind in disjointed fragments: the campfire burned brightly; boot laces slapping against his face; muted screams; terrorized faces. He attempted to get to his feet but the mountainous and malodorous man who had beaten and raped him again swatted him to the ground as if he was nothing more than a gnat. He could hear a child crying but it sounded far away. The crackle of the campfire exploded into his ears and the air filled with the scent of burning flesh. As Alan stared dumbfounded into the conflagration, the flames licked across the burning corpse it consumed. Its ligaments contracted, causing the dead man's head to turn at an unnatural angle and rotate slowly in Alan's direction. A ghastly mask of death now gazed back at him from the bonfire.

At the sound of heavy footsteps overhead, Alan's thoughts coalesced. His hold on sanity was tenuous at best, he realized as he struggled to get a grip on the loosed ends of his frayed psyche. Tears leaked down his cheeks. In an attempt to obliterate the appalling images embedded in his brain, he summoned Tia's face in his mind's eye. Was he too late?

Samantha finished reading what she had in her hand at almost the same moment that the typewriter went silent. She looked down at DeLucci. Disinterested eyes stared back at her. Extracting the remainder of DeLucci's efforts from the typewriter, she stood next to the bed and read the last page aloud to herself:

His resolve was disintegrating. If he was to proceed with any proficiency of effort, then the time to move was now. Otherwise, the predatory black vacuum that enveloped him would butcher the last of his courage and render his efforts futile. In an attempt to staunch the letting of his will and to steady his nerves, he took in a deep breath but the noxious atmosphere only further insulted his senses.

Above him, footsteps and muffled voices trailed away from the kitchen, followed by the clicking of lights switches. Alan extruded himself from between the wooden support columns under the stairwell and climbed the stairs with caution, listening for any misplaced sound that might warn him that the room was still occupied. His legs were rubbery and his tongue felt thick and chalky; he was parched. He was reliving a childhood fantasy in which a long dark passageway led him to either some heroic quest or his doom; he couldn't remember which.

He stood motionless at the threshold attending to the silence beyond until his breaths quieted. Reluctantly, Alan groped for the doorknob in the blackness, found it, and then pulled away. Locating it again with a brushing touch, he placed an ear to the door with angst, imagining it a coiled snake ready to strike. Something on the other side waited for him.

The metal knob seemed frozen on his skin. He twisted it in one quick movement, sucked in his breath and screwing the last of his courage in place, slid through the doorway.

A cold breath insinuated itself in DeLucci's ear, "Ad vitam revocare," the voice commanded, releasing him from his silent prison and summoning him to return to life.

Dream and reality converged, then disentangled. Images ran wild across Nick DeLucci's throbbing brain like terror stricken stallions escaping a burning barn: the groping desire of hands...and tongues...of human flesh pressing against his infant body to the background of rhythmic chanting. The metallic taste and smell of human blood...charred human flesh erupted in his mouth and nostrils, eliciting the memory of an endless orgy of flesh evoking both fear and ecstasy.

His flesh tingled with lust.

Nick DeLucci remembered who he was and how he arrived at this moment. There were still large gaps of time for which he could not account, where everything had slipped into a non-reality of disjointed images with black spaces in between. These black holes of memory not only obscured the past, but also buried whatever roots intimately connected him to the rest of humanity.

Things would be different this time and he would assume the role for which Fate had prepared him. Nick DeLucci broke through his cocoon of sleep.

When DeLucci's cold, waxy hand locked onto her wrist, Samantha expelled a half-stifled cry of surprise. She jerked back in reflex, but his stubby malformed fingers clung to her like crazy glue. His eyes glistened with life and turned their attention toward her. The hideous mask that was his face, infinitely strange and inhuman, twitched around the corners of his mouth. Samantha felt disoriented as if awakened suddenly from a deep sleep. She stood transfixed like a deer caught in headlights.

"Hi," DeLucci said. His lips curled menacingly around his large uneven teeth, but his diminutive voice conveyed no malice; it was full of sleep. He unfastened his hold on Samantha's wrist.

"Hello," Sam answered uncertainly, trying to decide whether she might be hallucinating. Then, she smiled, "Welcome back."

Chapter 24

The city reeked of decomposing garbage.

Bralich asked the cabby to wait for him.

"Sorry, Mister," The dark-skinned man said in a strong Indian accent, spitting out words in short, choppy syllables. "Bad neighborhood. No can do. Very sorry. You must pay now...as you promised."

Bralich doled out the required fare and a generous tip. Holding up another twenty he added, "Just wait until I try the keys. If they work and I go inside you can leave. If the keys don't fit, I'll want away from here as much as you do."

"Okay, boss. Try the keys."

Rain was turning to snow. Ordinarily Tony wouldn't venture into this section of lower Manhattan and he had to agree to pay the cabby extra to make the trip.

The building at the address DeLucci listed as home had seen better days. It looked like an old hardware store from the outside. The windows on the sidewalk level were boarded up; those above were coated over with grime. A derelict with a face made of leather and pus slumped in the doorway with a bottle wrapped inside a brown paper bag, seeming oblivious to the inclement weather. One doorway further down, a lady of the evening shivered a arrhythmic dance against the cold.

DeLucci was a cash cow for the Underland Empire. Surely his success afforded him better accommodations than this dilapidated structure. Then again, he hadn't even upgraded his old typewriter for a laptop.

Bralich stepped past the street dweller, ignoring the man's disjointed ramblings that did not appear directed towards him but rather to a distant memory. In the cold, he fumbled with the keys he had retrieved from among DeLucci's possessions before finding one that fit into the lock on the iron caging that protected the front door. The gate sprung open with a click. The door behind it opened as easily with a second key.

When Bralich looked back, the yellow cab had already driven off.

He reached inside the door for a light switch and flipped it. A single florescent tube came on above an elevator at the back of the building. It seemed a football field away. He turned and locked the cage and front door behind him. His nostrils twitched at the strong musty odor that assaulted him, imposing a bitter, unfamiliar taste on his palate. He tightened his throat to ward off the unsavory aroma.

The concrete floor held in the cold. Bralich's breath fogged in front of his eyes in the frigid air. He wrapped his coat collar more snugly around his neck and held it in place as he headed toward the elevator. His footsteps echoed hollow off the concrete and brick walls.

A palpable hostile presence permeated the suffocating silence. It had been ages since he last strayed from the protective environs that money and a good education afforded and his nerves were uncharacteristically raw. He imagined he could hear the calm, rational demeanor of his psychiatrist's armor chink. The fissure widened with each passing second.

Behind him, the tattered clothed derelict rattled the metal gate at the front door and accompanied the clanking with incoherent ranting. The sudden raucous sent a shrill of fear through Tony that turned his chilled bones to jelly. The man at the door concluded his exhortations as quickly as he had commenced them, but not before Bralich had broken into a cold sweat. He hastened his step.

When the solitary light that guided his way dimmed, flickered, and then went out entirely, he froze. Staring blindly into the black void, adrenaline pumped through his veins, pounding like a jackhammer. Hyper-sensitized, yet disoriented, he stood suspended in the vacuous silence.

The lights flickered on, then off again. Bralich thought he sensed movement out of the corner of his eye. He shifted to the right, waiting for his eyes to adjust to the blackness.

"Is anybody there?" he finally said into the emptiness.

There was no answer.

His heart hammered. "Hello?"

Nothing.

The lights flickered again.

Something moved, he was certain. He balled his fists and anchored his feet to the floor, knowing full well, however, that if someone was intent on doing him bodily harm, there was little defense his aged torso could render.

A sharp, clinking sound sent electricity through the air before dissipating into the black void. Milliseconds later, the quiet were shattered by the sound of exploding glass.

Bralich's chest and shoulder muscles knotted with dread.

His eyes searched in the direction of the noise. Two glowing yellow eyes looked down at him. Tony choked on his silent screams.

Then the light came back on.

A rat perched on a metal crossbeam scrutinized the old man with suspicion before scurrying away into the darkness. On the ground was a broken beer bottle.

Chastising himself for his irrational fear, Bralich emptied his lungs, relieved, and ran a forearm across his sweaty brow. He walked to the elevator, pushed the UP button on the wall, and slipped in quickly when the metal doors slid apart. Inside, he selected the second floor over the basement—his only other choice. The doors closed behind him and with a sudden jolt that buckled his knees, the four-by-six box began its ascent to a cacophony of un-oiled gears and droning machinery. His stomach somersaulted.

On the second floor, four-foot long florescent tubes illuminated a path from the elevator to a single room, which was carved from a large expanse of floor space that formed a U-shape around it. Light glimmered from beneath the room's closed door. Bralich again was overwhelmed by a permeating sense of solitude as the hardwood floors moaned beneath his steps. He used the third of DeLucci's keys to open the heavy-duty lock that secured the room. The door creaked open.

Two gas floor heaters burned from opposite corners of the room. The blue-yellow flames sputtered and hissed, but managed to bring considerable warmth into the confined quarters. A pervasive scent of cinnamon and cloves wafted through the living quarters. When Bralich found the light switch, a twenty-foot square living space materialized. A quick scan of the room noted a futon bed, bookshelves, a desk and chair, sink, refrigerator and stove, all of which hugged the floor, no doubt reengineered to accommodate DeLucci's diminutive stature. Little money had been invested in the furnishings. The walls were painted black, as was the large pane of window at the back of the room.

Bralich entered. Only one item adorned the walls. It was an old 1950's style movie poster of a scantily clad, buxom vixen, striking a pose of terror, hands raised as if to fend off an unseen assailant. "Satan's Web" was sprawled diagonally across the placard in red letters that dripped blood. "There's no escaping …" was printed above the title. The starlet on the poster bore such an uncanny resemblance to Samantha that Bralich actually rubbed his eyes as if he might clear away any illusion or misperceptions. His remedy changed nothing, however. A "Free 3-D glasses" sticker plastered over the bottom of the billboard obscured most of the credits. So his curiosity about the woman's name went unsatisfied.

He fingered the books on the shelves. They were mostly hardbound copies of Nick's novels. There were also a few erudite clinical psychology texts, and to Tony's surprise, a directory of licensed New York clinicians. He thumbed through the pages. A few names were highlighted; one was Robert Miller's. In the upper corner of the last page of names, "Zent" was written in an unschooled hand. Below that was scribbled "BioSyn." William Zent? Why, Tony wondered. And what was BioSyn?

Because the legs of the desk had been sawed off, when Bralich lowered himself into the similarly modified chair in front of it, his knees bumped hard into the desktop. He was virtually sitting on the floor.

The top of the desk was cleared, but papers protruded from the overstuffed desk drawers. Tony shuffled through the confusion. There were notes DeLucci made to himself regarding story lines, as well as mundane daily itineraries and reminders of where he had gone on any particular day and what he had seen. Bralich scanned the scribbling for mention of Zent. The best he could find was the notation: "Z: who is he?"

Apparently DeLucci also kept every receipt he had ever acquired—at least over the year prior to his being hospitalized. There were some for paper purchased from Office Depot, grocery bills from Food King, and the passenger's copy of an airline ticket made out to Stevie Cox. The name registered immediately in Bralich's memory banks as another character from DeLucci's novel. That made two characters that somehow were connected with DeLucci's real life; maybe three, if the unnamed malevolent dwarf was meant to be Nick, himself. Bralich noted that Cox had purchased a one-way ticket from LAX to Kennedy.

In another drawer, amidst a myriad of receipts, he found a yellowed Polaroid of a juvenile Nick DeLucci in the company of three other adolescents, two boys and a girl. The physical closeness of the foursome suggested that the youths might have been friends. They made a bizarre quartet, nonetheless. DeLucci's attempt to smile made more hideous the frozen mask that was his face. The pose was in striking contrast to the disarmingly handsome blonde-haired boy at Nick's right, yet struck an interesting balance with that of the pudgy girl on the other side of the photo. She had long strands of ebony hair, a face as cold as marble, and a smile laced with contempt and deceit. It was the image of the fourth child, however, to which Bralich was most drawn. He had seen the piercing dark eyes and finely chiseled features before. They had covered the front pages of newspapers and filled the airways, and now resided in the Rahway State Prison. Without question, the youth in the photograph was Lucius Sangre.

Bralich stowed the photograph in his pocket.

As he lifted a stack of pages from another drawer to examine their contents the dull thud of something falling to the bottom of the wooden pigeonhole caught his attention. Wading through the clutter with both hands, he spotted the ring that must have been the source of the noise. The red ruby was girdled in gold. An artistically engraved goat's head adorned the band, its horns wrapping around the jewel. Like lightning, it struck Bralich that Samantha wore a similar ring. No, not similar, identical.

There had been, he recalled, a passing reference to a Samantha in DeLucci's Embodiment of Evil. "My God," he mumbled aloud. As he contemplated the significance of yet another coincidence, the cell phone in his coat pocket jingled. He retrieved the phone and answered it.

Samantha's voice was excited. "Dr. Bralich. Nick DeLucci is awake. He's back!"

"Wonderful," he said cautiously. "It's impossible for me to get over to the hospital this evening, but I will check in with Nick first thing in the morning." He needed to visit with Zent before then.

"Can you handle the situation on your own?

"I'll be fine."

"You better contact Wayne immediately."

Chapter 25

While unconscious and inanimate, Nick DeLucci hadn't seemed real. Observers viewed the little man with a sense of curiosity and suspicion. Now, awake, it was hard to get past his ugliness. His face looked like a craftsman tripping on hallucinogens had cut it from marble. Bralich noted that most of the staff avoided eye contact. Only Samantha seemed capable of ignoring external appearances and related to Nick on a personal level. She continued her daily routine of exercising his leg although now there was a second cognizant party to participate in what had been for weeks only one-sided conversations.

Bralich had discretely considered Samantha's ring and didn't know what to make of it. It was, in fact, identical to the one he had located in DeLucci's room. The ring was far too unique and expensive for them both owning one to be coincidental. He watched their interactions with a new suspicion, but said nothing. Hopefully, these misgivings weren't evident in his communications with the duo. He realized that he had begun thinking of them as a couple since re-visiting Zent.

When confronted with the knowledge that Zent's name was handwritten in one of the books he had examined in DeLucci's apartment, Zent showed no outward signs that he recognized DeLucci's name, nor could he explain why the little fellow had taken any interest in him.

"Maybe he's familiar with my work with cult victims," Zent offered as a possible explanation.

That was certainly plausible, Bralich thought. "And what is BioSyn?"

Zent's response was simple. "I haven't a clue. It has the sound of a biotech organization and, if so, should be easy enough to find information about."

The real purpose for which he had ventured back to New Jersey was to quell his irrational fear that Zent, too, owned a large red ruby ring with a

191

goat's head engraved on its golden band. Bralich was greatly relieved to find that, true to his recollection, the semi-retired psychologist wore no jewelry at all, not even a watch. Bralich needed a professional ally he could trust, and he continued to believe that Zent's insights into destructive cultism would be invaluable to unraveling the web of mystery surrounding DeLucci.

He brought up the fact that both Samantha and Nick had the same ring. "As do members of most clubs—social, perverse, or otherwise. Coven initiates often share some external symbol of their membership. Rings or tattoos are common, and a goat's head is a common icon found among Satanic groups," Zent informed him.

How did Samantha figure into this scenario, Bralich wondered aloud. "It doesn't seem remotely possible for her to be involved with anything so incongruously kinky or self-deprecating. By all outward appearance she's an angel of mercy and the paragon of wholesomeness."

Zent's face seemed to tighten. His eyebrows had knitted across his forehead with a look of concern. "The rings could be betrothal bands," Zent said. "The marriage and ultimate deflowering of innocence and decency by evil has tremendous symbolic meaning in satanic ritual. The sacrifice of virgins and lambs predates recorded history. There is even greater significance if any such union is between blood relations, especially siblings. Could such be the case here?"

Bralich didn't know and said so. "Is it possible for the vestal virgin to be unaware of her pre-arranged nuptials."

"More than likely, as a matter of fact," Zent replied.

Bralich was shaken from his musings by Nick DeLucci's tinny voice.

"You are somewhere else, Dr. Bralich." DeLucci said. There was a semblance of confidence in the Munchkin's voice since his reawakening three days ago that Bralich hadn't expected.

"I apologize, Nick. I'm a little preoccupied. It's a hazard of the profession."

"Does it ever bother you that the founding fathers of your profession all suffered from psychological disorders? Freud battled depression and drug abuse. And who was the guy that sold the empty orgone boxes and went to prison?"

"Reich. Wilhelm Reich," Bralich answered.

"Yeah, that's him," Nick said. "Mad as a hatter, I imagine."

Bralich offered a look of noncommittal. Following his own instincts and Zent's advice, he was as supportive and non confrontational as possible during time spent with DeLucci each day, despite the leashed hostility in DeLucci's manner. Although he couldn't be certain, Bralich sensed DeLucci was toying with him, subtly issuing challenges. The photograph that Bralich had retrieved from Nick's ghetto domicile was burning a hole in his pocket and he desperately wanted to see how DeLucci might react to it. Not yet. Now that Nick had reentered real time, he couldn't risk the little fellow withdrawing again. Not until Bralich had all his ducks in a row.

"Well, does it bother you?" DeLucci repeated.

Bralich maintained a tranquil, nonjudgmental tone. "Not especially. The mistakes we make in life are not nearly as important as the lessons we learn from them. Does it bother you, Nick?"

DeLucci looked down the crooked bridge of his nose at Bralich. An obscene smile curled around his uneven teeth. "Not in the least," he said. Nick had anthracite black eyes that condemned.

Recollections of his visit to Sangre in prison rushed back at Bralich. There was an eerie similarity in the mannerisms of DeLucci and Sangre that Bralich found unsettling. He felt his skin growing tight and cold. Robert Miller had mentioned nothing of this almost predator-like quality in DeLucci's demeanor, nor had Jefferson Thorne, DeLucci's agent. Both had portrayed him as mouse-like, a pitiable character cowered by an unfeeling world in which everyone was suspect.

Zent had reportedly found a staggering correlation between developing multiples and spending the formative years in abusive cults. Was this perhaps a new persona; maybe an emergent personality, a fiery phoenix emerging from the ashes of weeks of psychological detachment? Or was the dwarf in DeLucci's novel a projection of DeLucci's real self, while the docile personality only a façade?

As yet, Nick had shared nothing of his past. And there was no justification for Bralich to keep him interred at the hospital. Alexander had already informed Bralich that DeLucci had to be discharged, his treatment returning to outpatient status.

As if reading Bralich's thoughts, DeLucci said, "I'm going home today."

"Yes, it's time to resume your life, isn't it?" Bralich responded. "We are all very happy for you." He looked to the portable Smith-Corona upon which DeLucci's hands were folded. Robert Miller had told Bralich how the typewriter never left DeLucci's side. It was more than a security blanket, Bralich concluded. It was an appendage. "I understand that you spent some time writing last night."

DeLucci said nothing. Nick was testing him, Bralich thought. This resistance seemed more than just a matter of trust to Bralich. It appeared as if DeLucci viewed their interaction as a battle of wills. Why?

"Tell me how you wish to proceed with our sessions. I think our meeting on an ongoing basis, as you did with Dr. Miller, would be beneficial."

DeLucci ran his stubby fingers over the wrinkled creases on his baggy pant legs with what appeared a calculated deliberation. His tiny feet poked straight out at Bralich, barely extending beyond the cushioned seat atop which he was perched. "I'll consider it and get back with you."

"Please, do," Bralich told him. "I'd like to see you resolve whatever issues initially led you to seek Dr. Miller's assistance."

"My dreams."

Bralich nodded. "And the underlying fears and anxieties from which they spring. We could coordinate our appointments with your visits to physical therapy until your leg is fully recovered."

"I'll think on it and get back to you," he said but DeLucci's words didn't ring true. He climbed down from his chair, hobbled over to Bralich, and extended his hand.

Bralich reciprocated the gesture. The little man's handshake was as powerful as a vice. He held his grip beyond normal convention before releasing Bralich's hand.

Headed toward the door, DeLucci said, "I'll call you," in a manner that conveyed. "Don't call me, I'll call you," as in "fuck off." He reached up for the doorknob, and then looked back at Bralich. "It has been said that each of us has deep within, the knowledge of all things. And when we ready ourselves to remember this, then the knowledge is there to be known."

"Yes." Bralich confirmed.

"I'll call you," DeLucci repeated as a warning as he exited the office.

Bralich followed him with his eyes as DeLucci limped down the hall to the elevator, pushed the button on the wall, and disappeared.

He went to his desk and sat down. Maybe it was somewhat unethical, he contemplated, but he would actively pursue DeLucci as a client. Furthermore, he intended to visit DeLucci's mother, and maybe Dante Underland, to glean whatever he might. As he absently looked over his desktop, brainstorming a plan of action, Bralich spied a large manila envelope standing upright against the back cushion of the chair that DeLucci had recently vacated.

He walked back around his desk, retrieved the envelope, and examined its contents. Recognizing the typed pages as the next installment of Embodiment of Evil, he read.

Flickering candles illuminated a macabre dance of ebony shadows overhead. Alan's eyes jetted helter-skelter across the room in anticipation of any onslaught mounted by the ominous shades. He pressed his spine into the cellar door through which he had just passed for support. His heartbeat thundered and he prayed that it was only his imagination that the vigorous pulsating of his heart echoed throughout the house like trains whistle in a tunnel. But the house was deadly silent except for a faint tapping sound behind him. When he looked to his hands at his sides, Alan saw they were trembling a spasmodic beat against the wooden door. He jerked his hands clear.

Get hold of yourself! He hadn't gone through all of this just to fall apart now.

Suddenly a rhythmic guttural chanting filled Alan's ears.

He started in the direction of the dirge; his mind spinning and terrified that the slightest sound might betray his presence.

A small dining room cluttered with candles gave way to a reading room lined with bookshelves. Lit in an equally bizarre manner, the room terminated at two huge oak doors that opened to the spacious, unfurnished room that Alan hadn't explored on his previous visit. It was from this room that the chanting emanated.

Like a circus performer on a high wire, Alan methodically placed right foot in front of left until he had traversed the distance to the portal. Shielding himself behind the doors, he peeked through the narrow crack left open between them.

"Now there's no use in pretending that you are not out there, Al. Have you come to join in or just watch?' The voice was that of Danny Cox—powerful and wild.

Oaken doors creaked open.

The passing moments were only impressions—a sea of masked faces and naked bodies: Danny, his gaze piercing, challenging every nerve ending in Alan's body; Evelyn at Danny's foot, nakedness accentuating her generously endowed form.

Alan, transfixed by Danny Cox's hypnotic presence, passed through the portal as if sleepwalking, mindlessly coming to a stop inches from Danny and Evelyn. His eyes blinked into focus.

Evelyn's arms caressed Danny's thickly muscled leg; her hands slowly slithered up his thigh. "He's come to watch," Evelyn said, propelling a sardonic smile that stuck Alan with a force that set his head reeling.

Alan was unable to summon a single word while, inside his head, he was screaming.

The chanting abated and the room fell eerily silent.

"You've always been uncomfortable with your own kind," Danny said. "Such foolishness! You miss out on all the fun." He turned his forbidding mien to Evelyn and slapped her violently across her face. Droplets of blood trickled to her lips and a rush of violet color to her cheeks.

Evelyn ran her tongue across the bloodied corners of her mouth, eyes locked on Alan, her contemptuous smile unyielding. Then, in an explosion of savage impulse, Danny pounced upon her.

The unclad congregation chanted their approval.

Alan had witnessed these pornographic acrobatics before in his nocturnal fantasies. Shame swallowed whatever anger stirred in him as he gaped dumbstruck at the two bodies' thrusting passions.

The earsplitting mantra amplified the bewailing cadence of sexual passion. Faster and faster a sea of bodies spun and twisted in choppy, aboriginal gyrations and distorted rhythms of dance around the uninhibited couple. The open-hearth fireplace and myriad of candles cast frightening shadows that clung to the walls and ceiling with an aura of evil.

Alan, his sense of despair deepened rather than invigorated into assault by the sexual acrobatics, was anchored to the floor, unable to act.

"Women are easily bored, and when left to their own devices, so easily encouraged to follow their most base instincts," a high-pitched voice said.

Looking down, Alan encountered the gargoyle-like interloper that danced in and out of his nightmares with disdain. His coal black eyes were those of a savage wild animal, intensely hostile.

The dwarf smacked his lips, arching bushy eyebrows up a thick-ridged, malformed brow. "But passions can be awakened through domination and degradation." He stretched his mangled fist toward Alan. The maimed appendage surrounded a crescent-shaped dagger that reflected the glimmer of wavering candlelight. "Cut out the blackguard's heart. Look at what he's doing to your woman!" he shouted in a voice filled with rancor.

Alan stared blankly at the knife.

"Do it now! Your little Tia is next," the gnome barked. Loathing seeped through his every pore.

It was only then that the breathless sobbing of a young girl flooded into Alan's ears. The crying belonged to Tia. Somnambulistic fantasy had imposed itself upon his waking reality.

The dwarf smacked his lips again. "Tell you what. I'm willing to strike a bargain, make a trade." He jabbed his stunted digits hard into Alan's side. When Alan flinched in pain, he was poked harder.

"Trade?" He was uncertain whether or not he had spoken the word aloud.

Alan's jaw muscles tightened. His lungs were heavy from the strain of suppressed anxiety. For the first time since entering the house, anger rose up in the pit of his stomach. With each new jab of the dwarf's finger, his ire grew. One cell of rage split in two and through mitosis became four. Four divided again into sixteen. Then sixty-four. Geometrically multiplying into a swirling, twisting maelstrom.

"Yes!" the evil little thing wailed, gripped with exhilaration. It probed more viciously at Alan's ribs.

"Daddy. Help me!" Tia's voice pleaded.

His good intentions dissolved. A tornado of anger ripped itself from Alan's breast, cutting a path through his fear, sending torrents of loathing into his arms. His clenched fists exploded into the creature's high-domed head, propelling it to the floor.

Eyes seething leprosy reached up to Alan from the creature's broad misshapen head. Then the troll smiled, offered the crescent blade once more to Alan. "You must learn which dreams to hold on to and which ones to let go. Which ones to act upon and which to nurse in silence."

His gaze returned to Danny Cox who had discarded Evelyn and now was dragging Tia by her hair across the floor. His daughter's cries echoed through the large chamber. "Daddy!"

A fury came upon him. Alan seized the knife and drew a wide sweeping arc in front of Danny Cox.

A thick spray of blood gushed from Danny's severed windpipe, spattering Alan's face. Incensed by the coppery smell of vital juices, Alan struck out with the blade again.

Danny's head crashed to the floor with the not quite solid squishing sound of a melon rolling off a tabletop. His headless body seemed to hang suspended in time, then crumpled into a puddle of flesh.

Alan fell to one knee, brandishing the knife overhead before burying it into Danny's lifeless form.

The dwarf's laughter mocked him. "Man is an unattractive creature that has become the dominant life form on this planet largely due to a lack of intelligent competition." Pointing at Danny he said, "This is nothing more than a bone to be chewed." He plunged his twisted claw into the carcass of flesh that was once Danny Cox, and plucked a heart from its remains. "Partake of this, for this is our body," he said thrusting the black organ into Alan's face.

"Eat it, Alan" Evelyn cooed as she crawled naked toward him, her face made more provocative by the lustrous tendrils of dark hair that hung to the floor, swaying hypnotically across her glistening smile as she moved cat-like to his side as he kneeled over the decimated corpse of Danny Cox. Her hands climbed up Alan's body. "Eat," she groaned, kissing him with an open mouth, licking Alan's tongue with hers. He neither welcomed nor resisted her lips.

The scent of blood was maddening.

"Do it," the dwarf echoed, having appeared over Evelyn's shoulder, kissing it. One of the creature's mangled hands reached under Evelyn's arms, found her breast, and cupped it. Evelyn tilted her head upwards and her open mouth sought out the dwarf's.

Their unholy touching repulsed Alan.

The abomination pulled his lips away. His other hand appeared holding Danny's heart. He raised the black mass of tissue to Evelyn's mouth and she bit into it. Blood gushed from the organ into Alan's face.

No longer able to resist, Alan surrendered to his primordial craving. He sunk his teeth into the unholy sacrament. Somehow the barbaric act defined the deepest parts of him.

The dwarf's face showed his pleasure. "Now we are one, Alan. You and I, one and the same."

He looked into Evelyn's eyes and saw what he always found there. Nothing. It was time to end this parasitic entanglement. He plunged the knife into his wife's torso and twisted. Her eyes showed her disbelief. It made him happy, very happy. She fell backwards onto her tiny companion, who screeched in panic.

As the dwarf struggled to free himself from beneath Evelyn's weight, Alan crawled over his wife's carcass. "You ugly little turd," he said with a sneer and the monstrous creature met with the same fate as Evelyn.

"Welcome back," Linda Windsor said, unmasking her face. Matthew appeared at her side.

Like automatons, the rest of the congregation followed her lead and unveiled themselves.

To Alan's astonishment, each and every personage bore his face.

"Now that you have slayed your demons, you can allow yourself to be who you really are, who you were destined to become," Linda informed him. Her robin egg blue eyes gleamed with excitement.

Alan stood. His breathes bellowed from his lips in rhythmic bursts like a powerful locomotive. His arms pumped with blood and chugged piston-like as he propelled across the room toward the foul twosome. He was struck with the realization that the evil he had found in the world was merely a projection of his own inner demons and corrupted soul.

As if privy to his deepest thoughts, the witch said, "Not only does evil prevail when so-called good men did nothing, but it flourishes because men rationalize their evil choices and justify them as virtue."

Alan stopped inches from the woman's face. "And what is it that I am destined to become." He challenged.

"You are the embodiment of evil, Master." She and her companion fell to their knees and bowed their heads.

*****

He could hear the hollow ring of footsteps as they echoed down the hall. They stopped outside the door. There was a clanking of the metal bolt followed by an explosion of light through a small rectangle opening in the metal portal. Alan shielded his eyes as light flooded his cell, stinging his retinas.

"Foods in, you piece of shit!" The prison guard informed him.

"How many days has it been?" Alan asked referring to the time he had spent alone in total darkness in the isolation box.

"What do you care? You'll never see the light of day again."

"How many days, asshole?"

"Fifty-six, not that it matters. If it were up to me, I'd let you rot in this hole. But if we ever do let you out, it's already been decided upstairs that you'll live out the rest of your pathetic life in isolation. You'll never be allowed to reenter the general prison population."

"You'll remain my personal servant then," Alan said with a chuckle. "That has to be a big career move for an ignorant, oversized piece of dung like you."

The guard banged his nightstick against the door. "You'll get yours, I promise you!"

"That's all I really wanted from you; some sort of commitment in this relationship, you inbred, fudge-packing faggot."

The door panel slammed shut with a clank as the bolt slid back into place, leaving Alan in the empty void.

"Hey, don't go away mad, Bubba. I have plans for us." He slapped his knee and howled like a wolf, the signature cry of the serial killer known as "the campfire carnivore."

Sitting motionless, alone again in the darkness, Alan slowed his breathing and allowed his physical body, a meaningless shell, to become dormant. In doing so, he would activate his inner body and no longer be bound by temporal constraints. His mind could travel at will as if in a living dream. This is where the spirit of Alan Ciani had existed for decades while his physical form was interred in a prison for the criminally insane.

It was not he, however, that was insane or shackled.

He was a free man.

Chapter 26

The same morning that DeLucci had left his office for the last time, Bralich finally connected by phone with Detective Augustus Morrell, who had done some investigative work for Robert. Morrell lived in Roselle Park, a stone's throw from Zent's office, and had pressed for a face-to-face meeting. They rendezvoused in Warrenecho Park.

Morrell had a sinewy physique and slow deliberate gait that seemed a crawl even for the elderly Bralich. With each step, Morrell seemed to rock back on his heels, linger a moment, as if in suspension, teeter forward onto his toes, then repeat the process; like a wise guy in slow motion, Bralich thought. As they strolled across a sun-dappled hill, the brick-paved path made slippery by fallen leaves from the massive maple an oak that defined their surroundings, the detective unwrapped a stick of gum and put it in his mouth. His eyes flitted across the landscape.

Morrell's thick head of red-brown hair that was slicked back meticulously into clearly delineated lines and tight waves. His boyish oval face, pink from the cold, sported a crop of freckles, a fleshy nose, and full lips that made him look like a middle-aged Howdy Dowdy. His voice was dockworker rough, strong. He wasn't a garrulous man; his comments were precise and well articulated, which told Bralich that Morrell was intelligent, insightful and exceedingly cautious.

Although the name was unfamiliar, he had seen Howdy Dowdy before. "We've met before?" Bralich had asked.

"Yes. At the wedding."

Bralich blinked his incomprehension.

"Robert and Lois. She was Lois Morrell before she became Lois Miller. I'm a first cousin."

"Of course," Bralich said, remembering that Lois had grown up in Jersey. "Her passing was so tragic. It devastated Robert. And now he's gone, too."

"So I learned only a few days ago." There was little affectation behind Morrell's thick accent.

"Robert and I were close." Bralich felt a catch in his throat, swallowed his sadness. "I have his crematoria urn at home."

Morrell looked down at him, said, "um-hum" in a manner that suggested he already knew. He stopped and surveyed their surroundings. "Let's go this way," he said, pointing away from the paved pathway towards a patch of trees. Bralich noticed the veiled curiosity with which Morrell took note of a man wearing a fleece cap and pullover walking an Irish setter behind them on the path. Then, the detective's eyes shifted to another fellow, reading a newspaper on a park bench. Bralich sensed that Morrell was taking quick mental snapshots, realized that in his circumspect manner Morrell had been studying him as well.

When they found an unoccupied park bench facing one of the park's baseball diamonds, Morrell signaled Bralich to sit. He scanned the surrounding area before sitting down himself.

Morrell asked, "Do you know why Robert was in Lakewood the evening he died?"

Under Morrell's careful scrutiny, Bralich explained.

"Any reason for you to suspect foul play?" Morrell asked.

His rhetorical question was unsettling. Bralich hadn't even considered the possibility that Robert's death was anything but an accident. But there had been Robert's phone message. "He left a series of messages on my answering machine the day he died. He joked about feeling that he was being followed."

Morrell's eyes narrowed in thought. Bralich could tell he was troubled about something and said so.

The policeman surveyed passersby over Bralich's shoulder. "I looked at the wreckage the other morning. The brake line may have been tampered with." He pulled at his nose, sniffled, before continuing. "I checked the phone records. He called you several times from his car the day of the accident. Why?"

"I told you, we were close." Bralich leaned in more closely, sought out Morrell's eyes. "Robert was like a son. Please, talk to me."

Although still guarded, the policeman's face softened a tad. "You first. If I like what I hear, then maybe."

Without mentioning his client by name, Bralich told him about DeLucci, the background he shared with Lucius Sangre and Linda Windsor, and the autobiographical references in his most recent fiction efforts. As a squirrel nervously nibbled on an acorn at their feet, Bralich related what he had learned from Zent about cults, ending with Zent's contention of a powerful satanic network. "That's everything I know to this point. Your turn."

Morrell hesitated briefly, and then expelled his apprehension with a sigh. "Robert was married to my cousin, Lo. Didn't know the man very well, except from a few family functions." He shrugged his shoulders. "And Lo's funeral. Thought he was an okay guy. He loved Lo, and she worshipped him, so that was good enough for me. Can't say I cared much for the way he made a living, coddling to losers, rationalizing their weaknesses with bullshit psychological mumble-jumble."

Bralich noted the rawness in his voice, nodded for Morrell to continue, but said nothing.

Morrell's irritation dissipated. "No disrespect intended, Doc." He massaged his Adam's apple with his left hand and continued. "Anyway, Robert asked me to run a check on this Linda Windsor because he couldn't trace her. A real sick bitch, I come to find out. I called Robert to report what I'd found out, but got nothing except answering machines both at home and work. Finally, I just left a message. Then your administrator, Alexander, calls back and tells me about the accident. I remembered how Lo used to tease Miller about being the slowest, most anal-retentive driver in the world. It touched a nerve. Figured I owed it to Lo to look into things." The corners of Morrell's mouth punctuated the end of his narrative in a singular twitch.

Bralich recognized hesitation n Morrell's mannerisms. "There's something else," Bralich stated with authority.

The detective's eyes widened in surprise. "I called up a copy of the accident report on the computer. Within an hour after I inspected the wreckage, my commander reams my ass for nosing around cases in which I have no business and tells me he's deducting the wasted time from my pay."

"That's unusual?" Bralich asked.

"Not unheard of, but it came out of left field. Part of the tongue-lashing had to do with sharing confidential police information with private citizens. Without saying so, he let me know that he knew about the message I left on Robert's machine. How he knew this, I have to wonder? Then yesterday, I picked up a tail. Not cops, not Feds."

Bralich asked, "And when I called?"

"I was curious, thought I'd play it out." Morrell's lips curled into the first resemblance of an authentic smile since they met. "Then, I recognized you right off from the wedding. You look like Sean Connery. Lo used to joke about it. Referred to you and Miller as Indiana and Professor Jones in quest of the wholly frail."

That made Bralich laugh. He'd heard the comparison before, but when he looked in the mirror it wasn't Sean Connery that stared back; just an older version of the frightened little boy who had played in the slag piles in Scranton. "What about Zent's satanic network angle?"

Morrell dismissed the supernatural overtones. "The world is full of evil, Dr. Bralich. Ask any cop, he'll tell you. There have been sewers and slime to crawl out of them since the beginning of time. You don't need a lot of conspiracy theories or mysticism to explain that! Do you? Perverts come in all sizes, shapes, denominations and occupations, so I'll never be out of a job. Pornography is a profitable industry. Windsor was part of that. There might be some connection."

Bralich said, "I think it's time for me to visit with my client's mother."

Morrell pursed his lips. "She's the last person to speak with Robert Miller. If what she knew got him killed, it's better that I do it. Give me the name."

Bralich informed him of the confidentiality dilemma.

"Bullshit! Do you think that child pornographers, Satanists, and murderers struggle with such issues?"

"That's one way to distinguish them from the good guys," Bralich answered. "When we divorce conscience from reason and action, we surrender to evil."

"Evil!" Morrell erupted. All his freckles melded together to form one large patch of red across his face. "Evil flourishes because good men do nothing. From my experiences, evil is impotent—a deformed, crippled entity whose only weapon is the willingness of the depraved or intellectually constipated to serve its ends by failing to act against it. What makes you think you're protecting your client by concealing his mother's name? How do you know that you're not just signing his death warrant, or for that matter your own, or, even worse, mine, by maintaining…confidentiality?"

It was the uncanny metaphor about deformity that changed Bralich's mind. He shared DeLucci's mother's name and her address in Lakewood.

"BioSyn," Bralich said as the two men were saying their good-byes. "I forgot about BioSyn."

"What about it?" the policeman asked.

"Do you know what it is?"

"Sure. It's a bio-genetics research firm in Dunellen. DNA research from what I'm told. Why?"

Bralich explained the connection.

Morrell craned his head to one side, and his hand absently stroked his Adam's apple again.

Bralich could see the wheels turning. "What?"

"There was a notice up in the call room last year, asking us to volunteer DNA samples to BioSyn for government funded research."

"What does it mean?"

Morrell either didn't know, or wouldn't say.

"I'll be in touch," Morrell told him, but as with Nick DeLucci, Bralich hadn't heard back from him. Both men seemed to have dropped off the face of the earth.

Bralich waited for several days, and then began calling Morrell at home; again without much success. Morrell had instructed him not to call at the station, but Bralich had grown impatient. According to his captain, Morrell had decided to use vacation time, reportedly to do some fishing in the Bahamas. That didn't ring true with Bralich, but nothing did lately, and he really didn't know Morrell well enough to have any rational reason to believe otherwise. He looked at his wristwatch; he was going to be late for class. Later that evening he had an appointment with Dante Underland.

Chapter 27

The elevator doors slid open and Tony Bralich stepped out on to the top floor executive offices at the Underland Towers. It was nine o'clock in the evening and, except for the security guard who allowed him entrance at the main door, the building appeared deserted.

Dante Underland had left instructions for Bralich to proceed directly to his office. It had been years since Underland had appeared in public and Bralich was surprised that the recluse had spoken with him on the phone, let alone granted him a meeting. He wasn't sure what to expect.

The Underland name was as old as Gotham itself, appeared to have an established presence since the first Dutch settlers swindled the Manhattan marshlands from its native inhabitants. The family's influence grew with the city, and while intricately ensconced in the political infrastructure, through the centuries had retained an uncelebrated propinquity, rather than a dominant demeanor, in city affairs. The citadel Underland Towers were as familiar a landmark as the Empire State Building to the native New Yorker, yet most knew little to nothing about the family to which the building owed its name.

Bralich rapped twice on the monolithic oak portals that bore the mogul's moniker. An ancient voice bade him to enter.

It had been a long time since Bralich had attended mass, but upon entering Underland's office, memories of draconian cathedral requiems become instantly salient. The décor was marked by a severe opulence that paradoxically inspired reverence and apprehension. Dark oak paneled ceilings framed in bulky, sculptured crown molding accentuated the oppressive chiaroscuro contrasts elicited by a single Tiffany lamp and the muted reflections it cast off the golden accessories that adorned a massive desktop.

"A pleasure to meet you, Dr. Bralich," Underland said from the shadows. "Please, take a seat."

Plush crimson and gold carpets cushioned Bralich's feet as he crossed the threshold into the sanctuary. There was little movement from behind Underland's desk, and Bralich could barely differentiate his host's outline from the thick, high-backed chair that surrounded the ancient mogul. However, Bralich felt the weight of the old man's gaze.

"Excuse my lack of manners for such an ungracious greeting at this ungodly hour, but the years have taken a debilitating toll on these old bones." Underland hacked on a phlegm-filled cough. "I hope you don't mind the dark. The doctors tell me that if I wish the delay the inevitability of losing my eyesight, then I must avoid bright lighting."

"This is fine, thank you," Bralich said as a social courtesy. "I am most appreciative that you could make time for me this evening."

"There is hot coffee on the credenza, if you desire." Underland's shaky hand emerged from the shadows, pointing Bralich toward the coffee. His skin was as yellow as parchment.

"No. Thank you."

Underland said, "You wish to speak to me about Nick DeLucci." His breathing sounded labored.

"Yes," Bralich answered. As he explained the reason for his visit, he strained his eyes hoping to obtain a better look at Underland. His attempts did little, however, to better define the old man's features. He ended his brief narrative with, "He needs ongoing psychotherapy, but I haven't heard back from Nick in two weeks. I hoped you might encourage Mr. DeLucci to contact me."

Underland's laugh was a gravelly rasp. "He's on the road again, no doubt," the codger said amused. "Besides, it's not terribly likely that Nick would heed any advice that I offered."

"Again?" Bralich asked. "Nick has disappeared before?"

Another hacking cough emanated from the shadows. "That's been his pattern. He's obviously worked out his next novel and now needs a setting dismal enough to finish it."

"I've visited his residence. He needs a place more dismal than that in which to write?"

Underland wheezed as much as chortled. "Apparently so. Nick goes from one dump to the next. He'll crank out an entire book in a few months, and then move on. One hour and ten pages a day is his motto. It seems to work for him. It's made him a bundle."

Bralich suspected as much. "Then his living arrangements don't reflect his financial situation?"

"Hardly," Underland responded in a tone suggesting insult. "With royalties under an assortment of pseudonyms, two movie deals, and a television mini-series, little Nick made over $40 million last year alone."

Bralich felt his mouth drop open. "What does he do with his money?"

Underland leaned forward in his chair. Bralich could now clearly discern the last remnants of white hair slicked back behind long conch-shaped ears that had grown to dominance on the antiquated face. A thin sheathing of yellowed skin tightly stretched across his patrician nose. His predatory eyes were made more sinister by the sands of time.

"You mean besides paying for psychiatric care," the worn magnate stated sardonically. Bralich wondered if the condemnation in Underland's tone was meant for him or DeLucci. If the old man didn't care much for the practitioners of psychology, what lay behind his intentions for agreeing to this meeting?

Underland reclined into his seat. "Ole' Nick has created quite the financial portfolio. He invests it."

"In BioSyn?"

Bralich felt suffocated by the brief silence his question precipitated.

Finally Underland continued. "Yes, among others. Nick is invested heavily in the high tech industry, especially in bio-genetics." Phlegm gurgled in his throat and Underland coughed it loose, spit it into a handkerchief, and then swallowed uneasily. "His genius extends far beyond the literary, you see. Because of his physical disabilities, some are tempted to think of him as an idiot savant. Such terminology is, of course, completely inappropriate and unjustified, for Nicholas is hardly an idiot. He is definitely one of a kind, however, and I've settled for the term "psychotic savant," Underland snickered.

Recalling Jefferson Thorne's comment about Nick being in and out of therapy for years, Bralich asked, "How do you mean?"

"The little bastard is as delusional as they come. He has completely obscured the lines between reality and fantasy. Still, everything he touches turns to gold."

Suddenly Underland was gulping for air with deep labored heaves that sounded like he was imitating a whooping crane. Bralich could just barely discern the old man pulling something from his lap to his face, heard the steady hiss of an oxygen tank, followed by a return to a less torturous breathing rhythm.

"Are you alright?" Bralich asked.

Underland pulled the oxygen mask away from his face and spat a "yes" that was thick with annoyance. A little more diplomatically he added, "These brittle old bones and degenerative organs are in constant revolt against my will to live forever."

He inhaled with greater efficiency through his oxygen mask and then continued his narrative regarding Nick DeLucci. "He checks himself in and out of psychiatric clinics and hospitals, undergoes psychoanalysis, hypnosis, primal therapy, and whatever other faddish treatment strikes his fancy. Somehow these inanities trigger both his artistic and business talents. He's been living this way for nearly twenty years—since he first started writing." Again, the mask was at the publication baron's nose and he was inhaling slow, even breaths.

"Tell me, what leads you to believe that Nick is delusional?" Bralich asked.

Hiss...ssss.

"Have you read any of his books?"

Bralich nodded.

Hiss...ssss.

Underland said, "Repulsive, no?"

Bralich nodded.

"He believes himself a prescient being. Whatever the little shit is writing, he thinks anticipates upcoming events in his life. I suspect that much of it is fabricated in the therapy process."

Bralich had discussed with Robert Miller the possibility of False Memory Syndrome. Sometimes, he reflected, the simplest answer is the best. "What can you tell me of Nick's personal history?"

Underland took a long time before he answered. The room seemed to vibrate with expectancy. Bralich folded his hands resolutely in his lap and waited.

"As his therapist, you are bound by confidentiality?" Underland finally asked.

"Absolutely," Bralich answered. He didn't feel the need to correct the misconception that a doctor-client relationship was still viable.

Hiss…ssss.

"Your intentions to help little Nick appear genuine."

Bralich nodded.

"Okay, then. His mother, Virginia DeLucci, was a Jersey girl with stars in her eyes. She went out to Hollywood in the early fifties, thinking that her big tits and tight ass were an instant ticket to stardom. She managed to land a few bit parts in low budget horror flicks and to get herself pregnant—according to her, by a rather famous leading man type." There was little sympathy in his voice. "But rumor has it she could have started a sperm bank with all the deposits that were made into her account. After a few years struggling to support her relish for fine cocaine and make ends meet, she gave up her dreams and the ghastly little creature she had spawned."

Underland erupted in another fit of spittled coughing. When he finished his hacking, he resumed. "She placed Nick in an orphanage in California and returned home to New Jersey. Several years later, apparently feeling guilty, she called upon her old Hollywood cohorts to use their influence to have Nick transferred to a New Jersey orphanage where she was doing volunteer work as penance for her sins and could see the boy on a regular basis. It was done. When at eighteen, Nick was no longer a ward of the state; he made his own way in the world. A few months later, his first book was offered to Underland Publications. It was published immediately and made into a movie after almost a year on the best sellers list. That was The Devil's Solicitor, have you read it?"

"Yes," Bralich answered, nodding.

"Still think it was Nick's finest most artistically crafted work. And he was just a kid when he wrote it," Underland said with what sounded like pride.

Underland leaned toward Bralich, folding his gnarled hands on the desk in front of him. His wizened, hawk-like face was a sea of liver spots and melanomas, which ordinarily would have captivated Bralich's attention. However, he was far more interested in the large ruby ring with a goat's head embossed on the thick golden band encircling Underland's finger. He looked up into Underland's eyes and saw in them a rapaciousness that made his throat grow tight.

Underland noticed his interest in the ring. With a macabre amusement on his face, he lifted the ringed hand near his eyes, fingering the jewel. "A beautiful little trinket, isn't it?"

"Yes," Bralich answered cautiously. "I don't think I've ever seen anything quite like it," he lied. He could see in Underland's eyes that the untruth was transparent.

"It's a family heirloom."

"Not quite a trinket then. What's that, an animal of some sort engraved on the band?"

Underland smiled. "A horned goat."

"Very beautiful," Bralich said. "Does it have any significance? The horned goat, I mean."

"It's our family crest. Beyond that, none that I'm aware of," Underland responded.

Bralich changed the subject. "So does Nick keep in contact with his mother?"

Underland again backed into his chair. Sounding disinterested, he said, "Provides her with a monthly living allowance that we distribute on his behalf. Out of obligation, I imagine, since to the best of my knowledge, they don't communicate."

"I see."

"I hope what little information I had was helpful," Underland said in a tone that left little doubt that their time together had come to an end.

He was no longer of use to Underland. Again he asked himself what purpose this meeting served the old man. He'd mull that over later.

"I would suspect that you've seen the last of Nick DeLucci," Underland added. "He tends to burn his bridges behind him and reinvent a new schizoid existence...and million seller, to boot." Underland tapped his heavy ring on the surface of the desk. "Be thankful for small favors," he said.

"How so?" Bralich wanted to know.

"Nick also tends to leave a trail of destruction behind him. You seemed to have survived his association intact...so far." It sounded like a warning.

A few parting cordialities passed between them before Bralich found himself again on the elevator. In his imaginings, the uncomfortable descent would take him beyond the main lobby and straight to Hell.

Chapter 28

"Stop howling at the rain, Wayne." Bralich had meant to sound flippant and, judging from the administrator's reaction, had exceeded his expectations.

Wayne Alexander slapped a sheet of paper on the desk in front of Bralich and leaned over the desk on balled fists. "What the hell is this?" The big blonde's face was flushed with anger.

Bralich recognized the letter without having to examine it. "Well, it looks just like what it is. A request for a few months leave of absence."

Alexander steamed. "Jesus H. Christ! You have to do this now! I'm already one psychotherapist short and you know damn well Mary Johnstone is going on family medical leave next week. If you take off, I'm minus fifty percent of my staff for this department."

Bralich said nothing. So shuffle people around he thought.

"Don't play that silent ambiguity bullshit with me, Tony. I'm not one of your Goddamn patients. What's this about? DeLucci right? Have you totally lost your mind?"

Bralich had begun to wonder the same thing himself. He was fixated on unraveling DeLucci's past. He both counseled and reproached himself for his obsession, but couldn't seem to stop from spending his every spare minute trying to unravel the mysterious circumstances surrounding the life and times of Nick DeLucci. He had dedicated an incessant number of hours in the university library absorbing whatever trivia about DeLucci's mother he might uncover. His efforts left him with the conclusion that she had used the stage name Virginia Cox while on the West Coast. Never graduating beyond minor appearances in B-movie, photographs confirmed that her physical attractiveness was as Underland noted, A-plus. She had been linked romantically to everyone but Dwight and Mimi Eisenhower. Furthermore, the physical resemblance between Samantha and young Virginia Delucci-Cox was uncanny.

"Request denied," Wayne Alexander said with a voice that sounded like falling glass. "And don't get sick, or broken, or die, or try any other shenanigans to weasel time off either!"

"What's really bothering you, Wayne?"

Alexander shook his head in frustration. "Don't psychoanalyze me, Tony. You know how that pisses me off."

Bralich cracked a smile. "So you're pissed off. Go with that thought."

The tension evaporated from Alexander's face. He smiled back. "You asshole. What, you graduated from the Bob Newhart School of Psychiatry?"

"Well, it appears that our time is up for today, Mr. Carlin. Let's pick up where we left off next time," Bralich said, doing his best to mimic the Newhart character from the old television sit-com.

The burly administrator picked up a folder from Bralich's desk. It was an annual report for BioSyn Corporation. "Thinking of doing some investing?" His brows knitted again and for a brief moment Bralich read something troubling in his voice.

"You familiar with BioSyn?" Bralich asked.

Alexander snorted a laugh. "All you brain-fuckers are alike; totally oblivious to the business side of what makes the world go round. Who the hell do you think paid for this nice office you're sitting in, and the comfy conference room where you do that voodoo you do?"

"BioSyn?"

Bralich's initial investigation into BioSyn had proved unsettling from the get-go. He looked across the desk at the folder in Alexander's hand and the company's logo, a horned goat, stared back at him. The California-based company was not merely into bio-genetics; it was cutting edge, a pioneer in the realm of cloning. It had made innumerable advances in decoding DNA strands. However, the fact that BioSyn paid his salary had totally escaped him.

"Duh, yes, Dr. Freud. BioSyn."

Bralich asked, "What does a bio-genetics company want with a psychiatric hospital?"

"DNA research. One of their subsidiaries does our blood work-ups."

Bralich found it disturbing that his clients might be part of research that neither he nor they knew anything about. His library research uncovered that BioSyn had been rewarded huge government contacts to work with police departments and the military establishment, identifying chromosomes linked to acts of both heroism and criminal deviance. He had learned that in addition to Nick DeLucci, Dante Underland was also a major stockholder.

Bralich said, "Don't we have some kind of ethical issue here? Shouldn't I be informed if my clients are being used as guinea pigs for some Frankenstein experiments?"

Alexander just shook his head condescendingly. He said, "You know what your problem is?" but before Bralich could be enlightened the phone rang.

"I'm waiting on a call, Wayne. I need to pick this up. Don't go, though, because a good psychiatric evaluation is extremely difficult to come by and I'd really cherish benefiting from the wisdom of a washed up professional football player turned inventory control clerk." He reached for the phone.

"Let's meet at DeLucci's mother's place," Morrell said over the line omitting any social courtesies and without offering any apologies for his elusiveness during the past weeks. Bralich had finally decided that if Augie Morrell wouldn't return his call, he would proceed without him, and had left one last message on Morrell's machine informing him that he was going to visit DeLucci's mother that evening with or without the detective.

"It's nice to talk to you again too, Augie," Bralich said. Across the desk, Alexander busied himself in the BioSyn report. "It'll be even nicer to see you again."

"Eight o'clock." Morrell's voice was hushed, but within its tones Bralich sensed the trepidation that the officer tried to mask.

"Yes," Bralich said. "Is something wrong?"

"I can't talk right now, but listen closely, Doc. Keep an eye over your shoulder at all times, understand?"

Bralich felt a mounting urgency. "What is it?"

"Zent was right. We'll talk tonight. Eight o'clock."

The line disengaged.

Bralich tapped a finger to his forehead.

"A problem, Tony?" Alexander asked.

"Hmm? What's that, Wayne?"

"A problem. Is there a problem?"

"No."

"You didn't forget about your group tonight, did you?"

"Rescheduled," Bralich answered, still distracted.

"How many times is that in the last couple of weeks that you've either rescheduled or just plain forgot about showing up for one of your groups?"

The psychiatrist was no longer listening.

Bralich was running twenty minutes late. He negotiated the insanely engineered cloverleaf intersection that offered entrance into the retirement village, and stopped at the security gate.

"Dr. Bralich to see Virginia DeLucci." He passed his driver's license through the window of the security booth for the guard, who looked too feeble to provide any kind of real security, to inspect.

"Yes, she's expecting you," the rent-a-cop said after thumbing through the papers on his clipboard. "Pass the lake, turn right. Follow that as far as it goes, all the way to the bay. Last house on the left." He buzzed open the gate and seemed inconvenienced when Bralich thanked him.

The starless October night was laced with the smell of salt water. Virginia DeLucci's single-story Cape Cod dwelling seemed to balance on a precipice, encircled by emptiness. Bralich parked across the street from a light colored sedan and approached the front door of the house.

He rang the doorbell. Had Morrell, too, discovered that Virginia DeLucci's stage name was Cox? It probably wouldn't have meant much to Morrell since he hadn't read DeLucci's manuscript. Still, the cop must have learned something that had him spooked.

When nobody responded, he knocked and the door creaked open on un-oiled hinges. "Hello. Ms. DeLucci," he called into the house. "It's Anthony Bralich."

No response.

He peeked into the hallway, ears perked for the sound of activity. There was none. In his current state of wariness, the quiet seemed ominous. His rational mind told him he was too old for such intrigue but he had become addicted to the adrenaline rushes this investigation into Nick DeLucci's strange world provided him.

Bralich stepped across the threshold, again announcing his presence. Still there was no response. The security guard had said she was expecting him. Where was the live-in nurse? Where was Morrell?

A large cathedral ceiling living room faced the bay through an expanse of floor-to-ceiling glass. Beyond, the universe vanished into an ebony void. He scanned the room, saw no one, and was about to turn to the hallway when a wall of expensively framed photographs caught his attention. One portrait of a beautiful young woman with long flowing black hair, stunning molasses eyes, and a familiar warming smile reached out to him. He crossed the room spellbound. For some moments he stood staring at the photograph, disbelieving, paralyzed by the harsh realities it proffered. It was a picture of Samantha.

Bralich surveyed the wall, following the trail of photographs across the room. There was none of Nick DeLucci.

Gradually he extrapolated a family lineage from the collage of glossy images. There seemed little doubt that if his absent hostess was in fact DeLucci's mother, then she must also be the ailing grandmother to which Samantha had alluded from time to time. That would make Samantha either Nick's niece or…his daughter. Bralich shuddered. He recollected Zent's comments about in-family unions. Was Samantha in danger?

In the unearthly stillness, a faint but malodorous scent insinuated itself upon his senses. Bralich sniffed with displeasure, then stalked the aroma down the home's central hallway.

With each step the pungency intensified. His heartbeats and pace quickened as he followed his nose in search of the source of the foul tang.

He peeked into a neatly and efficiently decorated bedroom. A nurse's uniform hung in the open closet. Live-in quarters, no doubt, but there was no caretaker to be found.

Next came a bath, meticulously attended to but uninhabited.

The hallway ended at French doors, most likely the master suite, he reasoned. Listening for nothing he could consciously name, he pushed the doors full open. A putrid odor stopped him short in his tracks. He retrieved a handkerchief from his pocket, and covered his mouth and nose but it did little to minimize the olfactory discomfort.

A woman lay in a canopy bed, motionless except for the almost imperceptible rise and fall of her shallow breaths beneath the sheets.

Candles arranged in a circle around the bed magnified and distorted shadows on the walls and ceiling.

"Ms. DeLucci? I'm Dr. Bralich."

She didn't respond.

"Ms. DeLucci," Bralich repeated as he walked toward the bed, uncertainly. "Are you all right?"

Her eyes were glazed over, staring vacantly as if in shock. The crone's face was an ashen gray.

As he leaned over and touched her shoulder, he could see the woman struggling to focus. Her mouth moved as if attempting to form words, but nothing except a small befuddled moan escaped her lips. A pleading materialized in her eyes. Her face twitched as she lifted a fragile hand to point toward the other side of the room.

Bralich's attention followed her finger.

Beside a seven-foot tall armoire of black walnut, a pentacle had been painted on the wall with little concern for aesthetics. Streaks of red trailed toward the floor.

Bralich cringed.

On the floor beneath the satanic icon, lay a disemboweled corpse marinating in its bodily fluids. He stepped across the room to examine the carnage. The stench of death thickened the air around the violated carcass.

What the hell happened here, he wondered.

The old woman moaned what seemed a random collection of unintelligible syllables as if she had heard his thoughts and wanted to respond.

Although the victim's face was turned away from him, it took little imagination to guess at the expression such a death would leave. From the way the entrails stretched out from the body Bralich could tell that the man's last moments were torturous. With trepidation, he turned the dead man's face toward him. It was Augie Morrell.

Vertigo overcame him and he reached for the armoire for support. When he got his legs back under him, he went back to the bed, grabbed the phone on the nightstand, and dialed 911. Still holding his breath to fend off the malodorous smell of death, he offered a brief and hurried report of his discovery to the police operator on the other end of the line.

"Hurry!" he said into the phone after providing the address and his name. He looked back to the old lady. She, too, was at death's doorsteps.

Her lips were dry, puckered and quivering as her throat gulped for moisture that it could not summon.

"I'll get you some water," Bralich said and turned towards the master bathroom.

However he and the old crone were no longer alone.

A portly woman, with long black hair and legs like turkey drumsticks, stood in the door to the hallway. "Good evening, Doctor," she said in a syrupy English accent.

The nurse? No. The unusual aquamarine blue eyes told him that this was Linda Windsor from Nick's manuscript and the Polaroid Bralich retrieved from DeLucci's den.

He had no sooner asked, "What are you doing here?" than a spidery, mustached man stepped passed the woman and struck Bralich full-fisted square between his eyes.

Bralich fell backwards, spinning, to the cold tiled bathroom floor. His head struck the surface with a crash, driving a spike of pain through his brain. An image of his skull splitting in two like an opened clamshell, and then coming together again as a whole, projected itself on the picture screen of his mind. A twinkling of stars exploded into the black recessed behind his eyes, then consciousness imploded into a black hole.

There were voices; a woman's, maybe two but they were muted as if someone had stuffed cotton in his ears.

The room spun as Bralich opened his eyes. Samantha's lips were moving but, at first, no words were coming out. As if someone had flipped on a switch to his brain, he heard, "Get up, Dr. Bralich. Hurry. Get up."

Candles flickered, casting elongated distortions on the wall. A warm wetness oozed down his forehead and into his eyes. His head throbbed. As the revolving room slowly came to a halt he raised his head, fighting off the pain.

Samantha knelt at his side. She said, "Get up. Quickly. They're here."

"Who?" he asked. His mind was a tangle of cobwebs. He wasn't sure whether Sam was really there or a delirious delusion.

Samantha pulled at his arm. "Hurry."

With her help, Bralich struggled to his feet.

His legs wobbled.

He leaned on Samantha's shoulder for support. They stumbled through the hallway. The walls seemed to expand and contract at his sides in unison with the throbbing ache in his head.

Thoughts formed with difficulty. "Your grandmother." He said.

"She's gone."

"She's Nick's mother."

"She told me," Samantha said. "We must hurry."

"My glasses."

Sam bent over to retrieve them from the floor.

He slid them onto his face but they were damaged beyond use rendering his surroundings a kaleidoscope of fragmented images.

The front door of the house loomed before them. Bralich could hear police sirens. The darkness beyond the door suddenly erupted into pulsating amber, blue and red lights played against the confounding rhythm of whining alarms.

"You know about the coven?" Samantha asked.

"Yes," Bralich answered.

"Can anyone else help us? Does anyone else know?"

"Just Augie." Bralich looked back toward the bedroom. Augie. "The police can help," Bralich said, returning his fractured gaze to Samantha.

Outside the din of sirens had reached frenzy.

"Yes, of course, the police are here to save the day." The sound of her voice chilled Bralich's bones.

She pulled his arm from her shoulder and pushed him away.

A cloud fell over Samantha's face as she reached to the neckline of her dress and tore the front of the cloth away. Swollen white breasts tumbled from the remnants of her clothing. Bralich stared confounded.

It was then at the blurred edges of his vision he saw the crescent-shaped dagger in Samantha's hand.

In one quick swipe, she sliced the dagger across her palm and followed that up by striking a blow to his arm. He blocked her next charge with his undamaged arm but she parried with a blow that found flesh at Bralich's throat. A thin spray of blood spurted from his wound and splattered across Samantha's face and chest.

Bralich's hands went to his neck. He sucked in air.

In what felt like a dream, Samantha forced his fingers open and around the knife. He felt helpless to resist. Her face contorted into a scream that the sirens muted. Then, she opened the front door and ran out, pulling at Bralich's belt so that he stumbled across the threshold behind her into the suffocating night air.

Feeling detached from his surroundings, Bralich watched ambivalently as Samantha, looking horrified, pointed at him. The rotund woman he had seen in the bedroom rushed up to Samantha and led her away from the front door. The hawkish scarecrow that had knocked him unconscious earlier was at her back just as Nick's manuscript had described.

Guns were raised and angry faces mouthed words that didn't register. Everything happened too fast for his brain to comprehend. His mind drifted back to his childhood, the streets of Scranton, Pennsylvania, and his father.

Bralich stumbled forward, one hand on his throat; the other outstretched still clutching to the knife.

Amber glimmered off the cutlery's metallic surface.

Then, searing white-hot daggers of pain exploded into his body. Everything went black.

Chapter 29

Nick DeLucci gathered up the fruit of his most recent labors. He only had little time to spare, so he grabbed a can of Coke from the refrigerator and reviewed what he had written.

Pieces of Hate
A Novel by Nick DeLucci

Bobby Della Rosa nervously drummed his fingers on his muscled thigh, waiting for the small plane to rev up its engines and head down the runway. He didn't much enjoy flying, especially the shuttle, and being paranoid about rolling a medicinal joint and smoking in the airport restrooms, he would rely instead upon jerking the chains of fellow passengers for distraction during the thirty-minute flight. As yet, there was a paucity of fellow passengers seated near enough to afford him any opportunity for mental diversion.

Left unaccompanied, there would be no way he could avoid the assault of unpleasant remembrances. Denial had somewhat helped him cope over the last few days, but that defense was weakening and the intensity of the brutal images that preoccupied his mind would magnify with the stress of flying. The first meeting with his new therapist wasn't until tomorrow. That did him little good right now.

A young heavy-set man in a three-piece suit, carrying a briefcase, appeared in the aisle. He checked his boarding pass ticket stub against the number posted above the seats, "My seat," he said, pointing to the aisle seat adjacent to Della Rosa. Bobby detected a trace of a German accent.

"Please," Bobby answered before returning his gaze out the porthole in order to conceal his glee from the man who had unwittingly volunteered himself as a sacrificial lamb to Bobby's perverse flying ritual. In the window, Bobby caught his own winsome reflection. His beguiling smile and expressive eyes created the illusion of perpetual enthusiasm, a look of youthful innocence that had served him well over the years—fifty to be exact, in January—especially in disarming potential targets. He had a memorable face. Framed in thick black curls, it was gentle and still boyish when his mood was festive, yet transforming into a frightening and menacing expression when the inner demons that scraped away at his peace of mind soured his disposition. Then, the paper-thin scar that ran vertically down his forehead to just in between his eyes became a deep ominous furrow that even scared his own mother. He viewed it as merely a minor imperfection that added character.

He patiently waited as his new traveling companion got comfortable. Although he knew that he would hate himself later for the mischief he was about to instigate, Bobby couldn't help himself. He had learned early in life that this unusual expression of the self-preservation instinct, and comedy, took precedence over everything else. Both demanded a target...no, a victim.

"This is your first time, isn't it?" he finally said to the man in the next seat.

"What do you mean?" the German asked.

"This is your first time flying the commuter. I can tell," Bobby said, confirming his diagnosis with an exaggerated nod and pursing his full lips.

"Yes, as a matter of fact. I go to Franklin on business to the new BioGen Research Facility. From Munich." He opened the briefcase on his lap and removed a folder.

"First time. I thought so." Again he reinforced his assertion playfully with exaggerated body language.

"How do you know this?"

"You don't look frightened." Bobby turned away, smiling to himself.

There was a brief silence. Outside, the engines started up.

The German chuckled. "Should I be?" he asked with a confident air that bordered on arrogance.

"Should you be what?"

"Frightened," the businessman said, raising his voice as if startled by the sudden movement of the plane.

"Probably, but it won't do you any good now." Bobby refocused his gaze out the window as the plane began to taxi down the runway. "The weather conditions look good; there's nothing to worry about." He returned his attention to the blue-eyed Aryan with the rolls of baby fat under his chin. "This pilot is probably okay."

"What do you mean?"

"The pilot looked like he was okay. Not like …" He left his sentence unfinished.

The businessman appeared uncomfortable with the silence. "I don't know your meaning."

Didn't they teach him any colorful American colloquialisms in language school, Bobby wondered?

"Just pray that the pilot isn't some pervert who finds entertainment in seeking out pockets of air currents. Trust me, I've been there. Transforms this little twenty-seater into a large blender that joggles your eyes around in their sockets until they feel like they're going to pop out of your ears."

The German looked at him incredulously, mumbled, "full of shit."

Bobby knew he was on a roll. "Take some friendly advice from an experienced commuter patron." He took on a more serious air. "There are only two precautions known to modern science with which to combat the natural tendency to empty one's internal organs in-flight."

The German pretended to ignore him and absently clicked his ballpoint pen.

"Good idea! Take notes," Bobby added. He held up his index finger. "First, avoid looking at the barf bags they've tucked into the pockets on the back of these paisley print, poop brown seats. The seats alone set into motion the body's craving to expurgate, but when viewed with the puke bags, it's unavoidable. Are you getting this down?"

The German looked confused.

Bobby liked that, gestured that his traveling partner should take notes. He waved a second finger in the businessman's face. "Second…and this is very important…chew gum; a whole pack at once, if you are carrying. That not only provides relief and expression to your internal discomfort, but it also serves as a buffer to minimize the damage that a violent gnashing of teeth would inflict on your fillings. I always travel with Trident. Allegedly, it's sugar free…if we can believe the advertisements. Not that we can, Adolf."

"Victor," the German said. "Victor Reich."

"Bobby Della Rosa. Trust me, Victor. I know of what I speak." His mother always used that expression; Bobby tried to mimic her seriousness. Now there's a scary thought, employing his mother as a role model.

The engines rattled as the plane lifted off the ground. The German shifted his weight, looking uneasy.

"Hey, just try and relax, Herr Reich. If you toss your cookies, you toss your cookies. I do it myself occasionally. Oh! FYI: I tend to regurgitate to the right. I can't explain it; it's just the way I'm wired, I guess. So at the first sign of my gagging cover yourself. I wouldn't want to mess up that nice suit of yours."

The cabin of the plane shook as the landing wheels were drawn up. Bobby's hands went to his mouth.

The larger man shoved the folder back into his briefcase and snapped the valise shut. "No reason for we being all cramped up in this little space. I will move…across the aisle."

"Suit yourself, Victor."

The man relocated.

Bobby watched amused. "Hey, it's okay, Victor. I understand. I'm not gonna' make an international incident out of your slighting me."

The German opened his mouth as if to respond but nothing came out.

"Was it something I said? Or is this some kind of German culture thing?"

Bobby turned away before the man could answer.

Both the weather and the pilot were superb. In what remained of sunlight, Bobby Della Rosa turned his attention to the shadowy landscape below. Having escaped the perimeter of Pittsburgh, the terrain below suddenly appeared as uninhabited wilderness; beautiful but isolated. The lush greenery was in sharp contrast to the cream-colored sands and ocean blue that predominated the California coastline from which he had departed several hours earlier. Heavily forested rolling mountains were suspended only by long stretches of roadway and the wide muddy waters of the Allegheny River, which snaked back and forth across the countryside. Rust colored outcrops speckled the higher elevations, and the occasional mining areas scarred the otherwise pristine earth. The forest was abruptly interrupted by the yellow and green checkerboard pattern of farmland that insinuated itself against the landscape. A few scattered residences with huge backyards appeared, then a couple of golf courses. As the earth below was swallowed up in darkness, Bobby played a few imaginary holes of golf as a pleasant mental diversion.

The fantasy round of golf proved to be his undoing. Through a series of mental free associations, his thoughts arrived at Eddie Maggio. It had been during their senior year in high school when the jocose Eddie had vanished into the woodsy rough of the New Jersey golf course, on which the boys had grown up playing, to retrieve an errant golf ball. Bobby and the other members of the foursome had begun to wonder where the hell Eddie had vanished when the boy reappeared completely naked, screaming, "Wood nymphs, wood nymphs! Run! Save your virginity!"

That's the way he always remembered the good-natured, easy friendliness of Eddie Maggio—the precocious kid who wore sunglasses, silk scarves and long red underwear to wrestling practices; the mischievous graduate student who contrived bogus audio tapes of counseling sessions to present as class projects and drove his professors crazy with wild stories of bizarre clients. Always animated and easily spotted in any crowd, Eddie was a scamp, most happy when engaged in acting out some silly, and usually irreverent, melodrama to an audience of laughing and sometimes stunned spectators.

The "Prince of Put-Ons" is what everyone had called Eddie back then, but now, Eddie Maggio was being touted a human monster. The gruesome Maggio Mutilations were receiving national coverage and his one-time best friend postured as the embodiment of evil. As much as Bobby Della Rosa didn't want to believe it possible, he was nearly certain that Eddie was guilty of the crimes for which he was accused. For as disturbing as the murders themselves and Eddie's involvement were, it was the way Bobby had first come to learn of them that terrified him—the night before they happened.

It had to be the hashish Bobby smoked on the sailboat coming back from Catalina that precipitated his most recent episode of portentous hallucinations. Hashish always played tricks with his head, which was why he seldom indulged in that particular delight. The modern market variety was laced with PCP and, by comparison, made the stuff he smoked during his youth as innocuous as cotton candy.

A mild southwesterly filled the Horned Goat's sails as he sat naked beneath a velvet night canopy speckled with stars as clear as diamonds. The pipe passed from Denny Doss, his California research partner, to the two bimbos that had hitched a ride back to Lido Isle in Newport Beach. They were identical twins, except for the hair coloring; fantasy clones straight out of the pages of Penthouse.

Bobby couldn't seem to take his eyes off the brunette's breasts, hypnotized by the hardened nipples as large as milk duds, standing erect and pointing skyward. Made him want the whole box! But, as fascinated as he was by her mammary perfection, the blunt feeling of narcotic torpor had already set in and he harbored little interest beyond an intense ogling. Succulent mounds of white flesh jiggled as the brunette nudged Bobby's arm and giggled. "You want a toke or not?"

He accepted the pipe, inhaled deeply, and succumbed to an even greater dulling of sensation. The boat rocked like a cradle to the undulations of the sea as the night closed in on him. The woman's breasts now seemed unreal and he reached out to finger a cigar-length nipple.

The passing moments were only impressions: Her tongue in his ear, then his mouth, then his lap.

That's when Eddie Maggio had inexplicably come up from below deck and walked right past Bobby to the bow of the ship. They hadn't seen each other in years. "Wow!" Bobby uttered in surprise. The brunette mewed in agreement and walked her fingers up across Bobby's chest to his lips.

At the bridge, Eddie stopped short and screamed, "You bitch! You worthless, pathetic bitch!"

Bobby jerked to attention, straining to see what had so angered his old friend. The brunette apparently further inspired by his tensing, moaned her delight and increased the suction.

Jeannie Maggio, Eddie's wife, appeared naked from behind the bulkhead. Next to her was a golden-haired teenage boy, also nude, with the physique of an athlete and hung like a stallion. They both looked terrified.

Now, Eddie, Jeannie, and the golden Adonis were standing directly above Bobby. Eddie was screaming so loudly, Bobby couldn't make out any of the words.

Mellow out, amigo, Bobby thought, but could not find his voice.

Eddie's face went from a scarlet rage to a malevolent black that raised gooseflesh on Bobby's skin. Bobby had seen that look only once before and gasped at what horrors it presaged.

The visceral images that followed were like ancient frames of eight-millimeter celluloid, flickering in unsynchronized herky-jerky actions. A baseball bat appeared in Eddie's hand. Eddie's arm sweeping upward. The young boy's face wide-eyed with disbelief. A spray of blood, brains and vital fluids jettisoning in rhythmic pulses into the night air. Jeannie's contorted screams. Eddie's face contorted into a monstrous mask of death as he turned his rage upon his high school sweetheart.

Even now, as the plane swayed from side to side like a porch swing, its pilot attempting to line up the aircraft with the evasive runway, like terrible pictures of a bad dream, Bobby could not escape the ghastly images.

The small craft cruised neatly to a traditional three-bounce landing at Lamberton Airport. The runway passed by the rudimentary terminal, and Bobby craned his neck in an attempt to spy his wife, Marcie, and their two Labrador retrievers, but was unable to do so in the dark. A speedy deceleration ended at a cow pasture, followed by a 180-degree turn and a slow-paced trek back to the single-room terminal

As the engines shut down, he looked over at the German businessman. The man was dabbing his forehead with a handkerchief. Even in the dark, Bobby could tell the man had suffered through the flight.

"Hope you enjoy your stay in Franklin," Bobby said, standing up and grabbing his carry-on satchel. "Don't eat any seafood in town; it's all poisoned from the toxic dumping in Lake Erie. Trust me, it'll make you sick as a dog." As he headed down the aisle toward the door, he could hear the man gagging.

*****

Nick closed the lid on his Smith-Corona. If he didn't hurry, he would be late for his first appointment with Dr. Harrison, a psychotherapist he hoped would help him sleep. Lately, his emotions had become confused again; confused, yet heightened. His nightmares were progressively more terrifying. The horrors hidden beneath his consciousness had resurfaced with the impact of a sledgehammer shattering cinder block.

His dreams seemed a nightmarish parade of perversions, a fogged delirium, distorted and unreal, in which Nick could not gain a firm foothold. He drifted through a labyrinth of disjointed images, sometimes like a shadow, yet the sensual residue so tangible he could not distinguish between his sleep and wakeful states.

In his dreams, Nick had been his mother's offering to the coven. She crawled naked on top of him, followed by scores of other men and women, until the world imploded into nothingness.

Each evening, although delirious from sleep deprivation, he feared to close his eyes, certain that demons would again fetch him from his bed to undertake the responsibilities of an Initiate at the bloody altar. Initiation rites. The Master placing a crescent dagger in Nick's crippled fist and doing what, at first, Nick alone was unable—plunging the steel deep into the chest of one of the children from the cages. The coppery taste of blood painted his lips.

A little boy begged him not to let the bad people hurt him and had made Nick promise to take care of him. So Nick protected him in the only way he could, he incorporated the sacrificed child into his own being. There the boy would be safe, to be jointed later by the personages of all the others whose hearts and spirits Nick would consume. He did so with ambivalent feelings of dread and pleasure, learning to kill without compunction, reveling in degradation.

A curtain dropped over his imaginings and they were again lost.

Maybe Dr. Sam Harrison could help him sleep without the nightmares.

He put out the cat and padlocked the rear door to the antique store in which he rented a basement apartment. Outside, the day was like any other in Southern California; sunny, warm and hazy. Very hazy, he thought as he headed toward the South Coast Plaza.

Passersby pretended not to notice him, a reality to which Nick had long grown accustomed. His success offered little solace for the years of solitude and anguish he endured. It seemed a very high cost had been extracted from him in exchange for his good fortune; years adrift in a surrealistic hell in which few humans acknowledged his existence, turning away with disgust, repulsed by his ugliness. He was an outsider, an observer of people, living vicariously through them and through the fantasies that guided his lumpy, thick-fingered hands across the typewriter keys. God seemed not to care for him, had abandoned him in infancy. Or perhaps, He had never acknowledged Nick's existence at all.

"Well, Fuck Him." Nick thought aloud. It didn't much matter what God did or did not acknowledge. He had done without God's help for as long as he could remember, and probably before then too. He didn't need anyone.

His ire boiled, a raging cauldron of wretched emotion, overflowing, cutting molten pathways of rancor across his brain. As abruptly as they had emerged, his dark feelings subsided.

He patted the portable typewriter nestled to his chest as if it were a small child. He had more money then the Pope—God's own banker—and it just kept flowing in. Embodiment of Evil had been number one in the bookstores for several months, and Underland had already negotiated a nice seven-figure movie deal.

The image of a black haired beauty that filled his dreams flashed across his mind. Such naughty dreams they were, yet so real. His body stirred. In his dreams, the girl's name was Samantha. His mental picture of her was so real, they elicited salient smells and tastes…and obscene cravings.

His breaths came in short, harsh gasps. Suddenly, Nick felt dizzy. The boundaries between now and then and when disintegrated. His thoughts churned, writing his next book on the pages of his mind, dreaming his dreams.

A gangly man with a hawk nose and brooding black eyes craned his neck into the front seat of the rust-pocked burgundy Corvair, "Dr. Sam Harrison," he said to the portly woman, who sat in the passenger's seat as if a queen on a throne.

She parted her lips, painted the color of tar, into an obscene smile. "Very well then," she said in a soft voice, eloquent in its English accent, incongruous with the face from which it had emanated.

When she returned her gaze out the window, her lanky escort contorted himself into the coupe and put the key into the ignition. The Corvair hiccupped, groaned, and then spat a noxious cloud of blue smoke from its hind end. "Fucking piece of shit!" he protested.

"Did you make sure DeLucci saw you?" Linda Windsor asked through her heavy mask of makeup.

"What the fuck do you think? He knows I'm here. He always knows I'm around." Then Matthew snickered with a glee that actually made him tingle. "He just doesn't know whether I'm real or not."

Chapter 30

"Dr. Bralich," a voice said from far away, distant galaxy. "You have a visitor."

There was a hard hand on Bralich's shoulder. It weighed a thousand pounds. Don't they know they're hurting me, Bralich wondered?

He wanted to lift his head, but it was just too burdensome a chore. They'd do it for him. There, see. A hand raised his chin until the crown of his head rested against the neck brace at the top of the wheelchair. His head rolled to the side, came to rest with a thump.

Bralich felt as if he was covered from head to toe with spiders that scurried furiously back and forth across his mind, spun webs to capture his thoughts and ensnare his body. Layer upon layer, a cocoon of binding silk woven into a protective net so the world could not reach him; nor he, it. Such hallucinations were the by-products of the pantheon of sedatives and narcotics he ingested against his will each day, he reasoned.

"How's he doing?" It was Wayne Alexander's voice.

"I'm in here, Wayne. Can't you hear me?" Bralich screamed in his mind. Air hissed through the tube protruding from his trachea.

"There's no change."

Alexander was down on his knees now, eyeball to eyeball. Bralich could tell the big guy was looking for some spark of life in his eyes. He struggled to provide it. A twitch, some glimmer of recognition. See it Wayne, I'm here.

"Hey, Buddy. How's it going?" Alexander asked.

Don't humor me, Wayne. You know how that pisses me off.

Alexander looked up to the attendant. "I'm going to trim his beard today. There's no reason he should look like a degenerate," he said, pulling the Norelco beard trimmer from his pocket and showing her.

The attendant issued a disrespectful snort and walked away.

That fat bitch! You see that, Wayne. Call her on it! Tell the pig off!

As if reading his mind, Alexander growled at her as the attendant walked away.

Inside Bralich laughed—roared.

"Nice place you got here, Tony." He straightened Bralich's head. There was sorrow in his eyes. "I told them you don't belong on a psychiatric ward, but…you know how the system works." He ran a small comb through Bralich's mustache.

A steady stream of saliva flowed from the corner of his mouth. Hey, can you get that, Big Guy?

Alexander stemmed the flow. "Can you close your mouth for me?"

Bralich tried but it was beyond his reach.

Alexander chortled. "No, I guess you can't. I never could get you to shut your mouth." He reached up and squeezed Tony's lips closed. "Don't want you to swallow any hair." He turned on the trimmer and lifted it to Bralich's face.

It sounded like a million bees.

"I'm trying for the Sean Connery look. Okay? Like in Russia House with Michele Pfeiffer. Man, how I love Michele Pfeiffer; and I'm pretty sure she really wants me. She just doesn't know it yet."

Alexander drew his own lips into a tight line as if looking into a mirror to manicure his own face. "Anyway, like I said, I told them you don't belong here. You deserve a private room. There's no reason, you couldn't be shipped back to Presbyterian, surrounded by friends and associates, where our staff can take proper care of you. I mean, what harm would it be. But no go, sorry."

Alexander combed through Bralich's beard. "Ew! Did I hurt you there, ole' buddy?"

You lummox. I'm not a collie, dammit.

Buzz …z …zzzz.

"Let's see, what's new?" Wayne said above the monotonous drone. "Samantha's doing fine. Moved to a little town in western Pennsylvania." Alexander pulled his head back, surveyed his work.

Like you're a fucking artist, you dull-witted behemoth.

He continued. "Nick DeLucci's latest book is another blockbuster. It's called Pieces of Hate, and there's a psychiatrist in it that just has to be based on you—a real royal pain in the ass. Rumor has it that Sean Connery has signed on to play the part in the movie."

He turned Bralich's head from side to side and brushed his beard with quick choppy strokes.

"Looking fine, Tony. People judge by appearances, right? Now maybe you'll get a little more attention."

I'm in here, Wayne. Please find me.

"Damn, look at this mess!" His white shirt was covered with black and gray hairs.

Alexander stood, leaned forward at the hip and brushed the hairs from his chest and shirtsleeves.

"You drooled on my shirt sleeves, Tony. I tell you, the more things change, the more they stay the same. You're fucking with me, right?"

Tony laughed in his mind, even though Wayne wouldn't be able to hear him.

Alexander flicked the hair off his sleeves. His lips tightened with displeasure. "Guess I'll just have to roll them up."

Bralich watched with amusement. Mr. GQ is rolling up his sleeves. Lord have mercy on those of us less properly attired and coifed, if one could find such a vagabond. Can you count bedpans with…what's that on your forearm, Wayne?

Alexander flipped up another turn of his sleeve.

You have a tattoo, Wayne. I never knew that. What is it? Come on, one more roll.

Alexander acted as if he had heard Bralich's request and exposed the horned goat emblazoned on his skin.

Bralich screamed. Nobody heard.

The End